"GET OUT OF HERE IMMEDIATELY!"

Alison's voice was shrill with outrage. How dared he barge in while she was taking a bath?

Jason chuckled softly. "You aren't in any position to threaten me at the moment," he replied, glancing deliberately at the rounded swell of her breasts.

Alison sank lower in the bubbles. "Okay, Jason Morgan," she said through clenched teeth, "get out of this bathroom—and out of my life!"

"Alison, Alison!" he sighed, sitting down on the edge of the tub. Tenderly, hypnotically, his hand cupped her chin, traced the outline of her lips. She couldn't move as he dipped one finger into the water between her breasts....

The spell was broken with Alison's gasp. Water splashed in all directions, and Jason fled. But his laughter echoed back at her, ringing with seductive promise.

WELCOME TO...

SUPERROMANCES

A sensational series of modern love stories from Worldwide Library.

Written by masters of the genre, these longer, sensual and dramatic novels are truly in keeping with today's changing life-styles. Full of intriguing conflicts, the heartaches and delights of true love, SUPERROMANCES are absorbing stories – satisfying and sophisticated reading that lovers of romance fiction have long been waiting for.

SUPERROMANCES

Contemporary love stories for the woman of today!

A PERSISTENT FLAME

LINDA TURNER

A SUPERROMANCE FROM WORLDWIDE
TORONTO • NEW YORK • LOS ANGELES • LONDON

Published May 1983

First printing March 1983

ISBN 0-373-70065-2

Printed in Canada

CHAPTER ONE

ROAD CONSTRUCTION snarled the early afternoon traffic, bringing it to a slow crawl. More than one driver was impatient with the delay, but Alison Bennet's agitation stemmed from eagerness, not frustration. After a week of driving across the United States she still couldn't believe she was here.

San Antonio! A sparkle of excitement flashed in the depths of her velvety brown eyes as she gazed around her. If only Susan, her roommate, could see it.

Alison chuckled. Secure in the concrete-and-steel forest of Manhattan, she and Susan had confidently pictured San Antonio as a sleepy, dusty town that had somehow been left behind in the nineteenth century. Nothing could be further from the truth.

On each side of the highway, suburban housing stretched as far as the view allowed. Alison had, of course, heard of the migration of people to the Sun Belt, but somehow she had associated the vast population explosion with Houston and

Dallas. Obviously she'd been wrong. Construction was rampant, with major road improvements and modern commercial buildings testimony to the health of the economy. The downtown district stood out boldly in the distance, golden in the afternoon sun. A space-age needlelike tower contrasted sharply with the older, more traditional buildings. Growth was evident everywhere. Several large office blocks were in various stages of completion, changing the city skyline forever. The area was a mixture of old and new, a blending of the twentieth century with the timelessness of Spanish architecture to create an atmosphere of permanence. It was a city Alison was eager to explore. Thanks to the largess of a grandmother she had never met, she would have that chance.

Her old but reliable Mustang barely inched along, but Alison hardly noticed the traffic. This move west was the answer to her dreams. It had all the makings of a modern-day fairy tale: a long-lost grandmother, an inheritance that was still a mystery to her, the chance to pursue her writing career. Behind her was another life, one she didn't want to go back to even though she had been more or less content with it before she'd learned of her inheritance. Until now she hadn't realized how stifled she had been in New York. She wanted to write—she had always wanted to write—but the daily grind of supporting herself had taken time and energy, and her writing had suffered. Going to the same job day after day, fraternizing with the same circle of friends were among the reasons her imagination had atrophied. She needed to expand her horizons, meet new people, get out in the world and live. Her inheritance would make that possible.

The entire situation was bizarre. Things like this didn't happen to ordinary people. She was just an average girl supporting herself as a copywriter during the day while she spent her evenings pounding out a novel on her old manual typewriter.

From the age of three Alison had been raised by her father's sister, Gwen, after her parents' death in a car accident. She'd been totally ignorant of the fact that her maternal grandmother was alive and living in Texas. Before she herself died Aunt Gwen had told Alison of the estrangement that existed between her mother and grandmother, and why she had kept the information from her. She was only trying to protect Alison from the indifference of her grandmother, she'd explained, a woman who had never acknowledged in any way the death of her daughter and son-in-law. Nor had she attempted to contact her granddaughter. Not once in twenty-three years had Alison received a card or letter or even a phone call from her grandmother.

After Aunt Gwen died, Alison had written to Texas, to the address her aunt had saved for all those years, but even then the barrier of silence had remained unbroken. Several months had passed before she'd received a response, and then it was not one she'd expected. Apparently her grandmother had died recently—shortly after receiving her letter, which had miraculously been forwarded to her current address.

The additional news left Alison more confused than ever. Why, after all the years of ignoring her existence, had her grandmother, Alison Ford Morgan, made provisions for her in her will? Certainly not just because she was her namesake. None of it made any sense, and it probably never would. With her grandmother and aunt both dead, Alison doubted she would ever have the answers to her questions.

And she couldn't even thank her grandmother for the unbelievable opportunities the inheritance had created for her. The letter from John Peters, her grandmother's attorney, could not have come at a better time. The historical romance Alison had been working on for the past two years had been rejected time and again by publishing houses. Each time it had been returned, she had again tried to perfect her fictional characters, but recently she had been hopelessly bogged down. Nothing was going right. Then the letter had arrived, and like the opening of Pandora's box, all her pent-up frustrations were released. This was her ticket to success. She'd be a fool to refuse it.

The inheritance itself was still a mystery. Her grandmother's will prohibited John Peters from disclosing any but the barest essentials. Alison was to receive a sizable sum, including a house. There was only one condition: she had to come to Texas for the reading of the will. Curiosity about her grandmother and the inheritance had quickly swept aside Alison's doubts, and almost immediately she was planning a trip to Texas. It was her writing career that made her decide to make the move permanent. The house and money she inherited represented independence. For the first time in her life she would be able to devote all her energy to writing. And now, in the next few hours, she would learn all the details that would make her career possible.

The traffic thinned, and suddenly she was moving again. With mounting excitement, she stopped at a gas station and left the attendant filling the car while she called her grandmother's attorney. Her fingers impatiently drummed out a staccato beat as she waited for John Peters to come on the line. It seemed interminable minutes but was in fact only seconds before he did. Alison sighed in relief and quickly identified herself. "Mr. Peters, this is Alison Bennet. I've just arrived in town, and I can't wait to find out about my inheritance. How about this afternoon? Will you be able to fit me into your schedule?"

Chuckling at her exuberance, the masculine voice exclaimed, "Whoa, Miss Bennet, not so fast! First give me a chance to welcome you to the city. When did you arrive?"

"About fifteen minutes ago. I didn't mean to rush you, but I've been dying of curiosity ever since I got your letter."

Regret deepened his voice. "I hate to put you off the minute you arrive in town but it can't be helped. You couldn't have come at a worse time. I've got to be in court in fifteen minutes...in fact, I should have left already. Why don't we meet sometime tomorrow? Then we won't be rushed and I'll have plenty of time to answer your questions."

"Tomorrow!" Alison cried, her tone shrill with disappointment. "Isn't there any way you can see me today? I realize you're busy, but I've waited over a month for this. The suspense is killing me!"

"I know and I'm sorry. But I can't possibly get out of my appointments this afternoon. I may be through earlier than I expected, though, if everything goes right. Why don't you give me a call later? I just might be able to squeeze you in."

Knowing he was pressed for time, she swallowed her disappointment and reluctantly agreed. "All right. But can you give me the address of my grandmother's estate? I know you were restricted from telling me anything while I was in New York. But now that I'm here in San Antonio, surely there's nothing to prohibit you from letting me see it. It really would be the best solution, Mr. Peters. Then I'll be able to ask all my questions at our meeting."

"John, call me John," he told her absently. "I really don't think you *should* tour the place before we've had a chance to talk. There are some things you don't know—"

"And I'm sure you'll tell me everything I need to know later," Alison interrupted him. "Please, John, what's the address?"

"Damn!" he muttered, "I wish I didn't have to appear in court this afternoon. I hadn't planned on things working out this way. Someone should be with you. . . ." With a sigh he told her the street and number. "But I wish you'd wait, Alison, until I can go, too. If you'd just leave it till tomorrow, I'm sure I'd be able to rearrange my schedule."

"That's not necessary. I'll be able to find my way," she assured him lightly. His reluctance to have her see the house suddenly penetrated the excitement she felt. "Is there any reason why I shouldn't tour the property today? I don't want to get shot for trespassing."

"No, it's perfectly safe that way. You can look around as much as you like. I'll warn you, though, you may be shocked by what you see. Just remember there's an explanation."

With a laugh, Alison promised him she would and hung up. He really did have the most distressing way of talking in riddles. Why was he so worried? Didn't he realize she would be happy with a two-room hut? She wasn't just inheriting her grandmother's estate. The deceased woman would never know it, but Alison was getting a whole career.

After receiving directions from the gas-station attendant, she climbed back into the reassuring familiarity of her car and plunged into the traffic. She had little chance to think of anything but her driving, though she could not ignore the tension that was building inside her. What would the property look like? And why had John Peters said she'd be shocked? Nothing could compare to the surprise his letter had generated, the letter that had restored all her faith in dreams. Of course, he didn't know that; he had no way of knowing she was embarking on an adventure that might very well change her life.

She was here! Exhilaration coursed through her as she found herself on the street where the property was located. Her stomach fluttered nervously and her eyes widened with sudden doubt as she looked at her surroundings in amazement. Had she made a mistake? Had John somehow given her the wrong address? She pulled over to the curb of the wide shaded street and braked to a halt before studying the address she had written down. Looking back at the street sign, she frowned. Surely this couldn't be the right street. Huge stately homes sat in the middle of equally large estates, their grace and elegance obviously the product of a bygone era. Well-tended lawns and gardens bespoke the presence of professional gardeners. This was no middle-class suburban neighborhood!

Absently she put the car in gear and slowly crawled past the old homes, savoring their beauty. Ancient oaks spread their arms protectively, casting lacy shadows. There weren't many houses on the street, for their size, plus the presence of tennis courts and swimming pools, necessitated spacious lots. Alison's eyes went back to the address John had given her. She was almost at the end of the affluent street, yet she hadn't passed the address she sought. In confusion she looked around her, then she noticed a driveway that was almost shrouded in overgrown bushes and low-hanging trees. Braking quickly, she searched for a house number and found it on the dilapidated mailbox. This was it! In her haste she had almost overlooked it.

Wide gates protested loudly as she pushed

them open. She got back into her car and slowly, almost hesitantly drove toward the house, which was barely visible through the thick foliage that lined the drive. No gardener here, she thought wryly. Large oaks and pecan trees shaded the approach to the house, providing a respite from the sun's heat.

The driveway continued up a small incline, where it forked. Nibbling her lower lip, Alison mentally tossed a coin and turned right. She emerged from the shrubbery to find herself on a circular drive in front of the house. Instantly she gasped aloud. A four-columned portico gracefully protected the front of the house, and carved double doors and long windows stared blankly back at her. Her pulses hammered wildly as realization hit her. The lawyer had said she would be shocked, but that wasn't the word for it. She was stunned! She had actually inherited this...this mansion! With its tall Grecian columns and twin wings, one on each side of the entranceway, it could have easily passed for a plantation of the Old South. It just needed a few hooped dresses and some mint juleps....

No, that wasn't all it needed. The rosy glow of excitement began to fade as Alison noticed the disrepair of the house. The paint was chipped and peeling, and several of the windows were broken. Screen doors hung crazily on their hinges, and Alison noted absently that the carving motifs on the wooden doors had been carried through to the screen doors as well. Even in its deteriorating condition, the house was obviously of excellent workmanship.

Suddenly angered by what she saw, Alison stomped up the few steps and tried to open the doors. They stubbornly refused to budge, but undeterred, she turned toward a gaping window. Thankful that she was wearing tennis shoes and jeans, she nimbly stepped through the shallow opening to find herself in the entrance hall of the formerly elegant house. What she saw brought a burning light of resentment to her brown eyes. So *this* was what John had meant when he said she would be shocked. How could her grandmother, how could anyone, neglect a home to the point that it had become a sad reminder of its former splendor? What possible explanation could excuse this destruction? Wallpaper had been torn from the walls in ragged pieces, to be thrown carelessly on the floor. Once-beautiful parquet floors were now dirty and dull, stripped of their shine. Gaping holes overhead spoke of the disappearance of antique light fixtures.

The stillness engulfed her, and suddenly her situation was achingly familiar. Unlike this mansion, Aunt Gwen's house had been in excellent repair. But it had been so Victorian, complete with doilies on the tables and lace panels at the windows. And then, as now, Alison's footsteps had frequently shattered the tomblike quiet, her inquisitive eyes had peered into secret corners. As a child she had stood in awe of the large empty rooms that echoed with her every movement. She had found it necessary to fill the attic with a family of friendly ghosts, their midnight wanderings responsible for the creaking of the old house. Aunt Gwen had laughed at her flights of fantasy, encouraging her to stretch her imagination to the limits, and in the process she had discovered the house was a home and not intimidating at all.

Besides the more obvious repairs, this mansion, too, was in drastic need of flights of fantasy. How strange that her grandmother and aunt had both lived in houses that seemed to be waiting for her to bring them back to life.

Shaking off the feeling of déjà vu that gripped her, Alison moved toward a doorway to the right of the entrance hall. Stopping on the threshold, she shook her head mutely at the sight that met her eyes. Designed to be used as a library or study, the room was now a shambles. Built-in bookcases had once lined the long length of the walls, but the shelves had been dismantled and were now littering the floor. A marble fireplace stood at the far end of the room, its grate full of ashes and empty beer cans left by intruders. The antique gold-and-green bamboo curtains that had covered the windows were now scattered in disarray.

Why? That one question kept running around in her head as Alison silently continued her inspection of the house, the echo of her movements seeming to follow her through the empty halls. Each room was a testament to the vandalism the house had undergone; none was spared. The upstairs bedrooms were huge, with tall ceilings perfectly suited for the canopy beds of another era; but they were bare of furniture, stripped of any beauty and grace. Sunlight streamed through the broken windows, and the dust stirred up by her feet floated in the bright rays. And always the silence taunted her.

When she reached the attic, Alison's shoulders tightened at the scene that met her eyes. Papers were scattered everywhere—obviously records of old business transactions. Bending down, she picked up a few yellowed pieces of paper, her eyes squinting to read the print. The signature "Edward Smythe" appeared on each of them. Who was Edward Smythe, and why were his business papers in her grandmother's attic? How was he connected with Alison Ford Morgan?

It was all so strange. Had her grandmother actually lived here, Alison wondered. If so, it must have been long ago because such destruction was the product of years, not months. Selling the place would have been more of a kindness to such a beautiful old house—and it certainly would have been a profitable move. The lot alone was worth a fortune. What had happened here to arouse such feelings? And why had her grandmother bequeathed the estate to her? There had to be a logical explanation.

Despair like a shroud dropped over her. Tears welled in her eyes, but she blinked hastily, forcing them back. She was not going to cry! Her dreams, all her wild, wonderful dreams, were gone, shattered like the glass that crunched under her feet. Aunt Gwen had often warned her she was too impulsive, but once again she had foolishly thrown caution to the wind. Like an idiot she had given up her job and used what little savings she had accumulated to come halfway across the country. For what? A run-down old house that mocked her dreams. In her naiveté she had believed that as long as she had a house, she could start living the life she had always hoped to. But this was no house! This was a pitiful remnant of the past, scorned and neglected. Why, even the banisters had been torn from the stairs! It was a ruin, a disaster, nowhere near livable.

No longer able to bear her disheartened thoughts, Alison fled the desolate scene and hurriedly made her way outside. There a cooling breeze whipped around her, lifting the chestnut curls off her neck and dispelling the clouded look from her eyes. The beauty of the grounds caught her unawares, weaving a spell about her that distracted her from the ugliness of the house. The years of neglect had given the garden a wild, untamed loveliness that no gardener could ever hope to copy. Wild roses grew in profusion, cascading from the trellis and fence in glorious disarray. From the front drive, granite steps led down to a fountain.

What a perfect spot for a rendezvous! For one spellbound moment time stood still for Alison. Then realization rushed in and she sank with a gasp to the stone bench beside the fountain. A rendezvous for two characters out of time. . .*her* characters in *her* manuscript! Suddenly she wanted to laugh and cry, to embrace the world in joy as wild thoughts buzzed in her head. For months she had felt stifled in New York. Her writing lacked the zest she knew she was capable of; something was wrong with her manuscript, an enigmatic "something" she couldn't quite put her finger on. She knew the characters needed more depth, especially Arabella, her heroine. That the problem included the setting had never occurred to her. And here it was—an old dilapidated mansion that could have easily fitted in the same neighborhood as Scarlett O'Hara's Tara. What an idiot she had been. She was from New York; how could she possibly write about a Southern plantation when she had never seen one except in the movies?

Write what you know; that was the advice successful authors always gave to aspiring writers, and that was just what she planned to do. Before long she was going to know every nook and cranny of the mansion, every garden and possible trysting place for her two fictional lovers. To be able to place herself physically in the setting of her manuscript was just the spark she needed, and it would make her writing so much easier. It might even improve her characterization.

Her fingers itched for paper and pencil, but she made herself get up and continue her tour of the grounds. Much as she would like to, she couldn't spend the rest of the day here. There were too many problems awaiting her, too much confusion. Her spirits were lifted by the improvements she planned to make in her writing, but what of the mansion? What was she going to do with it?

Thoughtfully she strolled around to the back of the house, where she stopped short at the sight of a good-sized swimming pool empty of everything but last fall's leaves. Widespread oaks hovered over the patio on the opposite side of the pool. Like an old shoe that had outlasted fashion, the mansion stood behind her, a silent testimony to another age.

How had this happened? What sort of woman had her grandmother been, allowing such a place to be treated so shabbily? For years Alison hadn't known anything about her mother's family. Now that she had at last discovered her roots, there was no one left to provide the answers she sought. Her only clue was a broken-down mansion, which only created more unanswered questions.

She was trying to put together a puzzle with half the pieces missing. It was so frustrating! But she could only blame herself. She had learned of her grandmother's existence two years before, when Aunt Gwen had died. And then Alison hadn't written for another year and a half, she had felt so miffed. But she should have put her feelings aside. Instead she had let valuable time slip away, waiting till the hurt had lessened before writing her only living relative. And now it was too late.

She tilted her head back to stare at the imposing edifice before her. It was being destroyed, if not by the elements of nature, then surely by the occasional trespassers who wandered in in search of shelter or a place to party. What secrets did it hold? If only the walls could talk! The papers that littered the attic floor might possibly explain her grandmother's ambivalent feelings with the property. Alison had to find out what had happened, if for no other reason than to stop the questions tumbling around in her head. But first the decay must be stopped before any more damage was done. The house could be saved; it had to be! It was an extension of her grandmother, something that had obviously meant something to the unknown woman at one time. Why else would she have kept it instead of selling it?

And Alison could not disregard her own writing. She had hoped the inheritance would give her the independence she needed to really launch her writing career. But the mansion represented much more than freedom. It was an inspiration, a sudden catalyst that had her mind reeling. It called to a romantic part of her that she couldn't ignore. She would never have writer's block if she lived in such a house. . . .

The sparkle that usually lurked in the depth of her eyes sprang to life as ideas began to buzz in her head. Why not? John Peters had mentioned that a sum of money was included in the bequest. Would it be enough to repair the house? Surely basic renovations wouldn't cost *too* much. Of course, the place looked awful, but a coat of paint would do wonders. She could almost see her fictional characters gliding out onto the front portico to greet the visitors who drove up in horse-drawn carriages. Why had she never realized how inspiring the proper setting could be?

Caught up in her thoughts, Alison abruptly realized that her aimless rambling had led her to a small two-story house located near the gates of the estate. Situated so near the entrance to the property, it was obviously a gatekeeper's or caretaker's house. The building was small and of simple design—white clapboard with black shutters. A low-railed porch ran the length of the house. Glancing at the place uncertainly, she stepped onto the porch. Although the paint here, too, was peeling and cracked, the building was in much better repair than the mansion was. Honeysuckle clung to the lattice at one end of the porch, engulfing her in its heady scent.

Stiffening her shoulders, she knocked gently at the screen door. Seconds passed in silence, causing her to shift her feet in sudden indecision. Should she go in?

Then her dimples flashed. The house was on her property, so therefore she owned it. And John had assured her that the estate was deserted. She turned the doorknob cautiously.

On silent hinges it opened to her touch. The silence that greeted her as she stepped inside soothed her jumpy nerves, and she looked around with interest. The living room was small, running the width of the house, and was furnished in the rich woods and warm colors of early American decor. A flowered couch with padded arms, two maple end tables and a coffee table and a rust-colored wingback chair near the small fireplace gave the room a comfortable, cozy atmosphere. Uncluttered and free of sophisticated trappings, it was much more appealing to Alison than the fashionable elegance she was used to in New York.

Her first impression was that the house really was occupied, but closer inspection revealed otherwise. A thin film of dust covered the furniture and bare wood floors, and a certain mustiness prevailed in the air. Obviously the house had been closed up for some time. There was nothing to show who the last occupant had been; no newspapers littered the floor and nothing was out of place.

A tiny kitchen opened off the living room, its ancient yellow tile, gas stove and small refrigerator shining dully in the sunshine that filtered through the closed windows. Stepping back into the living room, Alison noticed another door, this one near the stairway. Opening it, she grinned in delight. An office. Perfect! Granted, it was small; an ancient oak desk darkened with age seemed to fill the small room. But it would be more than enough space to write in. She would work in a closet, she admitted wryly, though come to think of it, this wasn't much bigger. Like the rest of the house, it, too, was bare of personal belongings.

With eager steps she hurried up the narrow

flight of stairs that led to the second floor. Three doors opened off the small upper hallway. The first one revealed an old-fashioned bedroom, complete with iron bedstead, golden oak dresser and flowered carpet on the floor.

The star quilt on the bed drew her envious gaze, recalling to her mind a long-forgotten incident of childhood. It had been when she was very young. The first snow of the year had fallen one night, creating a winter wonderland while she slept. Early the next morning she had bounced out of bed and run to the frosty windows, longing to leave her footprints in the smooth unbroken field of white. Without waiting for permission she had slipped outside, laughing with delight as she stomped in the yard. She had been discovered, of course, but the scolding she'd received had lost its sting when Aunt Gwen had playfully pelted her with a snowball. The resulting free-for-all had left them both soaked to the skin but exhilarated. When they had finally stumbled indoors, Aunt Gwen had hurried her into a hot bath, wrapped her in an old star quilt and plied her with hot chocolate. It had been an incredible day of fun for both of them.

Although she and her aunt had had their differences, the years they had shared together had made a special closeness between them. That closeness was now gone, and in its place was a void of loneliness....

Resolutely Alison pushed the thought away by closing the door to the bedroom. She had just stepped toward the next door, intent on inspecting what she supposed was a second bedroom, when a sudden sound interrupted her progress, effectively halting her in her tracks. She stood rooted to the spot as the third door swung open.

In an instant her heart had caught in her throat. It was a man—and a nearly naked man at that. Alison gasped, her hand fluttering to her throat as he stepped into the hall.

The man's craggy brows lifted in surprise at the sight of her, but despite the unexpectedness of their encounter his amazingly blue eyes swept over her in a thorough examination.

Instinctively Alison retreated from his sensuous gaze, until she found herself backed up against the bedroom door she had just closed. Unable to stop herself, she returned his frank perusal.

Black curly hair, shiny with moisture, hung over a wide bronzed forehead. His square chin and chiseled cheeks were too rugged to be classified as handsome, but there was a sensuous animal grace to him that stole her breath. His thick lashes were indecently long, but far from effeminate. On the contrary, this man was all male.

Alison cautiously sucked in her breath, and as she did so the clean, spicy scent of him drifted the short distance between them. What a magnificent historical hero he would make, striding the deck of a fleet schooner, laughing as he outwitted pirates. The image came unbidden, but Alison quickly rejected it. To catch the vibrant magnetism of this fellow in words would take more skill than she possessed. No literary description could ever capture the bold sparkle of his eyes, the mischievous quirk of his lips.

His shoulders were broad, seeming to fill the doorway, and the white towel slung carelessly around his neck highlighted his deep tan. Crisp black hair covered his chest, which still glistened from the shower he had obviously just taken. His narrow waist and lean hips were wrapped casually by another white towel. Alison felt her pulse start to race at the sight of such a virile male in such a state of undress.

Startled by the direction in which her gaze had wandered, she glanced quickly upward again, to find that his indigo eyes were returning her look with burning intensity. Mockery sharpened his gaze to hard crystal blue, and his sensuous lips curled cynically when he noticed her heightened color. In that moment she knew he could see right down to the depths of her soul. Confusion was clearly visible in her eyes, she could tell; the blush on her cheeks was mortifying evidence of the effect he was having on her.

Alison couldn't have moved if she had tried

to. Her pulse pounded in her ears, and her senses were spinning with feelings that were totally foreign to her. Never in her life had she experienced such an instant attraction to anyone. She could attribute it only to his resemblance to the fictional hero she had been vainly trying to create. The experience was ridiculous, exhilarating, frightening. . . .

Her embarrassment obviously amused him, for suddenly laughter danced in the piercing blue of his eyes. "John said he'd send his new secretary over to pick up the latest contracts, but I had no idea he had the good sense to hire someone so attractive. How did he know I was back?"

His erroneous assumption sent another wave of color into her cheeks, and she found herself stuttering, "Sec-secretary? No, I'm not a. . . a secretary. Mrs. M-Morgan—"

"Mrs. Morgan?" he repeated incredulously, interrupting her explanation. "Is that why you're here?" His eyes were instantly devoid of laughter, the look he directed at her cool and distant.

Bewildered by his reaction, Alison frowned. "Of course. Why else would I be here?" New thoughts churned inside her head, suddenly robbing her face of color. John had said the estate was deserted, yet this stranger had evidently made himself at home. Who was he? Uneasiness gripped her. She was completely alone with a nearly naked man, and he was beginning to look decidedly hostile. Surreptitiously she glanced toward the stairs, trying to judge the distance. If she caught him by surprise, she might be able to outrun him.

Before she could make a move, he reached behind the bathroom door and grabbed a terrycloth robe. As he shrugged into it he frowned at her impatiently, displeasure clearly written in the lines of his face. "Look, I've been dodging your footsteps for the past month, and frankly I'm tired of it. Don't you ever give up? Any normal person would have taken the hint and made herself scarce. I thought if I refused to return your phone calls you'd get the message. Obviously you didn't. So I'll lay it on the line, and there won't be any misunderstanding. I'm not going to give you or anyone else an interview. I refuse to dredge up the past just so you can sell newspapers. Mrs. Morgan hated publicity. She avoided it while she was alive, and I'm sure as hell going to see she doesn't receive adverse publicity now that she's dead. So go find yourself another story to write. You're just beating a dead horse with this one."

"But—" He was talking about her grandmother! Without even stopping to rectify his misconception about her identity, Alison stepped toward him and asked breathlessly,

"Why did she hate publicity? And why don't you want to talk about the past? How can it possibly—"

"Haven't you heard anything I said?" he cut in ruthlessly, his impatience giving way to anger. "I didn't want to take any action against you, but your constant harassment has left me little choice. Your editor's an old friend of mine, and he owed me a favor. I called him this morning, and he agreed to kill the story. If you want to keep your job, you'd better forget you ever heard of Alison Ford Morgan."

"I can't!" she almost snapped. Forcing herself not to grab him and shake him, she went on, "I don't know who you think I am, but you've got it all wrong. If you'll just let me explain—"

"There's nothing to explain." With one long stride he crossed the space between them, his fingers closing around her arm with all the strength of tempered steel. His grip was firm, refusing to release her despite her struggles. Before she could even offer a protest he was insistently pulling her toward the stairs. "You reporters are all alike—you won't take no for an answer. Well, this time you're going to have to. You're trespassing on private property, and if you're not out of here in thirty seconds, I'm going to call the police."

Feeling suddenly dwarfed, for her head barely came to the top of his shoulder, Alison lifted her chin, her dark eyes snapping with fury. "You're going to feel awfully foolish if you do. The police can hardly arrest me for trespassing on my own property!"

At his look of surprise, some of her anger dissipated, allowing her to say almost calmly, "I inherited the estate from my grandmother. I've just arrived in town and came immediately to see the property. It never entered my head that this house would be occupied. I really am sorry for invading your privacy."

The annoyance that had been visible on his face was gone, replaced instead by a devilish grin that Alison found potently attractive and far more dangerous than his ill temper. His eyes swept over her again with lazy interest, his hands reluctantly releasing their hold on her. He seemed completely unperturbed by the fact that he was wearing a robe and very little else. "So you're the long-lost granddaughter! I suppose you're entitled to look over the estate, though it's not in very good shape right now. I've been away for a month and things have sort of fallen apart. The cottage doesn't always look so... dusty."

Staring at him distractedly, Alison suddenly wished she had taken the time to go to a hotel and clean up. Next to him, fresh from the shower, she felt decidedly scruffy. The humid San Antonio wind had whipped her hair into wild disarray. Her white cotton blouse had lost its crispness hours ago and was now sticking uncomfortably to her shoulder blades. She felt at a distinct disadvantage, flustered and gauche instead of her usual composed self. As he started to open the door to his bedroom, she had an inexplicable urge to stop him, to continue their conversation. "I...I suppose you're the caretaker?" she asked hesitantly.

His blue eyes twinkled as he turned back to her. "I guess you could call me the caretaker." Laughter laced his voice, and she had a sudden suspicion she was the target for his humor.

Knowing she was missing something, Alison surveyed him warily. "Why would a reporter want to interview you about my grandmother? What do you know about her that I don't?"

As quickly as his smile had transformed his face, it was gone, with only a trace of it still lingering in his eyes. "Probably a whole host of things, but don't look to me to satisfy your curiosity. I'm not a gossip."

"Neither am I!" Fuming at his stubbornness, she tried to reason with him. "Look, I've got a right to know. She was my grandmother. If anyone is entitled to—"

"Darling? Aren't you coming?"

The feminine purr that suddenly called from his bedroom caught them both off guard. For one stricken moment Alison's eyes flew to the panels of the closed door before turning back to the man at her side. Embarrassment flooded through her, along with an illogical anger at this stranger for having placed her in such an untenable position. Her nails bit into her palms as she struggled for control. "I'm sorry," she said tightly. "I really didn't mean to intrude. If you'll excuse me. . . ."

"Damn! What's she doing here?" he muttered, the expression in his eyes turning to impatience. As Alison edged toward the stairs, he looked down at her almost distractedly. "You're not really intruding," he said in a low voice. There was a wicked glint in his eyes as they traveled the contours of her face, and he laughed shortly. "Well, I guess you *are*, but don't feel bad. You aren't the only one. I hope you'll excuse me for not showing you to the door. I seem to have a very impatient guest."

Heat surged over Alison's cheeks as once more her eyes went from him to the bedroom door and back again. Stammering an abrupt goodbye, she hurried down the stairs, the sound of his laughter ringing in her ears.

CHAPTER TWO

ALISON SPRINKLED a liberal amount of bath crystals under the running tap, then watched absently as bubbles foamed into the tub. With relative ease she'd found the hotel where John Peters had reserved her a room, but her thoughts were still several miles away, held captive by blue eyes and a wicked grin that even in retrospect could steal her breath away. She had acted like a first-class idiot, so mesmerized by a masculine physique that she had been tongue-tied. Not that he had been naked, but the expanse of his tanned skin had had a definite effect on her senses.... No doubt the sultry-voiced woman in the bedroom had seen him that way countless times, she thought grimly. But it was inexcusable of him to laugh at her just because she lacked the worldliness to pretend unconcern at the sight of a nearly naked man.

Switching off the tap, she stripped off her grimy clothes and slipped into the warm water, immersing herself until bubbles tickled her chin. The road dust that grated on her skin was easily disposed of, but not so the thoughts of the infuriating man whose laughter still filled her ears. She groaned, squeezing her eyes shut in a futile attempt to banish the memory of her embarrassment. But her senses refused to cooperate, and she could see the muscled firmness of his chest, the almost teak color of his skin, the arrogant light in his eyes that had mocked her blushes. With vivid clarity she heard again the feminine call that had interrupted their discussion. Would she ever be able to think of the incident without feeling her face flush with color?

And he had thought it a huge joke! What could be more flattering to a man's ego than to have one female panting after him while another waited for him in his bedroom? Of course, Alison hadn't really been panting—she didn't even know his name—but with one look he had set her heart pounding in her breast. Never in her life had she met a man whose sexual attractiveness was so blatant. It fairly oozed out of him, and she knew it would attract women like ducks to water. He probably had to beat females off with a stick. And she, like a starstruck schoolgirl, had queued up with the rest of the rank and file.

Had he dismissed her from his thoughts with a careless wave of his hand? If only she could do likewise. Instead here she sat, mooning over the caretaker of her estate while her skin shriveled and wrinkled in the rapidly cooling water.

Caretaker! She groaned as the realization swept over her. He must work for her grandmother—or rather, for Alison herself. What a fool she had been, and he had enjoyed every minute of it. Damn! She'd stood there like a dummy as he questioned *her* actions, when it should have been the other way around. He had a helluva lot of explaining to do about why the mansion was in such sad shape. Obviously he hadn't lifted a finger to save it. And he had the audacity to question her!

Once again she could see his dusky skin as clearly as if he stood before her. With his curly black hair and broad shoulders, he didn't fit any of her preconceived images of a caretaker. What was a man in his early thirties, one who was so self-assured and confident, doing with such a job? It didn't seem to fit him at all. The short time she had spent with him was more than enough to convince her he was used to giving orders and having them obeyed without question.

It was inconceivable to her how her grandmother could have employed such an arrogant man. Yet from what he'd said, he must have known the elderly woman quite well. Alison's anger evaporated as she tried to recall his exact words. What did he know about Alison Ford

Morgan that could be of any interest to a reporter? He had mentioned adverse publicity, something he seemed determined to avoid. He had even "had the story killed." But *what* story? Darn it, what was going on? There must be a skeleton in the closet somewhere.

Had Aunt Gwen known? Instead of protecting her from her grandmother's indifference, had she in fact been trying to bury a family scandal? The lawyer's infuriating hints about Alison's inheritance confused the issue even further, and the dark stranger, who obviously knew more than anyone, had flatly refused to tell Alison anything. She felt as if she'd mistakenly walked into the middle of an Agatha Christie mystery without being told who had been murdered. It was driving her up the wall....

With her chin stubbornly set, Alison quickly finished her bath. It was time she got a few answers. She was tired of playing twenty questions, and she would not be put off any longer.

She selected a white voile dress for its coolness; the heat was going to be quite an adjustment for her. The tailored collar emphasized her soft tanned throat while the wide scarlet belt at her waist drew attention to her figure. The circular skirt gently caressed the calves of her legs as she walked to the telephone on the night table near the bed and dialed the lawyer's office.

The phone rang twice, three times. Had John Peters completed his business early or would she have to wait until tomorrow to get some answers? Glancing at her watch, Alison was stunned by the lateness of the hour. She should have called him sooner. Disappointed, she was on the verge of replacing the receiver when a male voice carried easily across the wires.

Gripping the phone, she sighed in relief. "John? Thank God you're back! This is Alison... Alison Bennet."

His voice was warm and friendly. "Hello, Alison. I've been waiting for your call. Did you have any difficulty locating the property?"

"No." Her fingers twisted the phone cord in agitation. "The house is a disaster area, John! I was shocked. I never expected anything like it. How could anyone have let the place fall apart that way?"

Surprised silence greeted her criticism. Then the lawyer said, "I knew you shouldn't have gone by yourself. You were bound to be disappointed. Believe it or not, there *are* extenuating circumstances. Why don't you come over to my office and I'll tell you everything I can."

"Tonight?" she asked in surprise. Through her hotel window she could see that it was still daylight, but the shadows had lengthened considerably. It wouldn't be long before twilight.

A chuckle traveled the length of the telephone

wire, and she could hear the smile in his voice as he said, "Of course tonight. It's still quite early. The sidewalks won't be rolled up for another two hours."

Alison's laughter bubbled like a brook. "I didn't mean to imply anything, John. I was just surprised. You must admit this isn't normal business hours."

"No, but this isn't normal business. You're practically family. Mrs. Morgan was like a grandmother to me—I ate more meals at her house when I was a kid than I did at my own. And I didn't bring you all the way from New York just to abandon you. You're not completely without friends, you know. You just haven't met them yet."

"You've just banished one of my nightmares," she confided laughingly. "I had this horrifying picture of not having any friends but the mailman! And since you knew my grandmother so well, maybe you can answer some of my questions about her. There's so much I don't know."

"I'll be happy to." Briefly and concisely he directed her to his office, which he said was nearby. "If you get lost along the way, stop and give me a call. Though I doubt you'll have any problem."

Fifteen minutes later Alison drove into the parking lot of the small law firm. There was still enough daylight to reflect her image in the rear-view mirror. What she saw was reassuring. Her makeup, applied with a restrained hand, was flattering in its simplicity, drawing attention to her high cheekbones and her large brown eyes. She frowned in annoyance at the sprinkling of freckles, which no amount of makeup could disguise. She tried so hard sometimes to look chic and sophisticated, only to have those ridiculous freckles mock her every attempt. With a resigned toss of her head, she locked her car and walked toward the office.

The reception area, elegant in Spanish decor, was quiet and deserted. The typewriter was neatly covered and the front desk cleared of clutter. Unsure of her next move, Alison gazed searchingly down the short hall that obviously led to the offices. She had already been accused of trespassing once today, and she had no intention of making the same mistake twice. "Hello, is anyone here?" she called, feeling rather silly but knowing of no other way to make her presence known.

A door in the back recesses suddenly opened; a man strode quickly forward, gazing at her with a delighted smile. His blond hair was straight and conservatively cut, swept aside to show to advantage his wide forehead. Dimples on each side of his mouth flashed, giving him a boyish look that was belied by the masculine gleam in his green eyes as he boldly assessed her.

"Alison?" At her nod, he reached for her hand and enclosed it within his warm grasp. "I'm John Peters. I would have known you anywhere. You favor your grandmother a great deal, you know. Did you have any trouble finding the office?" He rushed on, "Good, I didn't think you would. I'm really sorry I couldn't go with you to the estate this afternoon. But I'm sure you're anxious to find out more about your inheritance. Let's go back to my office and we'll discuss it." His tone was warm and inviting, almost as if he had known her for years.

As she followed him down the hall, Alison struggled to find her voice. "I do have quite a few questions to ask, actually. And I want to thank you for seeing me tonight. I know this isn't your normal procedure."

She had prepared herself for a younger man, but not quite this young. And definitely not this attractive. John Peters was in his early thirties, lean and devastatingly good-looking. His low Texas drawl was pleasant to her ears, and he treated her with a natural friendliness that she found impossible to resist. Even if she'd wished to protest, he gave her no time, naturally assuming that she wouldn't object.

A grin teased her lips into a smile, and she wondered if he tried this approach with every woman he met. How many had fallen for his boyish grin and the smooth talk designed to sweep a girl off her feet before she had time to think about it? Probably too many to be counted, she decided wryly.

"After you phoned, I got in touch with Jason Morgan, the other beneficiary of your grandmother's will. Since the two of you will be working together, I thought it important that you meet as soon as possible." He pushed open the door to his office and gallantly waited for her to precede him.

A frown wrinkled Alison's forehead as she looked at him in confusion. "I don't understand, John. What do you mean, we'll be working together? Who is Jason Morgan?"

"The wolf in caretaker's clothes. Or perhaps I should say, no clothes at all." The deep voice came from the depths of the office, its owner shielded from view by the partially open door.

For an instant Alison froze in her tracks. She needed no glimpse of the speaker to identify that voice, for it was unforgettable. Her heart lurched in her breast; she could feel the blood drain from her face, and she hoped that her face wasn't as white as her dress. On stumbling feet she forced herself into the room.

Color surged back into her cheeks as she met mocking blue eyes for the second time that day. Her composure fled and she groaned inwardly. How could she possibly be expected to discuss business with this man in the room? Every time she looked at him she was reminded of the embarrassment of their first meeting.

That he was perfectly aware of her discomfort was evident by the knowing look he was giving her. Tall and lean, a sardonic grin slashing the sharp angles of his face, he stood across the room from her, drawing her gaze despite herself. The towel had been replaced by conventional clothing, but it did nothing to distract from his animal attractiveness. A light blue pinstripe suit covered his tall frame elegantly, the jacket stretched taut across his broad shoulders. The deep blue diagonal stripes of his tie exactly matched the blue of his eyes, which were lazily assessing her figure, missing nothing in their sweep from her sandaled feet to her curly head.

Alison stiffened, desperately trying to ignore the tug of attraction she did not want to acknowledge. His challenging stare mesmerized her, and much to her horror she realized it would take more than a concentrated effort on her part to make her forget their first meeting. Resentment for her own wayward emotions lifted her chin and drew her toward him. "I'm glad you're here, Mr. . . . Morgan. There are a few things I'd like to discuss with you. And first on the list is the mansion." All the frustration she had experienced came rushing back as she demanded, "What kind of a caretaker are you? In case you hadn't noticed, the place is falling down around your ears. Don't you even care?"

"Of course I care," he defended himself smoothly. "That's why I'm here—so we can discuss it."

"What's there to discuss?" Alison retorted. "By your own admission you abandoned the estate for over a month. If you used to do the same thing while my grandmother was alive—and from the state of the place you must have—it's a wonder you didn't lose your job. Did she know your amorous pursuits were interfering with your work?"

Jason Morgan laughed. "Oh, she knew all right. She complained for years."

How could he laugh about it, she thought angrily. He obviously found great satisfaction in knowing he had taken unfair advantage of an old lady. Alison turned to the attorney accusingly. "Were you a part of this?"

John Peters's eyes were wide with surprise. "Part of what? Will somebody please tell me what's going on?"

Chuckling at the lawyer's bewilderment, Jason Morgan replied, "Alison's a little confused. We met this afternoon when she came out to see the property, you see. She thinks you're partly responsible for the destruction of the mansion."

"Me?" John choked, startled by the accusation. "I had nothing to do with it! I tried to advise your grandmother, I admit, but she wouldn't listen. She even threatened to get another attorney if I didn't quit harping about that place." Moving behind his desk, he motioned for Alison and Jason to be seated. "Really, Alison, I had nothing to do with the fact that that house is in such a shocking state. You do believe me, don't you?"

His sincerity could not be doubted. Although Alison felt her anger lessening, she was still confused, however. Did he condone Jason Morgan's behavior? Didn't either one of these men have any scruples? "Yes, of course I believe you, John. But—"

"Good!" he interrupted. "Now, since you two already know each other, I'll just go ahead and read the will. As you know, Alison—"

But Alison, far from satisfied with the answers she had received, stubbornly refused to be sidetracked. "I'm sorry, John, but I don't think we *should* continue until a few things are cleared up. As Mr. Morgan explained, we did meet this afternoon. But I still don't know why he's here now."

Again the attorney seemed momentarily speechless. Casting a questioning look at Jason, he finally replied, "Because he's your grandmother's grandson!"

"Stepgrandson," Jason corrected calmly

before getting to his feet. He leaned his bulky frame against the polished wooden bookcase. "I know you're probably confused right now, but this isn't really as complicated as it sounds. The story goes that grandmother was married twice, first to your grandfather, then to mine, a widower. I don't know too many of the details, just that her first experience gave grandmother bad feelings about marriage. She didn't marry again for many years after that, even though she had a small daughter and it couldn't have been easy supporting her child and herself. Anyway, she met my grandfather while your mother was still a teenager. He tried for years to get grandmother to marry him, but she always refused. When your mother eloped with your father and moved to New York, she finally accepted my grandfather's proposal. They were married for almost ten years."

Alison's mind was reeling. In five minutes he'd told her more about her mother's family than she had learned in her entire lifetime. "My parents eloped?" she asked in surprise. Why had Aunt Gwen never told her?

Jason nodded. "I take it you didn't know."

"No. You evidently know more about my family than I do. Why did they elope? Is that why my mother and grandmother weren't speaking to each other?"

"Partly. Apparently your mother was very

young; she'd just turned seventeen. Grandmother didn't approve of her seeing your father. He was stationed here in the service, and she was afraid he would take advantage of your mother and then be shipped out. She forbade them to see each other. And just as grandmother had feared, your father was transferred. Before he left town, they eloped. Grandmother was a proud woman. She couldn't forgive your parents for getting married without telling her. As it turned out, they never spoke to each other again."

Regret washed over Alison, regret that she had missed out on a relationship with both women, regret that she had to learn of them through strangers. "Your grandfather," she asked tentatively, "he's dead, too? I don't mean to pry, but you've got to remember this is all new to me. I never even knew my grandmother's name until two years ago!"

Jason walked across the room and sat down beside her. Alison thought she detected a flicker of emotion in the depth of his eyes as he explained, "My grandfather died while I was in college. After he married your grandmother, I lived with them until I graduated from high school and left for college. They more or less raised me while my own parents were off traipsing the globe."

The very apathy with which he spoke of his

parents revealed a wealth of feelings hidden beneath his audacious mien. There was a certain bitterness, however, that couldn't be concealed, and Alison wondered if he, too, had missed out on parental love. "You don't have any brothers or sisters?"

He laughed shortly, without amusement. "No. That's one mistake my parents didn't make." Before she could ask any more questions, he glanced at the lawyer. "I think you should go ahead and read the will, John. It's getting late."

"By the way, why would a reporter be interested in interviewing you about my grandmother? How could she have been newsworthy?" Alison asked suddenly, hoping to catch him off guard.

Jason's blue eyes narrowed, thoughtfully studying her before he replied, "You're not familiar with the city yet, but the Southwest Medical Center is located not far from the mansion. The University of Texas Health Science Center is there, along with a large number of the city's hospitals and medical office buildings. My grandfather owned part of that land before it was developed. The reporter wanted to do a local-interest story. She wanted more information than I wanted to give, so I had the story killed."

Alison eyed him speculatively. Was he lying?

His explanation seemed plausible, but it could also be a half-truth designed to satisfy her curiosity. His recitation was just a little too pat, a little too well rehearsed to ring true. Such a story would not create adverse publicity, as he had claimed at the cottage. Whatever he was hiding was much more serious than a local-interest story.

She glanced at John, but his boyish, open face concealed nothing. He obviously accepted Jason's tale. The shuttered expression in Jason's eyes, however, was enough to make her suspicious. She couldn't let the subject rest, not when her instincts warned her that his answer was nothing but a lie. "Are you sure that's the only reason? It all sounds pretty fishy to me."

Before Jason could respond, John intervened. "It's the truth, Alison. Mr. Morgan really did own that land. We used to play there as kids."

Alison was smart enough to know when she was beaten. She sighed in apparent surrender. "I just wish you hadn't killed the story. I would've liked to have read it." She turned to John. "I'm sorry I keep interrupting you. I promise. . .no more questions until you've finished reading the will."

John picked up the legal document, his green eyes serious, locking with hers. "First I want to explain a few things. You're probably wondering why your grandmother never answered your letter. She was very ill—in fact, she was in the hospital at the time—but your letter did her more good than any medicine. She was delighted to hear from you; she was making all sorts of plans. The coronary bypass she needed, however, came too late. She died a month after receiving your letter."

Alison blinked back the tears that suddenly threatened. "I should have written sooner. I had had her address for a while, but I didn't write."

John tried to comfort her. "Don't blame yourself, Alison. There was nothing any of us could do. Just be glad your letter reached her in time. It meant a great deal to her."

The meaning of his words finally registered, etching a frown in her usually smooth forehead. "But she died three months ago. Why didn't you contact me sooner?"

John's light complexion flushed with color. He looked at Jason, who didn't seem the least disturbed by her suspicious question.

"Unlike grandmother, we could hardly accept your letter at face value," Jason stated bluntly. "Your sudden appearance was more than a little bit suspect. I couldn't stop grandmother from changing her will, but I could make damn sure she didn't change it in favor of an impostor."

"You mean you had me investigated?" Alison exclaimed indignantly.

"Of course I had you investigated. Anyone who knew the least bit about her family circumstances could have written that letter. She was a wealthy woman. I had to protect her interests."

"And your own," she retorted angrily. He certainly didn't lack nerve! "Regardless of what you think, I wasn't after her money."

"But you must admit it will come in handy."

Alison gasped, too angry for an instant to think of a fitting rejoinder. Before she could protest John cleared his throat, eyeing his two clients warily. "I'm sorry about all the secrecy surrounding the inheritance, Alison." Determinedly he brought the conversation back to the will. "It was strictly your grandmother's idea. She felt your curiosity, if nothing else, would bring you to Texas. That's why I could only give you the barest of hints. She hoped that once you saw the estate and the city, you would want to stay. That's not a requirement, though. You can leave tomorrow if you like, but I hope you won't."

"The will, John," Jason reminded him dryly. "Alison would probably like to know the details before she makes a decision. I'm sure she's dying to find out."

John opened the folder before him and began to read the last will and testament of Alison

Ford Morgan. As he did so, Alison sat on the edge of her chair, trying to decipher the legal terms of the document. The meaning of the will gradually seeped through the jargon, however. Before long she was practically staring at the attorney in disbelief. She studiously avoided looking at Jason Morgan; she knew he was watching her with his hooded gaze. Silence reigned when the last words were read, a silence the three of them seemed loath to break. Finally John lifted his eyes. "Do you have any questions, Alison?"

"Do I have any questions?" Hysterical laughter bubbled in her throat; fiercely she pushed it back. She forced herself to relax, to release her grip on the arms of her chair. "To make sure that I heard correctly, could you go back over it, this time in English?"

"Of course." A smile lighted his green eyes as he contemplated her. "To put it simply, the estate and the buildings on it belong to you and Jason jointly. A sizable sum of money was left to each of you, as well. You yourself will receive your grandmother's personal diaries and some letters. As for the property, if at any time one of you wishes to sell, the other must either buy you out or agree to the sale. Do you understand?"

Alison's glance went from him to Jason and back again. "That's what I thought I heard." Unable to sit still any longer, she stood up and walked restlessly across the office. Then she turned to John. "Why? Why did she leave the property to us jointly? Don't get me wrong, I'm not complaining. It's just that this makes everything so difficult. Jason and I don't even know each other, and now we own property together. It's going to be awkward, especially if we disagree. Why didn't she divide the estate or leave it to just one of us?"

This time Jason spoke. "Perhaps you should tell her, John. You're much more diplomatic than I am." The mocking light was back in his eyes and there was a cynical lift to his mouth.

Nodding in agreement, the lawyer eyed Alison speculatively, as if weighing the most delicate way to put his next words. "You and Jason were Mrs. Morgan's only grandchildren. Of course, Jason wasn't related by blood, but that was just an accident of birth. He was her grandson for all practical purposes. You have to understand, Alison, that your grandmother was a very fair person. She wouldn't ignore your existencc and leave everything to Jason, nor would she forget all the years she had spent with him and leave everything to you. So she left it to you jointly, hoping that the two of you would be able to work out a compromise. Her diaries will probably help you understand her feelings better than I can. As for the clause about selling the mansion, she wanted to make sure the estate didn't become a source of contention between the two of you. Evidently she had had firsthand experience in a similar situation, though she never did tell me about the circumstances. In any case she would rather that you sell the mansion than argue about it. She had become disillusioned with the place herself, obviously. I never understood why she bought it anyway. The house was already unlivable and needed drastic repairs. Jason and I both tried to talk her out of it, but she wouldn't listen."

Alison's gaze shifted unwillingly to Jason. "You mean she didn't live there? But I thought it was her home!" Confused by this sudden revelation, she tried to sort out her thoughts. "If she didn't live at the mansion, where did she live? And why did she buy the estate?"

"She lived in an apartment," Jason replied. "Several years after my grandfather's death she sold their home—she felt it was too big for just one person, and I was overseas at the time. She bought the estate a few years after that. She had lived there as a teenager, apparently; her father had been the gardener. She'd even fallen in love with the owner's son, but for some reason it didn't work out. He eventually married someone else, and it was his heirs who sold the estate. They all had homes of their own and didn't want the place. Grandmother was heartbroken when she saw how they had neglected it, so she bought it. I think she had fantasies of revisiting her lost youth. But she never moved in, and she never fixed it up. Basically she just let it go.''

Alison blinked back the tears that misted her eyes. What an unhappy life her grandmother must have had! For some inexplicable reason she'd been unable to marry the man she loved. Her first marriage had ended in divorce. She'd been separated from her only child by an irreconcilable argument and then by death, and she had never known her grandchild. The woman had certainly had her share of tragedy.

''What happened between her and the man she loved? Why didn't they marry?'' Alison asked finally.

Jason shrugged, his expression shuttered again. ''You'll have to read her letters and diaries. Maybe they explain everything.''

Alison instinctively suspected he knew more than he was telling. From the moment she had encountered him in the cottage, he'd been dropping infuriating hints about the past. But the minute she asked for more specific details, he clammed up. How were they ever going to come to terms with their joint inheritance if he wouldn't be frank with her? She had come all this way believing she had finally acquired a home and she didn't want it to be wrested from her solely on the whim of one man.

And Jason could be so maddening! Covertly she studied him from beneath lowered lashes.

His chiseled face with its square-cut chin told of strength and determination, his tenacity tempered by the glint of mockery in the depths of his eyes. But she knew from experience that those same eyes could take on the hardness of steel. She could expect no leniency from him should he turn against her. His mockery was a double-edged sword, yet to her consternation she was discovering she was vulnerable to the charm he seemed so unaware of. If it came to a battle, she was no match for him. Men of his stamp were completely out of her league.

Pushing these thoughts aside, she addressed John Peters. "So what happens now?"

The attorney looked at Jason, who stood up and moved away from the desk. He turned to Alison, a wary expression on his face. "Since you've seen the estate, you'll obviously agree it needs to be sold."

"I will not," she denied promptly. Golden sparks flashed in her brown eyes. "I gave up everything in New York—my apartment, my job, my friends—to move out here. Surelv you aren't suggesting that I give the house up, too? And return to New York without giving all this a chance? No, never!"

"Look, I'm not suggesting you move back to New York," he said quietly. "After we sell the estate, you can easily use your share of the money to buy another house in San Antonio.

But you might as well forget about the mansion. It's a dry hole." At her puzzled look, he explained, "A dry hole is an oil well that never pays off. You can pump thousands of dollars into it, but it won't make a bit of difference. The mansion needs too much work—we'd never be able to get our money out of it."

When she remained stubbornly silent, he sighed in exasperation. "You realize I can get a court order permitting the sale, don't you? But I don't want to do that. If you'd just think for a minute, you'd see it would be better for both of us if we got a reputable agent to handle the property—and that we sell it as soon as possible."

"No," Alison said obstinately, refusing to budge from her position. How could she make him understand how important the house was to her writing? It was the house of her dreams, the one she had been vainly trying to recreate in her book. If she could only live there, she knew it would be a constant source of inspiration. With so much historical atmosphere, it would take very little imagination to picture her characters walking the halls. But would Jason Morgan understand? At the moment all he could see was dollars and cents. "I will not agree to sell the mansion, Jason. Of course, the place doesn't mean anything to you. You're lucky—you have your own memories of grandmother. All I have is my half of the mansion and her diaries—those are my only links with her. I'll never have the special relationship that you two had."

From the stubborn set of his jaw, Alison knew she wasn't getting anywhere. Impatiently she added, "Aren't you going to allow me anything at all of my grandmother's?"

For a moment he almost looked stunned. Then his jaw tightened, and she could see he was physically trying to restrain his anger.

"You had your chance with her, but you didn't take it," he said almost accusingly. "For twenty-three years she was denied any knowledge of your existence. Do you have any idea how much that hurt her when she found out? As far as I'm concerned, you've got no right to put in your two cents now. You can't ignore a person during her life and expect to profit from her death."

"What are you talking about?" Alison demanded angrily. "She's the one who ignored me. I never even know I had a grandmother until two years ago."

"You don't honestly expect us to believe that, do you?" Jason didn't even attempt to conceal his disbelief. "Talk about farfetched! Didn't you ever ask any questions about your mother or her family?"

"Of course I did. But Aunt Gwen always said they were dead. She didn't tell me the truth until just before she died. And the only reason she said anything then was because she didn't want me to be alone in the world."

"So why did you wait two years before you wrote?"

Alison winced inwardly. She couldn't begin to describe how she had felt when she had learned of her grandmother's existence. At first the hurt and anger had overshadowed any joy she had felt, and it had taken her a long time to work that out of her system. But she refused to feel guilty for what was only a natural reaction. "If she didn't care about me, I didn't see why I should care about her. And I still haven't heard you offer an excuse for her indifference."

"She wasn't indifferent, she just didn't know you'd been born." At Alison's own skeptical expression, he sighed. "Obviously your mother never told her about you. They weren't speaking to each other at the time."

"But how. . . ." Alison frowned in confusion. His story made absolutely no sense. "Aunt Gwen told me she notified grandmother of my parents' death. She found the address on a letter."

"Yes, your aunt did contact her. But the telegram came two weeks after your parents died. There was no mention of a child."

Alison was stunned, unable to believe that Aunt Gwen would have deliberately misled her grandmother. All the years that had been wasted! "It must have been a mistake. I know Aunt Gwen resented the fact that grandmother never tried to contact me. She must have thought she knew about me but just didn't care."

Now more than ever she was determined to keep the mansion. Her grandmother was not the heartless creature she had imagined her to be! "Don't you see, Jason, that I have to keep the house? I've finally got the chance to really share something that was hers, to get to know her in some small way. You have no right to interfere in that."

"I'm not interfering," he objected. "Don't start throwing accusations at me when you don't know the situation."

"So tell me!" she cried in frustration. "Ever since I learned of my inheritance, I've been tormented by innuendos. First John couldn't tell me anything about the estate, and now you won't tell me anything but the barest essentials about grandmother. What are you hiding? Why won't you tell me?" Her eyes flew to John, who was watching them silently. "Do you know what he's talking about?"

"Leave John out of this," Jason warned her. "Whatever grandmother wanted you to know, I'm sure she's mentioned in the papers she left you. You'll have to read them and see for yourself."

Lifting her chin, Alison met his gaze. The light of battle was in her eyes. ''I suppose that's your not too subtle way of telling me to mind my own business. Well, it won't do any good because I'm going to find out everything I can about Alison Ford Morgan. And I'll never agree to sell the mansion. Don't think you can bully me, either. I won't knuckle under to pressure.''

Jason's eyes were diamond sharp. ''Girl, I'll have you know—''

''Hey, you two, time out!'' Laughingly, John interrupted the heated words, his glance taking in both their angry faces. ''If I'd known there was going to be a fight, I would have sold tickets!'' He leaned down to Alison, a warm smile lighting his features. ''Are you all right? Jason can be a pretty tough opponent. Do you want to throw in the towel or go on to round two?''

A little appalled at her own vehemence, she grinned shamefacedly, allowing his laughter to ease the suddenly tense atmosphere. ''I'm sorry, John. I didn't mean to turn your office into a battlefield. I guess I got carried away.''

Patting her on the shoulder, John smiled reassuringly. ''Don't worry about it. You've had a rough day—you're entitled to blow off a little steam. Why don't you go back to your hotel and get a good night's sleep? You'll feel a lot better in the morning. Things won't seem nearly so bad when you're rested."

"Have you had dinner?" Jason's voice, now devoid of anger and slightly aloof, cut through the air, once more drawing Alison's gaze back to him. When she shook her head, he said, "Get your purse and I'll take you to dinner. No wonder you're in such a bad mood. You're hungry!"

"Dammit, Jason!" John protested indignantly before she could reply, "I was going to take her out."

Unperturbed, Jason laughed. "Sorry, the lady's already spoken for. You should have asked sooner."

Well, he certainly was confident, Alison fumed. He and John obviously expected her to fall in with their plans without a word of protest. For a minute she was tempted to turn them both down and go back to her hotel. She glanced up, intending to tell Jason exactly that, but the words died in her throat. The look he was directing at her surprised her, reminding her of the unexpected emotions she had experienced at their first meeting. Her cheeks flushed with color before she could drag her gaze away. Silently she admonished herself for being so susceptible to a virtual stranger, especially one who had other women beating a path to his door. Granted, he was extraordinarily attractive, but that was no reason to act like a complete idiot. They had business to discuss, nothing more.

With that resolve firmly fixed in her mind, she picked up her white clutch purse and turned to John, offering her hand with a charming smile. "Thank you so much for all your help. I understand why you had to check out my story, and I just wish I'd written sooner. Maybe then I'd have had a chance to meet grandmother. And even though the mansion isn't exactly what I was expecting, I don't regret coming."

Warmly shaking her hand, he grinned boyishly. "Believe me, it was my pleasure. I have a feeling we're going to be great friends. And before I forget—" he reached into his lower desk drawer and handed her four small leather-bound volumes and a stack of letters tied with a faded blue ribbon "—your grandmother's diaries and letters."

Alison reached for them eagerly, then spontaneously clutched them to her breast. "Thank you. You have no idea what these mean to me. I just wish she could have given them to me herself."

Jason moved to her side, his previous expression replaced by a warm smile of understanding. "This is the best she could do, Alison. Almost as soon as she got your letter, she notified John to make changes in her will. She wanted you to have these. I know it doesn't make up for all the years you missed out on, but maybe it will help."

His glance fell on the attorney and his smile widened into a grin. "Sorry to steal her out from under your nose, John, but we really do have things to discuss." When his friend only snorted in disgust, he laughed, "You always were a sore loser." Flashing him another grin, he ushered Alison out of the office.

John's parting shot as they walked down the hallway was, "Let me know what you decide to do. Alison may need the services of a good attorney!"

CHAPTER THREE

IT WAS ALREADY DUSK as they left the office. Alison drove the short distance to her hotel, with Jason following her. In the parking lot she locked her car, then climbed into his sleek silver sports car, the powerful engine of which was purring like a contented cat. Once she was seated, the seat belt snug around her hips, the car leaped forward with a snarl.

In silence she watched Jason's strong brown hands control the vehicle. Through her lashes she studied his set face, his wide brow, chiseled cheeks and firm jaw. He was an enigma, a contradiction that seemed totally baffling.

Obviously the mansion represented an investment to him; the bottom line was all he saw. There were no emotional entanglements to cloud his vision. Selling was the only practical thing to do. Yet despite this pragmatic side of his nature, she had not imagined the emotion she had seen on his face when he spoke of his parents and grandparents. He was not a cold man, even though he refused to reveal what he knew of their grandmother's link with the mansion.

By his very secrecy, she knew that that link involved a tragedy. Alison wouldn't be satisfied until she discovered what it was. But even then she couldn't agree to selling the place. Living there would be a constant stimulus to her writing. How could she voluntarily give that up?

"Why are you frowning?"

Startled, Alison looked up to find him gazing at her. A shrug of her shoulders sent his eyes back to the road, but he shot her another quick look when the silence remained unbroken. Finally she spread her hands before her, a defiant expression on her face. "I was thinking about the mansion and all the problems it's presenting."

"Forget it." Pulling into a downtown parking lot, he switched off the engine and turned to her. As he did so his thigh momentarily brushed against hers, setting her nerves atingle. "Forget the estate and everything else until after we've eaten. Hopefully we'll both be a little more objective. Okay?"

At her hesitant nod, he grinned, a slow devastating smile that went straight to her heart and sent her blood pounding in her ears. She watched, still under the spell of that smile, as he got out of the car and came around to open her door.

Taking her hand, with a gentle tug he pulled her out beside him. "C'mon, I want to show you one of San Antonio's prettiest sights. I doubt if you've ever seen anything like it, even in New York."

Laughter sparkled in Alison's eyes. Tipping back her head, she gazed up at him challengingly. "Now *that* I find hard to believe. New York has everything."

"No, you just think it does." He pulled her arm through his and walked several yards to a waist-high stone wall that ran parallel to the sidewalk. Turning her toward the wall, he leaned against it expectantly, watching her face as she gazed over it to the view beyond.

Her dark brown eyes, wide and appealing, turned back to him with a look of surprised delight, then drifted again to the scene before them. The San Antonio River, lazy and slow moving, was meandering past, its green black depths catching and reflecting the lights that were cleverly concealed in the trees. Sidewalk cafés with umbrella-shaded tables crowded each bank like colorful jewels; their multicolored lights gave a festive, almost holiday spirit to the entire area. Enviously Alison noted the couples strolling along the stone paths that followed the river's curve. A cooling breeze whipped up, casting running ripples on the water and shattering the ribbons of reflected lights into a thousand diamonds. English ivy covered the stone walls that bordered the river and twined around the base of ancient magnolia, pecan and cypress trees that graced the banks.

After a moment Alison dragged her gaze away and grinned impishly at her companion. "Okay, so we don't have sidewalk cafés along the Hudson. We can't have everything. We're content with the Statue of Liberty and Central Park and Broadway, Times Square and the Yankees and—"

Jason clamped his hand over her mouth, laughingly cutting off her staunch defense of New York. "All right, all right! You win. Let's quit arguing and go eat. I'm starving." Once again his hand was there, guiding her with gentle pressure toward the circular stone stairway that led to the river level. When they reached one of the restaurants a hostess dressed in a colorful peasant skirt and blouse approached them. When Jason stated their preference for outdoor dining, she showed them to the riverside, where a candle flickering behind a red globe stood in the center of their Mexican tiled table.

Alison looked at the menu in confusion. The derisive laugh she gave immediately drew Jason's questioning gaze, and she closed the menu and handed it to him, an impish grin on her face. "You'll have to order. This is all Greek to me."

"Not Greek. Spanish!" he joked. "It won't take you long to pick up a few words, especially for the common kinds of food. Don't worry, though—all foreigners have trouble at first."

Before she could reply, a waitress appeared to take their order, which Jason gave clearly and fluently, not stumbling over the Spanish words as Alison knew she would have. "The lady will have *chiles rellenos* and a *guacamole chalupa*. And I'll have the *cabrito*." He glanced at Alison. "Is beer okay with you or would you rather have a margarita?"

Knowing she would need a clear head when they got around to discussing the mansion, she asked for iced tea instead. When they were left alone again, she said playfully, "I don't understand. Why did you call me a foreigner? I was born in the United States. I'm as American as you are."

He chuckled softly, his gaze lingering on her face. "Ah, yes, but you weren't raised in Texas. That makes you a foreigner and a Yankee!"

A smile began at the corners of her mouth. "This all does seem a bit foreign to me!" Her hand gestured to their surroundings, encompassing their fellow diners, the river and its beauty, the tall trees with the Gulf breezes whispering through their branches. "You know, people in New York would never believe this. Susan, my roommate, would be shocked! I guess we were both guilty of falling into the typical stereotypes: deserts and cactus, and, of course, cowboys. I don't know why, but I wasn't expecting a large city, especially one with a river and sidewalk cafés. It looks almost European."

"The city has always been centered around the river," Jason answered, "but it wasn't until this century that its potential was noticed. In the early 1920s, a flood devastated the city. A lot of people felt that poor flood control in this area, which is called the river bend, was the problem. They wanted to fill in this part of the river to prevent a recurrence of the flooding. A group of outraged citizens protested such drastic measures and proposed that proper flood control be built, along with the walkways, bridges and the lighting you see now. The Paseo del Rio, that's River Walk to you Yankees, became commercialized in the sixties, gradually developing into what it is today. The entire length of the River Walk is maintained by the city's Parks and Recreations Department."

Gazing around her, Alison drank in the beauty of the area, mentally storing details for future use in one of her novels. "They must spend a fortune on all these gorgeous plants. They're beautiful!" Wistfully she rested her chin in her hand. "I must remember all this. It would be a wonderful setting for a scene in a book."

"I beg your pardon?"

His question invaded her daydream, bringing her back to the present. She felt a faint blush steal over her cheeks as she explained, "I'm a writer, you see...though as yet an unpublished one. That's one of the reasons I was so excited about inheriting grandmother's estate. I hoped to finally have a place of my own, rent free, so I could devote all my time to writing. The mansion, to say the least, was something of a shock."

"I don't doubt it."

The arrival of the waitress interrupted their discussion, and Alison's eyes widened at the sight of the plate set before her. "I'm not sure I really want to know what all this is. I recognize beans and rice, but that's about it."

Jason laughed. "Your education has been sadly neglected. On the left is *chiles rellenos*, which is really just a pepper stuffed with cheese and dipped in a batter. And that green thing you're frowning at is a *guacamole chalupa*. It has avocado salad, refried beans and cheese on top of a fried corn tortilla."

Alison looked across at his plate. "And what are you having? I think you called it *ca... cab*—"

"*Cabrito*. The *i* is pronounced as a long *e*. It's the Spanish word for kid." His lips twitched at the horrified look on her face. "It's baby goat, Alison."

"Oh." Her cheeks flushed with color again as she laughed lightly. "Is it good?"

"Delicious." He made a movement to push the plate toward her. "Would you like to try it?"

When she hastily declined, he chuckled and they began to eat in companionable silence. It was only when they had finished the excellent meal that he returned to the subject of her career. "What kind of writing do you do? Magazine articles?"

"No, fiction. Historical romances."

"Romances!" Jason scoffed teasingly. "I should have known."

"Don't knock it," she advised him. "One out of every four books sold in a bookstore is a romance."

"So you're in it for the money."

"No. . .I mean, yes." She sighed, smiling in spite of herself. "You're deliberately twisting my words. Sure, the money is important, but since I haven't sold anything yet, that really doesn't come into it. I write what I like to read. And there's nothing better than a good old-fashioned love story, though I don't expect you to agree with me. You probably don't have a romantic bone in your body."

"You'd be surprised." Easily he sidestepped her attempt to put him on the defensive, turning the conversation back to her. "Why historical instead of contemporary? Isn't it more work, what with the research and everything?"

"Yes, but I don't mind. I love history. I was even going to major in it before I had to drop out of school."

"Why did you quit?"

"My aunt had a stroke." Deliberately she glossed over that part of her life, not wanting him to think she was looking for sympathy. After all the years Aunt Gwen had spent taking care of her, Alison hadn't hesitated to return the favor. Even though her aunt had protested about her leaving school, she had needed her, not only emotionally but also financially. Alison had never regretted the sacrifice.

Jason seemed to sense her reluctance to discuss the past. He leaned back in his chair, all traces of teasing gone. "Have you finished your manuscript or are you still in the planning stages?"

"For the last two years I've spent all my spare time working on a novel. I thought I was finished—I even sent it to a few publishers. But it still needs a lot of work. After I make some changes, it's going back in the mail. It won't sell in a desk drawer."

She could see the next question hovering on his lips, and she suddenly wanted to cringe. She had heard it so many times that she was heartily sick of it. "Do you know how hard it is to break into print?" God, how she hated that question! Jealous of her inheritance, a few of her so-called friends in New York had made no secret of their skepticism. She was crazy to give up a good career to go whistling off in the dark for a dream that would never materialize, they said. Oh, they gave her credit for being a fairly decent copywriter. But books? Never! Cynics, they were all cynics. She had hoped people in Texas might be different.

Before he could say a word, she held up her hand, cutting him off. "Please don't say it. If you only knew how many times I've been asked that question. I know the deck is stacked against me, but it doesn't matter. Writing is all I want to do. I've got to try."

Surprise was evident on Jason's face, the glint of amusement back in his eyes at her outburst. "I wasn't going to suggest you wouldn't be able to find a publisher for your work. I only wanted to know what era of history you're most interested in. What's your book about?"

"Oh." Chagrin washed over her; she really must learn not to be so touchy. "I. . . I'm sorry. It's just that I've had so much discouragement from well-meaning friends that I forget some people are truly interested. As I said, it's a romance, set in the Civil War. You know—Southern belle meets and falls in love with Yankee spy. It's not *Gone with the Wind*, but

I've had some encouragement from an editor in New York. If I can only make the right changes, I know it will sell."

He leaned back in his chair to study her thoughtfully. "Have you always wanted to write? Almost all the major publishing houses are in New York. Wouldn't that have been the logical place for you to stay? I'm not saying you shouldn't have come to collect your inheritance. I'm just surprised you moved away from all the action."

Alison glanced across the table at him, then she looked away. "I wasn't getting anywhere in New York. At least, not with my writing. I couldn't write much before my aunt died—there just wasn't time. And afterward, well, it just sort of grew stale. I had to work all day, and I guess at night I was just too tired to produce anything brilliant. I realized I needed a change, and what with this windfall, San Antonio seemed the logical place. Since I won't have to work at a job, I'll have plenty of time and energy to write." Her eyes met his again. "What about you? I know you're not the caretaker, so you must do something."

He grinned, unabashed by the trick he had played on her. "I really do look after the estate, at least as much as my job permits. I'm a geologist, in fact. I've got my own exploration and drilling company. That's why I've been gone this past month—I was out in the field drilling a new well."

Alison's eyes widened at his offhand explanation. "You're really in the oil business?"

He laughed at the surprise in her voice. "I haven't given Exxon or Texaco anything to worry about yet. But I've been doing pretty well, especially this last year. I no longer just sell oil leases to the more successful independents. I'm able to take a few chances, try to hit upon an undiscovered field. That's what it's all about, really—taking a gamble and hitting pay dirt."

Alison found herself sitting on the edge of her seat, caught up in the exuberance of his words. His whole face was alight, and it was obvious he loved what he was doing. "It must be pretty risky. What happens if you don't hit oil?"

"You pack it all in and go home. And kiss three hundred thousand goodbye. Enough mistakes could ruin a company within a year's time. So far, I've been lucky. Out of eighteen wells, I've come up short only twice." His explanation—and his enthusiasm—came to an abrupt end as he reached into his pocket for his wallet. A minute later he rose to his feet. "C'mon, let's get out of here. We've got things to discuss."

Mutely Alison allowed him to guide her away from the restaurant along the river. Sneaking a glance at his profile, she flinched at the shuttered, impassive set of his face. The filtered lighting cleverly hidden in the tree branches cast stark shadows on the planes of his chiseled face, creating angles that seemed to rob his expression of understanding or compassion. She had no knowledge of this man, no clue as to the best way to approach him. Would an impassioned plea soften his heart and weaken his resolve to sell the estate? Or would it only harden him against her, and in the end, bring about what she sought to prevent? Earlier he had given little thought to her feelings. . . .

Somehow she had to make him understand just how important the mansion was to her. He couldn't be totally insensitive—he was so concerned with protecting her grandmother's reputation, for one thing. But from what, she didn't have the slightest idea. It was all so confusing.

With a sigh she dragged herself out of the reverie she had slipped into and looked up to find him waiting for her, impatience drawing his brows together in a frown. "What's the matter now?"

"Jason, about the mansion. . . . I know you want to sell it. But couldn't you consider for a moment how I feel? I told you I was having problems with my manuscript. Well, that's an understatement if ever there was one. My heroine's a paper doll—she's got no depth. While I was in New York, I couldn't seem to correct the problem. I didn't even know where to begin—"

"And now you do," Jason interrupted flatly. He seemed no more receptive than he had earlier.

She twisted her hands in sudden agitation. "You're probably going to think I'm crazy, but the mansion is the perfect setting for my manuscript. After I saw it, I thought of a hundred ways to improve my story. It's given me all sorts of ideas, ideas that would never have even occurred to me in New York. Don't you see? It's like stepping into the pages of my novel."

"If what you say is true, then you already know what changes you're going to make in your book. You don't need the mansion anymore. It's served its purpose."

"I can use it in more than one book. And I will write more than one." His obvious skepticism irked her, and she flared, "This isn't just wishful thinking on my part. Not when I've had a personal letter from an editor."

"What's so special about that?"

"Editors don't write personal rejection letters," she explained patiently. "They send form letters. So any kind of communication other than that is special. That letter means as much to me as a personal letter from the president of Exxon would to you."

He grinned at her analogy, but Alison had a

sinking feeling he wasn't moved at all by her entreaty. She was suddenly exhausted from her trip, and he was being deliberately stubborn. Why couldn't he understand? Tears of frustration pricked her eyes. "The mansion is my legacy from grandmother—a woman I didn't even know. I can't just sell the estate as if she'd never existed, Jason. I want to get to know her, how she thought and felt. I want to find out why she bought the house in the first place. And I don't think what I'm asking is so unreasonable. Selling it will only result in money. Sure, I can always use more cash, but neither you nor I is exactly destitute now that we have the inheritance she left us. The mansion is history, a heritage we could never hope to buy. Don't ask me to give it up."

Jason's blue eyes flickered with a strange emotion as he studied her. A hand, lean and tanned from hours in the sun, came up to caress the tear that slipped down her cheek. Then he led her to a nearby stone bench surrounded by wide-leafed banana trees.

"Sit." Firmly he pushed her onto the seat and stared down at her, a withdrawn expression on his shadowed face. "Do you have any idea how much it would cost to restore the mansion?"

At the negative shake of her head, he named a figure that brought a shocked gasp to her lips. "Now you can see why it's expedient for us to dispose of the property. The longer we hesitate, the more the value drops. Selling is the only logical thing to do."

"Why must men always be so practical?" Alison shot at her feet, gold flecks of annoyance lighting her eyes. "That old house is nothing more than brick and mortar to you, isn't it? Just a mass of wood, plaster and cement that can be conveniently turned into a profit. It could become a beautiful home so easily, but all you see is dollar signs!"

"Easily?" he scoffed. "Come off it, Alison. You must be wearing rose-colored glasses if you think all that that house needs is a few coats of paint. It needs major renovating, and that costs money! If it can be done. It may be so far gone nothing can save it."

"Want to bet?" she challenged. "You're right, a lot of work is needed. But the place is hardly falling down. In fact, I'll bet it can be saved for half the figure you named."

"Oh, really? Would you care to put your money where your mouth is?" Jason leaned toward her. "If you can have the house restored for half the sum I named within, say, two months, I'll drop the issue of selling. But if you can't, we sell. What do you say? Are you willing to risk losing the house to prove your point?"

His mocking tone unnerved her. She wavered uncertainly, torn between her love for the house and the desire to show this arrogant man that she could not be so easily dismissed. Her eyes pierced the shadows in her effort to determine his mood. "Are you serious? Where would I get the money for such an undertaking?"

"From the inheritance. We'll each contribute three-quarters of our share. That should work out to about half the sum you say is necessary. At the end of two months, if the repairs haven't been made with the stipulated money, you agree to sell. With no arguments!" He held out his hand to her, his teeth flashing in the darkness. "What do you say? Is it a deal?"

Without a second's hesitation she placed her hand in his. "It's a deal." She smiled confidently. "I hope you don't live to regret it."

"If you win, we'll both be winners. After all, that's one of the reasons grandmother bought the house in the first place. And I'll be the first to congratulate you. If you win."

"Are you always this doubtful of a person's abilities? Or is it just me?" Alison asked boldly, irritated by his skepticism. "I realize you've just met me, but is it necessary to be quite so negative? I haven't reached the age of twenty-three without having acquired *some* knowledge of the world. At least give me the benefit of the doubt."

"I don't question your common sense, I question your ability to restore a run-down mansion within a limited budget and without the guiding hand of a man.'' Grinning at her gasp of outrage, he took her hand and tugged her to her feet. ''It's getting late. I'd better take you back to your hotel.''

In silence Alison walked beside him as they headed back to the car, impotent fury seething through her veins. He was still living in the dark ages if he thought a woman needed a man to guide her every move. His audacity knew no bounds! She was no empty-headed female who was devastated without the strong shoulder of a man to lean on. She knew her capabilities, and she deeply resented his scoffing. She'd show him if it was the last thing she did!

When she surreptitiously glanced at him, she discovered he was lazily studying her face, a knowing twinkle in his eyes.

''I suppose you'll want to start looking for an apartment tomorrow,'' he said. ''Give John a call. If he doesn't have time, his sister, Nancy, will probably be free. I'd take you, but I'm tied up in business meetings all day tomorrow.''

Smiling rather smugly, Alison shook her head. ''Thanks just the same, but it's not necessary. I've already found a place.''

''You have? Where?'' Jason looked at her with narrowed eyes.

''The caretaker's cottage.''

''Oh, no!'' His momentary surprise quickly

turned to grim determination. "That's where I live, and under no circumstances will I agree to share it with you. You'll just have to find someplace else. The cottage is taken."

Alison stopped in her tracks, determined to go no farther until they came to an agreement. "Aren't we equal owners of the cottage?"

At his curt nod, she shrugged. "Then what's the problem? I have as much right to live there as you do. It's really the only logical place. Being stuck off in an apartment somewhere won't help my writing. And once the repairs start, I'll need to be near at hand. It's ridiculous for me to pay rent when I already own a house." She took a shaky breath. "Why should you be privileged and live rent free, anyway, when I have the same rights you do? It's my house, too."

"The only reason I'm living there is because grandmother wanted someone on the property. The house had already been vandalized, and she thought my presence would discourage trespassers. Which it did. But that doesn't mean I'm going to share that house with you, because I'm not!" The slim hold he had on his temper seemed to snap, and he stared at her angrily. "My God, you're brazen! How many other men have you moved in with?"

A surge of red fired her cheeks. "None! What do you think I am?" she asked hotly. Breathing deeply, she valiantly sought to extinguish the flames of her anger in order to reason with him. "Jason, I'm not asking you to share your bed with me, just the house. After all, we're practically cousins. The house has two bedrooms; it's definitely large enough for two civilized people to share without being at each other's throats all the time." Feeling as if her words were falling on deaf ears, she abandoned diplomacy altogether. "If you don't agree, I'll simply go to John tomorrow and get a duplicate key. You can't keep me out of my own house, Jason," she said quietly.

"Dammit, Alison!" he exploded angrily. "I'm only doing this for your own good, and you insist on casting me as the villain! But you're right. I can't keep you from moving in; I won't even try. It's all yours, because I'm moving out. You may not care about your reputation, but I do. I'm not going to repeat history by having your name on every wagging tongue in San Antonio." He took her arm almost roughly. "C'mon," he said, practically pulling her down the walkway. "What's the matter now?" he growled impatiently as he caught her curious look.

Alison was undeterred by the angry scowl that darkened his face. "What do you mean about history repeating itself? You might as well tell me this awful secret you're trying to hide, because I'm going to keep asking questions until I get some answers."

"You can ask till you're blue in the face, but it's not going to do you any good," he snapped. "Now let's get going. I'm taking you back to your hotel. Or were you planning on moving in tonight?" he added sarcastically.

"I. . . I thought I would," she said hesitantly, suddenly leery of pushing him further. She placed her hand on his forearm, halting him with her touch. "Please don't be angry, Jason. If you'd only try to see things from my point of view! Why do you have to be so stubborn?"

"You're the stubborn one, not me. I'm just trying to be practical. I can see now I might as well save my breath."

The drive to the hotel was accomplished in silence. Despite her insistence, Jason refused to abandon her there to find her own way home. Instead, while she packed her suitcase again, he went to the front desk to pay her bill and met her back at the car. By mutual agreement she followed him back to the mansion, waiting patiently while he got out to open the gates before driving in behind him. They both parked in front of the cottage; then he went over to take her suitcase from her. The sardonic look in his eyes brought a flush to her cheeks; hastily she lowered her gaze and followed him onto the porch, standing behind him silently as he unlocked the door of the darkened house. Anyone would think he was the injured party, Alison thought indignantly. She hadn't asked him to move out, he had volunteered! Which was just as well. With any prolonged exposure to his sexual magnetism, she knew her indifference would begin to crumble. He was too potent for her peace of mind; the greater the distance between them the better.

Preceding him into the blackness of the living room, she halted just over the threshold, afraid of proceeding farther for fear of running into the unfamiliar furniture. Jason stepped forward confidently and switched on a light, effectively dispelling the shadows. Then he headed for the stairs. "I'll put this in your room," he said, gesturing with the suitcase.

With a wildly beating heart, she followed him up to the room she had admired earlier that day. The scene of their first meeting flashed before her eyes, and along with it the embarrassment she had suffered. What an idiot she had been—carrying on a conversation with a nearly naked stranger while his girl friend waited for him in his bedroom! She cringed every time she thought of it. If she'd had any sense, she would have turned tail and run.

She glanced up from the doorway to find a look of mocking amusement on his dark face. His mouth broke into a wicked grin. Was he remembering her fascination with his body?

Her eyes fled from his to chase about the

room. "Thank you for bringing up my case," she managed. Suddenly tongue-tied, she searched for something else to say. "Did this furniture belong to my grandmother?"

"Yes. She made this quilt and the one in my room. She was an excellent seamstress. In fact, that's how she'd supported her father and herself after he'd lost his job as head gardener here. She always had that skill to fall back on when times got rough, though I think leaving the estate was one of the roughest things that ever happened to her—that, and your mother's death. Is there anything else you'd like me to bring in for you?"

"Just a box of books. They're kind of heavy. The rest of the stuff I can get tomorrow."

A few minutes later Alison held open the screen door while he struggled in with a cardboard box filled to overflowing with books. As he set it down on the desk in the office, the topmost book started to slide. He caught it quickly, reading the cover as he placed it back on the stack. "Abigail Peyton. Are you a fan of hers?"

"Oh, yes," Alison laughed. "She's my favorite author. If I ever come close to writing half as well as she does, I'll have it made. She's terrific!"

Jason laughed, a strange note of disbelief in his voice as he added, "It figures." When Alison looked at him quizzically, he shrugged.

"You write historical romances, and Abigail Peyton is the queen of the genre. I suppose it's natural for you to admire her." Advancing toward her, he placed firm hands on her shoulders and turned her around. "Come out with me so you can lock the gates after I leave."

As they stepped outside, Alison tried to see Jason's face in the darkness. "Why do you want the gates locked?"

"To discourage any wayward visitors who might decide to do a little midnight exploring. We've had more than our fair share of trespassers, although lately they seem to be diminishing."

Alison felt the blood drain from her face. "You mean I have to worry about prowlers?" she squeaked in alarm. She wouldn't be able to sleep a wink! As Jason started to get in his car, she grabbed his arm. "Jason, do you have to go? It's so late. Why don't you stay here tonight, after all?"

"Is that an invitation?" Laughing at her stunned look, he lifted her chin with his finger, effectively closing her mouth. His eyes were dark with an emotion she couldn't identify as they skimmed lazily over her face. His fingers moved to trace her jaw before falling to his side. "Believe me," he chuckled, "you'd be safer with a prowler."

Helplessly Alison watched him get in the car.

"But. . .where are you going? It's so late—"

"Don't worry," he interrupted. "I have a small efficiency apartment behind my office. I usually spend the night there when I have to work late." He started the motor and turned to look at her, grinning wickedly. "Don't look so upset, Alison. There's nothing to worry about if you lock the gates after I leave."

"That's easy for you to say," she protested. "I'll try telling myself that when I have to contend with a burglar."

"I tell you, you're perfectly safe," he laughed. "Even if a prowler does decide to pay you a visit, all you have to do is plead with those gorgeous brown eyes of yours and you'll have him doing whatever you want. Take me, for example. I'd much rather stay here to see if you're as innocent as your eyes say you are instead of driving halfway across town to a lonely bed."

"You've already had one woman in your bed today. Isn't that enough?"

"But it wasn't you," he replied. "Don't forget, lock the gates!" With a flash of his devastating smile he drove off, leaving her to watch his disappearing taillights.

A few seconds later Alison walked on trembling legs to the gates, automatically shutting and locking them. Her heart pounded in her breast, and she wanted to scream in frustration. She had no defenses against Jason Morgan. Just the lift of his mouth in a smile set her senses spinning. She had never met a man with such sex appeal.

That he enjoyed his effect on women was obvious. He was such a handsome devil! But she had met handsome men before and never experienced this reaction. What was it about Jason Morgan that caused her to see red one moment and the next to feel weak at the knees? He was every woman's dream—perhaps that's why she found herself responding so readily to him, despite her better judgment.

He was a romantic hero, she decided, a character in her manuscript come to life. He was bold, laughing, daring her to deny her attraction to him. It was probably a game he played with every woman he met....

That thought brought Alison back to earth with a jolt. He could save such antics for the obviously willing woman who had infiltrated his bedroom this afternoon. Alison herself would leave her fantasizing for her writing.

CHAPTER FOUR

THE LATE MORNING SUN streamed through the window, flickering over Alison's closed eyelids until she awoke. For a minute she lay there, refusing to abandon the sleep that had been so elusive in the darkness of the night. She could cheerfully have killed Jason Morgan. All night his reference to prowlers had had her jumping at the slightest sound. She'd been on the edge of sleep innumerable times, only to find herself jerked back to wakefulness by the rustling of the wind through the trees or the scrape of a tree limb against the house.

Reluctantly her eyes blinked open, her glance immediately lighting on the package of her grandmother's letters on the nightstand. All thought of sleep fled. She bounded up and reached for the bundle, the yellowed paper crackling stiffly beneath her fingertips. She had a thousand things to do—unpack the car, start the groundwork for the repairs of the mansion, begin her corrections on her manuscript—but she couldn't do anything until she read those letters. Breakfast and all other minor details fled in the face of her eagerness to discover more about her grandmother.

Settling back against the pillows, she gently eased the faded ribbon from the bundle of letters. The envelopes were tattered, the ink faded but still legible. Hastily Alison flipped through them, studying each envelope carefully as she put them in chronological order by their postmarks. They were all addressed to her grandmother in the same bold scrawl, all carrying dates from the summer of 1928.

Thoughtfully Alison examined the writing on the first envelope. What could these letters contain that had made them so important to her grandmother? Would they answer any of her own questions? Apprehensively she slid the letter out of its envelope, almost holding her breath as she carefully unfolded it. "My darling Alison." The words fairly leaped off the paper. Alison blinked in surprise, expelling her breath in a rush. It was a love letter! For over half a century her grandmother had kept love letters!

Cautiously she smoothed the creases of the fragile missive, trying to ignore the funny feeling that had come over her. Love letters were so personal. To read those addressed to someone else made her feel uncomfortable, almost voyeuristic. Her grandmother had obviously wanted her to read them, but Alison couldn't help feeling as if she was prying. It was very disquieting.

She steeled herself to ignore such ridiculous notions and began to read the letter. Gradually her uneasiness faded, eclipsed by the beauty of the words that seemed to wrap a spell around her.

> Each time we meet, my love for you increases. We are both courting disaster, but I cannot stay away. When we are separated, the hours of the day drag and my heart is encased in unrelenting loneliness. Thoughts of you are with me always. I see your sweet smile with the rising of the sun and hear your joyous laughter in the tumbling waters of the fountain. Only you can relieve my abject misery. Meet me in the moonlight, my darling. This torture will end when I again hold you in my arms.

How had her grandmother felt, receiving such a letter? Could she have resisted such a poignant entreaty? Alison's eyes dropped to the closing and signature, "Love always, Edward." Could this Edward and the Edward Smythe whose papers littered the attic be one and the same man? Probably. Her grandmother must have fallen in love with the son of the man who owned the mansion. But why were they courting disaster by falling in love?

Alison carefully returned the letter to its envelope and reached for the next. Its contents were similar to the first, the unknown Edward again professing his undying love. Another assignation was made, and he again entreated his love to meet him and relieve the torment of their separation. Alison wondered if her grandmother had complied. Their trysting place was not disclosed; obviously it was one they were both familiar with.

Automatically she reached for the third letter and then the fourth, unable to tear herself away from the one-sided love story. Each missive was more eloquent than the last, and not even the coldest heart could have remained immune to them. Time had not diminished the depth of feeling revealed—they were just as persuasive today as they had been in her grandmother's time. How had Alison Ford Morgan responded to them?

The last letter was much the same as the previous ones, and Alison finished reading it with a feeling of frustration. It ended just as the others did, with the suggestion of a secret meeting, leaving Alison hanging as to the outcome of their romance. That they had never married was obvious. Yet it was doubtful Edward Smythe would have poured out his feelings to her grandmother without some expectation of having them returned. The romance must have turned sour. What events had precipitated the split? And what was her grandmother's purpose in leaving the letters to her? What was she trying to tell her?

Alison's brow furrowed in a frown as she tenderly gathered the letters together, tying them with the blue ribbon. A broken love affair was something she herself hadn't experienced. She had had her share of fun, and she had a number of male friends, but few of the men she'd dated did much to her heartbeat. Invariably her thoughts had drifted back to her writing. Writing was the most important thing in her life, and until she found a man who would understand that and share in her dreams, she would have to keep dreaming alone.

She could only wonder at what her grandmother must have gone through. Even though this Edward and she had parted, such intense feelings couldn't have vanished with the blink of an eye; they must have lingered despite the best intentions. Through two marriages and the innumerable tragedies that had touched her life, Alison Ford Morgan had cherished the letters of her first love. It was possible the love she once felt for him had never died. She had, after all, kept his letters for the rest of her life. Had their breakup been his doing?

The growl of Alison's stomach disturbed the quiet of the room. With a start she realized she had spent the better part of the morning engrossed in her grandmother's love life. It was a story without the benefit of an ending. Of course, she knew that nothing had come of the affair, but it was that very lack of details that was so tantalizing. Would the diaries provide more clues?

Alison glanced at them thoughtfully, tempted to pick one up and satisfy her curiosity. But the rumble of her stomach again interfered, and she decided to leave it for another time. Instead she got dressed and went to the kitchen in search of food. The peanut-butter-and-jelly sandwich she fixed appeased her hunger but did nothing to satisfy her inquisitive mind.

The summer of 1928.... It was almost impossible for Alison to picture the life her grandmother must have led. That was the time of cloche hats, bobbed hair and speakeasies. The depression was right around the corner, and the world economy was racing toward disaster. Her grandmother, too, had been headed for personal disaster, but she had been young and in love. Sultry summer nights were not conducive to rational thinking—she had probably given little thought to the future. Like ripples on water, however, the consequences of that summer were far-reaching, easily crossing the barrier of time.

Letters once sent to Alison Ford Morgan were now in her granddaughter's possession, their message anything but clear.

The ringing of the telephone rudely interrupted her pondering, and Alison hurried to answer it. "Hello?"

"Alison?" Jason's unexpected laughter suddenly caressed her. "Evidently the bogeyman didn't spirit you away during the night. How are you? Are you settling in all right?"

"I'm in one piece, but it's no thanks to you," she retorted dryly. Her heart was responding crazily to his voice. He had no right to sound so attractive over the phone. With an effort she recalled the lack of sleep he had caused her. "Since you weren't too concerned about me last night, I doubt that you're calling about my health. Which means you have another reason for calling. What is it?"

"It wasn't that I didn't care," he protested. "I knew you'd be perfectly safe. You were just being paranoid. And stop being so suspicious. Can't I call just to be friendly?"

When she only snorted in reply, he laughed again. "I guess not. Well, actually I did have another reason. My car's out of commission. I don't know what's the matter with the damn thing, but I'm stuck out here on foot. I wouldn't mind if I didn't have an appointment to keep, but it's too important to cancel. So I was wondering. . . are you doing anything important this afternoon?"

"Why?" she asked suspiciously.

"I thought you might like to take a ride around town," he replied promptly, deliberately choosing to ignore her less than enthusiastic response. "And while you're at it, you could give me a lift to my meeting."

"Aha! Now we're getting to the real reason for this call." The nerve of him! Last night he'd nearly scared her to death with his casual reference to prowlers, and now he expected her to drop everything to do him a favor. She studiously ignored her clamoring senses to ask, "Why don't you call a taxi?"

"This isn't New York, Alison," he reminded her teasingly.

"Well, what about the bus? And don't tell me San Antonio doesn't have a bus system because I won't believe you."

"Of course we have buses. They just don't run out this far." As if suddenly realizing she was reluctant, he said contritely, "Look, if you'd rather not, I understand. Normally I'd have caught a ride with someone in the office, but I'm the only one here today. Don't worry about it, though. I'll just call and cancel the appointment. I'm sure they'll understand."

Absurdly, his reassurances only served to make her feel guilty. She *had* practically thrown him out of the cottage. "It's not that I don't want to help you, Jason," she objected finally. "It's just that I don't know the city very well. I'd probably get lost, and you'd miss your appointment completely. Isn't there anyone else you can call?"

"Not a soul," he retorted cheerfully. "And don't worry about getting lost—my office is easy to find." Blithely, before she could offer any further objections, he gave her directions. "It's going to take you a while to get here," he advised, "so don't be discouraged when it begins to look as though you're on your way to Houston. My office is quite a way from town—that's why I have an apartment here. In fact, you probably should leave as soon as possible. Since you're not familiar with the city, you'd better allow extra time to get here."

When, she wondered wryly, had she agreed to his request? "All right. I'll be there as soon as I can. But don't say I didn't warn you if I get lost." At least this would give her the chance to ask him something about Edward Smythe and his relationship with her grandmother. If Jason would cooperate. Up to now, he had been incredibly closemouthed.

"One more thing, Alison," he said before she could hang up. "Your moving into the cottage caught me unprepared. I didn't realize until this morning that most of my things are still at the cottage. Since you're coming out here anyway, would you mind bringing me my clothes?"

"Of course not," she said sarcastically. She was definitely the victim of a setup! "Is there anything else I can bring you?"

"No," he laughed. "Just your sweet self will be enough."

Several minutes later she entered his room. As she did so she tried to forget the woman who had been there the day before. A woman obviously in pursuit of Jason. . . .

She shook herself impatiently. Why did she continue to dwell on the matter? What Jason did in his spare time was none of her business, especially what he did in the privacy of his own bedroom!

Forcing her thoughts back to the matter at hand, she glanced around curiously. His room was similar to hers except for the brass bed that seemed to dominate the decor. Had he and his sultry-voiced girl friend. . . .

She groaned, angry with herself for the persistent thoughts that taunted her. In a spurt of determination, she marched to the closet and jerked it open. A suitcase was stored at the back of it, so she hastily pulled it out and opened it on the bed. She turned back to the closet, noticing the familiar robe that hung on the back of the door. Steeling herself to ignore the memory it evoked, she reached instead for a handful of shirts.

As she folded his clothes and packed them in the suitcase, she was unprepared for the feelings that washed over her. The entire room retained a lingering scent of him. And packing Jason's clothing intensified the feelings—it was such an intimate act. That thought burned, and she slammed the lid of the suitcase down with a bang. She was too imaginative—she needed to start writing again so she could channel all this creativity into a productive project. And from now on, Jason could pick up his own clothes!

After dragging the suitcase downstairs, Alison quickly reread the directions Jason had given her. Picking up her purse and the suitcase, she opened the door, then stopped abruptly. Standing on the other side of the screen, her hand upraised to knock, was a raven-haired woman.

Startled, Alison inspected the stranger inquisitively. She was several inches taller than Alison, her jeans and cotton blouse showing off her slender figure to perfection. Her huge blue eyes were widely spaced, the dusky lashes that surrounded them darkened by nature instead of mascara. Unconsciously, Alison found herself smiling in answer to the girl's mischievous grin. She couldn't have been much older than eighteen. "Yes?"

"Oh, Lord," the girl muttered wryly. "You aren't supposed to be here...I mean, I'm not supposed to be here. Jason's going to kill me. But I honestly thought you'd be gone." As if that explained everything, she shrugged good-naturedly. "The only thing to do is make the best of it. I'm Lana—Lana Harper. I'm here to clean the cottage, but you're not supposed to know that."

"I'm not? Why?" Alison asked in bewilderment. This was getting to be a habit of hers, stumbling over Jason's women, though this girl hardly seemed old enough to qualify. How did he keep them all straight? "I'm Alison Bennet. I guess Jason didn't tell you, but I'm living here indefinitely. Jason has moved into his apartment at the office."

"Yes, I know. I thought you were there, too. That's why I'm here." She laughed suddenly. "This sounds crazy! You see, I always clean the cottage for Jason after he's been out in the field for any length of time. I was supposed to wait until you left, though, before I came over today. Jason didn't think you'd let me clean up if you knew about it. Once the job was done, though, there would be no argument."

Alison opened the door, motioning for the girl to come in. "He's right. It's nice of you to offer, but it's not necessary. I was just leaving to go to Jason's office. I'll clean the cottage when I get back."

Even before the words were out of her mouth,

Lana was interrupting. "Please let me do this. Jason has been awfully good to me and my family, and this is just one of the ways I can pay him back. Believe it or not, I like cleaning. And you shouldn't have to clean a whole house before you unpack your things. So you just go on with what you were doing, and I'll have the place spotless before you get back." She flashed Alison a reassuring smile. "Oh, and would you tell Jason I'll be out to the office later? I wish he'd let me straighten up the mess he's made out there, but he won't let me touch it. He claims he knows where everything is, even though it looks as if it's been hit by a tornado."

Alison felt herself weakening. How could she object to such sincerity? "All right. I really do appreciate this, Lana. I hate to clean house. I'll give Jason your message, but I'd better hurry or he's going to be late for his meeting."

Conflicting emotions warred within her, disturbing Alison's concentration as she drove away. Lana seemed very fond of Jason. Didn't the man have any scruples? The girl was an infant, her experience practically nil compared to Jason's. How could he take advantage of such innocence? The seductive woman in his bedroom was more his speed. *They* no doubt understood each other very well. Any woman who wanted more than a casual affair should avoid him like the plague, Alison decided caustically. And that included herself.

Caught up in her own thoughts, she almost missed the correct exit from the expressway. She made an effort to pull her attention back to her driving.

This part of San Antonio was sparsely populated. The suburban housing was gradually giving way to farms. She was almost convinced she had driven right past his office when she spotted a small stucco building that fitted the description he had given her. As she pulled into the empty parking lot, she spied his name on the door and sighed in relief.

Her eyes traveled over the small building, and she had to admit it wasn't at all what she had been expecting. Oil exploration seemed so exciting. It conjured up pictures of rugged wildcatters and gushers spewing forth Texas tea. With any luck it was a very lucrative field, one which would eventually lead to corporate offices in a towering, smoky-glassed building. Somehow this small structure with its plain facade and pothole-ridden parking lot didn't at all fit the image. There were no windows, only an unimposing single glass door. No outward sign, other than the name on the door, indicated the profitable business located there.

Alison stepped inside and stopped short. The room was not overly large, and every available inch was utilized. Maps and photographs were pinned haphazardly to the walls, with geographical logs and a wide assortment of books jammed onto the metal shelves that lined three of the walls. A serviceable black vinyl couch was pushed up against the fourth wall, facing a desk that was more or less centered in the room. The desk was littered with papers that probably should have been filed in the cabinet at the end of the couch. From the top of the filing cabinet, a radio blared the news.

Alison grimaced and walked over to turn down the volume. Just as she touched the knob, the door that obviously led to Jason's private apartment opened. She turned quickly to find him standing on the threshold, his shirt unbuttoned to expose the muscled firmness of his chest. Her heart lurched painfully in her breast, her gaze drawn to him despite herself. She seemed destined to come across him in various stages of undress!

She forced her breathing to return to normal, but the blush that stole into her cheeks did not escape unnoticed. His eyes glinted with acknowledgment of it, but before he could say anything, she distracted him. "Your office is literally out in the sticks, Jason. Isn't it inconvenient?"

"Not really. I don't usually drill for oil in downtown San Antonio." Chuckling at her heightened color, he proceeded to button his shirt. "You brought my clothes, didn't you? This is the last clean shirt I've got."

"Y-yes." Alison cursed her stuttering tongue, angry with herself for not being more blasé. She was altogether too aware of him, and to make things worse, he knew it. Studiously she dragged her gaze from his, forcing herself to look around his office. "This place is a mess. How do you ever get any work done?"

He laughed at her expression. "If I'd wanted to be a file clerk, I'd have stayed with the large oil company I worked for after college. Having an office is one of the necessary evils of this business, but I spend as little time here as possible. I like to be in the field."

"I didn't know you worked for one of the big companies," she said in surprise. "What happened? Why didn't you stay with it?"

"It was a combination of things. Right after college, I had a field job at a drilling site. It was a good learning experience—it's important to know how to meet a production schedule and still stay within the budget. After a while, though, I was transferred back to headquarters and stuck in a staff job. In a large organization, that kind of work is essential, but I hated it. The executive merry-go-round is a bore. It just doesn't compare to the work done in the field."

"Is that why you quit?"

"Eventually." He motioned for her to sit on the couch while he made himself comfortable behind his desk. "I finally got the higher-ups to let me out of the office, and I was shipped off to Libya. It didn't last, however. After a couple of years they wanted me back at headquarters. I couldn't stomach the thought of another desk job, so I revolted and came home to start my own company." His eyes met hers. "You did the same thing. You didn't like your job, so you gave it up to come to Texas to write."

"But you're right back in an office," she reminded him.

"Only part of the time. Oh, there's paperwork, but that's only a small percentage of the actual effort involved in discovering a new field. There's a lot of self-satisfaction in searching through past drilling records and doing my own seismic testing. When a well pays off, it's through my efforts, no one else's."

Alison marveled at the change in him. As he talked the mockery was gone, and his eyes were dark with interest. His work was obviously close to his heart. Alison discovered to her surprise that she liked this side of him. How had she ever thought him unapproachable? With very little prompting from her, he seemed willing to talk for hours despite the fact that he had an appointment to keep. "It must have been difficult, starting your own company."

"The hardest part was getting the money to drill. The banks wouldn't loan me a nickel. Exploratory drilling is not exactly considered a sound business venture. So I had to turn to private investors. Grandmother was one of my first backers."

At Alison's start of surprise, he laughed. "She always did like a good bet. I explained to her the chances she was taking; there was a good possibility she'd never see her money again. But she insisted. And she made a nice profit from it, too."

He rose to his feet and walked around the desk, a mysterious smile relieving the hard angles of his face. "I'll be right back. I just remembered something I want to give you."

Alison barely had time to blink before he was back, placing a large, frayed volume in her hands. Her fingers trembled as she traced the letters imprinted in the faded maroon leather. "This is her album? A family album?" At Jason's nod, she lifted the cover, gasping at the image staring back at her. The picture was yellowed with age, but it was readily apparent that she favored her grandmother a great deal. Alison's face was narrower, her hair several shades darker, but their eyes were the same. And their smiles. The picture must have been taken when her grandmother was in her late teens or early twenties. Her mischievous grin and sparkling eyes almost lighted up the photograph. Alison grinned in response, elation flowing through her. She had found herself in her grandmother! Alison Ford Morgan was no longer a disembodied name, but a woman with a face much like her own.

She glanced up from her study of the picture to find Jason watching her. "Would it be vain of me to say she was very attractive?"

He laughed. "Not at all! If you've got it, flaunt it, I always say. I had a feeling you didn't realize just how much you resemble her. That's why I thought you'd like to have the album."

"Oh, I would. I do!" Realization swept over her. He was actually giving her these irreplaceable pictures! Unable to contain her excitement, she jumped up and hugged him. "Thank you so much! I never expected you to give me the family album. How can you bear to part with it?" Her eyes were dancing as she slipped out of his arms, which had returned her spontaneous embrace. She sat on the couch and pulled him down beside her. "Come and tell me who all these people are."

Laughingly Jason complied. "All right, but we can't stay long or I'm going to miss my appointment." Soon he was pointing out pictures of his grandfather, of himself much younger, with her grandmother, and even brown-toned snapshots of Alison's great-grandfather. They didn't have time to look at the entire album—that would have taken hours—but the brief glimpses momentarily appeased Alison's curiosity about her mother's immediate family. When Jason announced it was time to leave, she suddenly remembered the letters.

"What about Edward Smythe?" she asked. "Is his picture in the album? I spent most of the morning reading the letters he wrote to grandmother. He must have loved her very much. Didn't she have a picture of him?"

With a snap Jason closed the album and stood up. "No, his picture isn't in the album," he replied shortly. "As to whether or not he actually loved her, I don't know. Actions speak louder than words. But if someone loved me the way he supposedly loved grandmother, I'd run long and hard to get away from her."

"Why?" Alison asked, startled by his vehemence. "I haven't read the diaries yet, but from the letters I thought he adored her."

Jason shrugged, his expression once again closed. "Who knows? Maybe he did. I just think he had a funny way of showing it." He held out his hand. "If you'll give me your keys, I'll get my clothes out of your car, then we can go."

Automatically Alison handed him the keys and watched him stride out the door. Evidently the subject of Edward Smythe was closed. Jason was the most exasperating man! He could be incredibly thoughtful: he knew how curious she was about her mother's family, for example, so he unselfishly gave her pictures that must mean a great deal to him. Yet with the blink of an eye, he could be as stubborn as a mule. It was infuriating!

He came back into the office several minutes later, shrugging into the lightweight tan sports coat that matched his camel-colored slacks. "C'mon, let's go." His lips twitched at the malevolence of her glare. "Don't cloud up like a thunderstorm, Alison. Sulking won't get you any answers."

"I'm not sulking!" she denied indignantly. "Anyone would think I'm asking for top-secret information. Which is ridiculous. My God, Jason, it's ancient history! Why are you being so secretive?"

"Call it family loyalty if you like," he retorted nonchalantly, gesturing for her to precede him so he could lock the office door. "This isn't my secret to tell. Personally, I think it would have been better to let it out of the closet years ago. But as I said, it's not my secret."

Alison stalked to the car and huffily slid into the passenger seat. She wasn't ever again going to ask him anything. After all, she didn't have to be beaten over the head before she got the point. If he wanted her to know something about her grandmother, he'd have to volunteer the information, because she certainly wasn't going to ask! Crossing her arms across her chest, she stared moodily out the window, not even bothering to look at Jason when he got in the car.

"Damn!" The quiet curse broke the silence, and Alison looked at him in surprise. He was looking at the dashboard, his frown intensifying to an irritated scowl when he turned the ignition key and it only clicked in response. He turned his head sharply, his eyes piercing. "Did you have any problems starting the car when you left the cottage? Was it making any strange noises?"

"No." Alison schooled her features to remain impassive. She had to try desperately to conceal the laughter that was bubbling up inside her. It served him right. This couldn't have worked out better if she'd planned it herself.

Jason opened the door and stepped out of the car. "Slide over here into the driver's seat. I'm going to lift the hood. When I give you the signal, try the ignition."

Alison did as he instructed, patiently waiting for him to signal her to turn the key. Her view was limited by the raised hood; she could see little of what he was doing. When he finally did motion for her to try to start the car, the only response was another click.

Jason frowned and wiped his hands on his handkerchief before coming around to Alison's side. He glanced down at her, a thoroughly perplexed look on his face. "I don't understand why you haven't had any warning, but it sounds like something's wrong with the starter."

"Yes, I know," Alison replied baldly.

"You know?" he exclaimed. "Then why haven't you had it fixed?"

Alison tried not to smile at his irritation. "At the time, I didn't have the money. And after the mechanic showed me how to start it, it didn't seem necessary. It only acts up occasionally."

From his towering position he gave her a measured look. "Since you obviously know how to start the car, I guess the next question is, will you?"

"I might," she chuckled. She really should feel guilty for teasing him so, but it was about time he got a taste of his own medicine. Now maybe he'd understand how irritating he was when he refused to impart information she needed. "What time is your appointment?"

"Cut the fun and games, Alison," he advised sternly. "We both know you're going to start this car. It's just a matter of my paying your price. What is it? What do you want?"

"Don't be mad, Jason. I just want some answers about you-know-who." Her conscience bothered her for breaking her resolve not to ask him any more questions. She was taking unfair advantage, but she couldn't seem to stop herself. It was such a heaven-sent opportunity.

"No!" His legs were spread apart, his arms folded unyieldingly across his chest. "We can stay here all night, but I'm not telling you another thing about grandmother."

"Why? Because of some promise you made a thousand years ago?" At his curt nod, she added, "Does this mean you don't break promises?"

His eyes, alight with a threatening glare, met and held hers. "That's right. And if you make me miss this meeting, I promise you you'll live to regret it!"

Tension fairly crackled in the air, and Alison was stunned to discover it wasn't all anger. The beat of her heart accelerated to a trip-hammer pace; the ambiguity of his threat was deliciously alarming to her heightened senses. Dear God, what was wrong with her? She was much, much too aware of this man.

Silently she cursed him and her traitorous emotions. An overwhelming sense of panic gripped her, and she clothed it in anger. She had to get away. "Oh, all right!" With jerky movements she leaned over to the glove compartment and extracted a large screwdriver. As she did so she mumbled to herself, "The whole world has lost its sense of humor! Things are pretty bad when you can't even tease anyone anymore."

She stepped out of the car and glared up at him. "You're no fun, Jason. I was just teasing you and you puff up like a toad! Get behind the wheel and turn the key."

When he did as she instructed, she leaned over the fender and did something to the engine that he couldn't quite see. The car started immediately. With a triumphant smile, she closed the hood and returned to the passenger seat. "Okay, let's go."

The expression on Jason's face would have been hilarious if Alison hadn't been so disgusted with the entire situation. As it was, she was in no mood for smart remarks. "Are we going or not?" she asked impatiently.

With an economy of movement, he put the car in gear and pulled out of the parking lot. Once they were headed toward the city, Jason's glance slid toward Alison. "I had no idea I was harboring a closet mechanic. If your writing doesn't pay off, you can always open your own garage."

"Oh, shut up!" Alison complained, laughing despite herself. "I'm not a closet anything. Haven't you ever heard of necessity being the mother of invention? I wasn't always an heiress, you know. And repair work costs a fortune. So I learned to make do with what I had. I just use the screwdriver to jump the starter. It works every time."

"I'll remember that in case I ever have to borrow your car again," he replied with a grin.

After that they slipped into silence, but it was a comfortable silence. Alison occasionally glanced at Jason's profile, but his eyes were on the road, and he seemed unaware of her scrutiny. It galled her to admit it, but he had been entirely right in refusing to succumb to her blackmail tactics. She didn't know what had come over her. Maybe she'd been revolting against the attraction she felt for him. Such awareness was new to her; she didn't know how to handle it. Even when Jason wasn't deliberately exerting his charm on her, he still couldn't easily be ignored. If he ever did turn the full force of his magnetism on her, she would probably go up like kindling.

Jason turned off the expressway, and several minutes later they entered a quiet, affluent-looking neighborhood. Alison sat up straighter, glancing around in surprise. Didn't anyone in Texas conduct business in the usual, conventional method? John had appointments at all hours of the night, and now Jason was having a business meeting at someone's home. And this wasn't your average three-bedroom-two-bath house. Her eyes lingered for a moment on the attractive Tudor-style house they pulled up in front of. She glanced at Jason questioningly. "You're having a business meeting *here*?"

"Believe it or not, more deals are put together over a few drinks than are ever discussed in the office." He got out of the car, motioning for Alison to move into the driver's seat. "Thanks for the lift. And for the lesson in auto mechanics."

She would never live that down! "Forget it. The ride gave me a chance to see more of the city. I can't wait to explore. One of these days when I've got time I'm going to play tourist."

The sudden sight of a taxi driving down the street surprised her. She turned to him accusingly. "I thought you said San Antonio doesn't have taxis."

"No, I didn't. I said this wasn't New York. You were the one who assumed there were no taxis. Which there aren't, really. None of the drivers were that anxious to come out to the office to pick me up. Those that were willing said it would be at least an hour before they could get there, maybe more. I couldn't chance it."

He leaned down and brought his face almost level with hers. The slow smile he gave her caused her heart to pound crazily. Despite her best efforts, she was finding it almost impossible to remain indifferent to him—or indignant.

"Still, it was a long drive," he continued. "And an inconvenience. Since I got you here under false pretenses, I'd like to repay you."

Why did he have to ruin it? She was just beginning to think he wasn't half bad when he insulted her by offering money. True, she hadn't wanted to offer her services at first, but once she'd put her irritation behind her, she'd enjoyed his company. And now he was putting a price on her enjoyment. She was hurt, and her eyes reproached him. "I'm not a taxi service, Jason. I didn't give you a lift for the money."

"Who said anything about money?" Without warning, he eliminated the distance between them, covering her startled mouth with his own. His lips took bold possession of hers, languorously taking full advantage of her stunned surprise. Alison was devastated, her defenses in disarray. His deliberate expertise left her gasping, her senses intoxicated with his nearness. Feebly she sought to summon a token resistance, but the effort wasn't necessary. Slowly, almost reluctantly, he released her trembling lips, pulling back a hair's breadth to smile lazily into her confused eyes. "That, my little grease monkey," he breathed huskily, "is much better than money."

Alison swallowed convulsively, hardly hearing his words for the rushing of her blood in her ears. With bemused wonder she watched him walk away, unable to tear her gaze away from his retreating back. *You have no pride, Alison*

Bennet, she told herself as she saw him knock on the door, her senses still reeling from his sensuous assault. She had to admit she had been disappointed when he ended the kiss. She—

With a heart-rending jolt, she fell back to earth. The man who had kissed her with such unexpected passion was now enveloped in the arms of a gorgeous blonde, who had just opened the door of the house. Alison's eyes widened in disbelief as she watched. The woman was pulling Jason's head down, was giving him a kiss that was guaranteed to knock his socks off. And he certainly wasn't complaining.

For a moment Alison was too stunned to move—but only for a moment. White-hot anger seared her, incinerating the sensuous feelings she had enjoyed only minutes before. Her foot pushed the accelerator to the floor and her car leaped away from the curb with screeching tires.

You idiot! she chided herself fiercely as she drove along. A business meeting—sure! Like a gullible fool she had let him use her so he could keep a date. How much proof did she need to be convinced the man was nothing but a playboy? And an unscrupulous one at that, the way he went from one woman to the next.

Her grip tightened on the steering wheel, her thoughts in a turmoil. Wasn't Jason satisfied with the string of women already dogging his footsteps? A reporter, the brassy woman in his bed, Lana, and now a so-called business associate—the list was apparently endless. And she had forgotten to tell him Lana was going to pay a visit to the office. It would serve him right if he found himself in a compromising mess. But Alison wasn't his social secretary—it wasn't her job to juggle the women in his life.

For a fleeting moment, an unfamiliar feeling of longing swept over her, but determinedly she hardened her heart against it. If he thought she was going to start chasing him, he was crazy! She may have been temporarily blinded by his charm, but it wasn't a permanent condition by any means. Her eyes were wide open. She didn't care what he did. Any contact between them would be limited to the discussion of the mansion. His women—it was definitely a plurality—were of no concern to her. She didn't care if he started a harem!

CHAPTER FIVE

THE CUPBOARD DOOR SLAMMED SHUT with a bang. Alison, her arms full of the cupboard contents, hardly noticed as she struggled toward the kitchen table. Halfway there, a can of tomato soup started to slide. She readjusted her arms, hoping to stop its fall, but her frantic movements only succeeded in upsetting the rest of her load. Helplessly she watched her entire armload of cans and boxes crash to the floor, then scatter in all directions. "Hellfire and damnation!" she muttered.

It had been her own crazy idea to clean out the kitchen cabinets. Her hands settled on her blue-jean-clad hips and her eyes swept the room in disgust. Talk about a disaster area! The table was piled high with pots and pans, cookie sheets and an assortment of utensils. Glassware and a less than complete collection of blue willow china took up all the available counter space. And most of the canned goods were on the floor. It would take her hours to rearrange everything.

Philosophically Alison immersed her hands in warm soapy water and began to clean the insides of the cabinets. She welcomed the physical activity—it required little thought process, and at the moment she was tired of thinking. Ever since the previous night her mind had been following along a single track: Jason and his women, Jason and his kiss. Damn! Why did she keep harping on the subject? She didn't care whom he spent his time with, but it wasn't going to be her! He was an infuriating man, trouble with a capital T. And that was something she didn't need right now. She had enough problems to contend with without adding Jason to the list. Alison's writing was her paramount concern, and she refused to let anyone or anything interfere with it.

The night before she had arrived home tired and angry—not only with Jason but also with herself. She hardly knew the man, yet he had disturbed her from their first meeting. She hadn't even been able to concentrate on her manuscript. Every time she thought of her hero, her thoughts would slip back to Jason—an annoying occurrence at the best of times.

And then there was the mansion. With only a two-month period to have the place repaired, she didn't have any time to spare for dalliance. For the time being, she would squeeze in writing time whenever she could, but her days would be occupied primarily with the mansion. Despite Jason's skepticism, or perhaps because of it, she was determined to make wise decisions concerning the renovations. During her childhood the adage, "Waste not, want not," had been regularly drummed into her head. In later years she had often teased Aunt Gwen of coining all proverbs. But now the maxim made more sense than ever. Following such sage advice was the only way she would ever remain within her budget. She hated acting like a skinflint, but she would do anything to keep her inheritance.

"Hello? Is anyone at home?"

The lilting feminine call from the front porch shattered Alison's contemplative mood. She frowned, quickly wiping her hands on a kitchen towel. Now what? She wasn't expecting anyone—she didn't know anyone. The beginnings of suspicion hardened her eyes. Almost aggressively she marched into the living room. At the sight of the attractive blond woman who had just stepped into the room, she came to an abrupt halt. Her worst fears were realized. Another one of Jason's women! And this one put Lana Harper in the shade. Not much taller than Alison herself, she somehow managed to look sophisticated in jeans and an apple-green blouse. In contrast Alison felt positively dowdy. In self-defense she lifted her chin, ignoring the woman's friendly smile. "Yes?"

"You must be Alison—you're the spitting image of your grandmother. Jason told me you'd be getting settled in, so I thought I'd drop by and give you a hand. I'm Nancy Sommers." At Alison's puzzled frown, she explained, "John's sister."

"Oh." Relief washed over Alison, along with sudden embarrassment at her cool greeting. Hastily she gestured for her to come in, a warm smile of welcome on her face. "I'm so glad you came. Sorry if I seem sort of out of it. I was just in the middle of cleaning the kitchen."

"Good. I'll help you." Before Alison could offer a word of protest, the older woman strode past her into the kitchen, rolling up her sleeves. She didn't seem the least surprised by the chaos, and went immediately to the stack of blue willow china, turning her dancing eyes toward Alison. "Don't you just love this stuff? I think everyone's grandmother must have had a set of it. I know mine did. It always reminds me of steaming hot oatmeal on cold winter mornings."

"And bacon frying."

"And fresh coffee."

Alison laughed. "Are you sure your grandmother didn't live in New York? You've just described breakfast at my Aunt Gwen's."

Other childhood memories were dragged out and shared, and the two women were soon laughing like old friends. When Nancy discovered Alison was a writer, they immediately launched into a debate over their favorite authors. It wasn't until several hours later, when the kitchen was finally spotless, that they noticed the time.

"My gosh, it's after twelve o'clock! Tony's going to kill me. I'm supposed to meet him for lunch in ten minutes, and I'll never make it." Swiftly Nancy untied the apron she had earlier wrapped around her waist. "And I wanted to take a tour of the mansion! Would you believe I've never been inside it? Rats!"

Alison followed her to the door, grinning. "Don't worry. You can always come back. You probably wouldn't want to see it right now, anyway. It's a mess."

"Oh, I don't care about that—a little dirt never hurt anyone." The other woman glanced at her watch. "I've got to go!"

"Thanks for helping me clean the kitchen. You saved me hours of work."

Nancy flashed her a teasing grin. "I'll send you my bill."

When Nancy had left, Alison felt the loneliness closing in around her. Determinedly she put her idle hands to work preparing a light lunch, her thoughts centered on the woman's friendly visit. Alison already felt as if she had known her for years instead of hours. She sighed in relief. She hadn't wanted to admit it to herself, but she had been uneasy about leaving New York for a city where she knew absolutely no one. Now she knew those fears were groundless. With friendly people like Nancy around she wasn't going to be buried in the sticks with only her typewriter for companionship.

After lunch she unpacked her car, her eyes straying to the mansion several times as she did so. Her grandmother's love letters had whetted Alison's curiosity, creating more questions. She was convinced the answers would be found in the diaries—and in the mansion. It sat almost broodingly in its shelter of trees, harboring the secrets she couldn't even begin to guess. Would she ever know what tragic events had happened there?

The last box was finally in, and within seconds, Alison was back outside, trudging up the hill to the mansion. With pad and pencil in hand, she studied the structure, noting the obvious repairs and then searching keenly for the more obscure flaws. The most conspicuous thing was the windows. Some were merely cracked, but many had gaping holes, and she couldn't find one without a flaw. Walking slowly around the house, she counted them and was staggered by the sum. Forty-four windows! And that didn't include the den, which was supposed to be solid glass but had long ago been shattered by careless hands. Dear God, the glass alone would cost a small fortune! And there was still the wiring and the roof to be checked out, not to mention the plumbing. Slightly dazed by the thoughts that were bombarding her, she entered the house with mounting dread. Wallpaper, floors, ceilings, light fixtures and eight bathrooms! How in heaven's name was she going to have it all repaired for the allotted sum of money, which seemed to grow pitifully smaller with each passing moment? Her hasty bet came back to haunt her, and she suddenly wanted to kick herself for her stupidity. She could still see the gleam in Jason's blue eyes when he had challenged her. That rat! Knowing she had let the dirt and litter blind her to the real repairs needed, he had tricked her into making an agreement he was positive she would lose.

Alison had an overwhelming urge to cry. What was she going to do? The renovations needed were extensive, much more so than she had initially realized. But she couldn't lose the place! Her grandmother, her writing—everything—was tied up together. And she wasn't going to let it be taken from her without a fight. Her eyes hardened with determination. If she had to, she would do most of the work herself. She didn't know anything about renovating a house, but she'd learn. Jason wasn't taking the mansion from her!

The telephone book became her ally when she returned to the cottage in the middle of the afternoon. The day had grown much hotter, and her blouse was sticking to her back, the curls at her forehead and neck clinging to her skin. Armed with the directory's reassuring bulk and a large glass of iced lemonade, she settled down to search out the services she would be needing.

Time passed quickly as she sought the advice of people more expert than herself. The list of numbers she wrote out was a long one, but purposefully she went down it, explaining the situation to electricians, plumbers and roofers. When she replaced the telephone receiver for the last time, a satisfied smile shone on her face. Not bad for a day's work. Tomorrow would see the arrival of the first workers. Granted, they would only be giving estimates and offering any advice she might need, but it was a very important first step toward the return of the mansion to its previous elegance.

Glancing at her watch, she started in surprise. So engrossed had she been in her work, she had hardly noticed the passing of time. The day was almost gone. Long shadows had crept into the yard, and along with them came an increased awareness of her solitude.

Loneliness engulfed her. Had she made a dreadful mistake in coming to Texas? Nothing was as she had expected. The mansion might very well be lost to her within two months. Her writing had, from necessity, been relegated to a part-time activity, superseded by the renovation work she had to oversee. She was frequently preoccupied by the mystery of her grandmother's life, an enigma she was still trying to explain. And thoughts of Jason and his string of women were constantly interrupting her peace of mind....

A twinkle appeared in her eyes. What a ridiculous way to describe him! Regardless of how she tried, however, she couldn't separate him from the women in his life. They were always there, waiting in the background, ready to step forward with the least encouragement.

Alison sighed. She had successfully closed her mind to Jason Morgan for most of the day. If she could only be so lucky tonight.

In a burst of energy, she entered the kitchen, determined to cook dinner and forget her problems. The refrigerator, the one place she hadn't scrubbed thoroughly that morning, yielded a varied selection of food, much to her surprise. Somehow she couldn't see Jason traipsing down the aisles of a supermarket in search of bargains. Taking out eggs, onions and a package of hamburger meat, she quickly mixed up a meat loaf and placed it in the oven to cook. She put potatoes on the stove to boil while she prepared a salad.

Cooking for one was going to be a problem, she realized. She would have to learn to cook all over again, or she would be eating a lot of left-overs. Idly she wondered if Jason had the same problem. It wasn't likely, not with all the women trying to catch him. He probably didn't even know how to cook.

Annoyance flickered briefly across the usually smooth features of her face. *You're at it again, Alison!* she told herself in disgust. The man had done nothing more than give her her grandmother's photograph album and kiss her. That didn't give him the right to monopolize her thoughts!

The aromatic smell of the meat loaf drifted through the cottage, tantalizing her. Supper was nearly done, and she was standing here like an idiot, mooning over a modern-day Don Juan! She had better things to do. Resolutely she walked to the cabinet where she had rearranged the china and extracted a plate.

"My, my, aren't we the busy homemaker. Is all this for my benefit?"

The caustic remark caught Alison completely by surprise. With a muffled cry she whirled around, and as she did the plate flew out of her hand to shatter in a million pieces at her feet. Jason stood in the doorway, a mocking smile on his face. His indigo eyes, quick and assessing, missed nothing as they swept from the stove to her apron-clad body, then to her cheeks, which were rosy from the stove's heat and his unexpected arrival.

Suddenly the memory of their last meeting came between them. The heat in Alison's cheeks intensified, then anger coursed through her at her own involuntary reaction. In self-defense she lashed out at him. "Now look what you've done! Sneaking up on a person without any warning...you scared the devil out of me! Haven't you ever heard of knocking?"

His eyebrows rose in surprise. "I did knock. Obviously you didn't hear me."

Her eyes were dark with fury, and she continued as if he hadn't spoken. "How dare you come in here and make cracks about me and my cooking! I wouldn't boil water for you, Jason Morgan! If you weren't so puffed up with your own importance, you'd realize I wouldn't go to all this trouble just for you! I wasn't even expecting you!"

"Damn it! If you'll give me a chance to explain...." He cursed softly under his breath, his hand reaching up to ruffle his hair in irritation. Carefully he stepped toward her, his shoes grinding the shattered china into the floor. "Didn't Nancy tell you I was coming by?"

"Nancy?" she asked in confusion. "What does Nancy have to do with this?"

"Everything. I told her to tell you I'd be by

this afternoon. I should have called. She obviously forgot."

"She did have to leave suddenly." Her eyes fell to the broken plate, and in sudden dismay she forgot his mockery and her anger. "Grandmother's china!" she moaned. "I can't even glue it back together." She dropped to her knees, her fingers reaching for the blue-and-white shards.

"Watch it, you'll cut yourself," Jason warned. In two strides he was at her side, his fingers closing around her wrist to pull her up beside him. The contact was electric. He eyed her warily, half expecting a resurgence of her anger, but Alison was too busy trying to repress the sudden response of her senses. With his fingers wrapped around her wrist, surely he could feel the effect he was having on her.

It's only physical, she told herself sternly as she tried to unobtrusively free herself from his hold. He was one of the most attractive men she had ever met. Any woman would have found herself responding to him. And every woman did; that was the problem. Her eyes flickered to his when he refused to release her. "If you'll let go of my wrist, I'll sweep up this mess."

"I'll do it. It's my fault anyway." His fingers caressed her wrist, creating an insidious warmth that shot up her arm to steal her breath. Her eyes fled from his, and he chuckled briefly.

Then he released her to get the broom from the closet where it hung. "I'm sorry I scared you. I really thought you heard me come in the front door. The only. . . ." He sniffed the air suddenly, his eyes moving to hers questioningly. "Is something burning?"

"My meat loaf!" She flew to the stove and pulled open the door, automatically recoiling from the oven's scorching heat. Grabbing for the pot holders, she hurriedly rescued her dinner and set it on the counter. "Thank heavens!" she sighed in relief. "Another few minutes and it would have been burned." She turned to find Jason expertly wielding the broom and dust pan. An involuntary laugh escaped her. "Aha! Your secret is out—you have been housebroken. What lady was responsible for that?"

"Grandmother, naturally." Deftly he deposited the broken plate into the trash. "She was one of the original women's libbers. She didn't believe in assigning household duties according to sex. Believe me, when I was growing up I did my share around the house."

His words conjured up pictures of him swathed in an apron, cleaning and ironing. "You'll make some woman a wonderful husband."

"Don't you believe it." His eyes skimmed over her teasingly. "Is that what you're looking for in a husband—chief cook and bottle washer?"

Alison shook her head, suddenly not wanting to continue that vein of conversation. Vainly she tried to remind herself he was not to be trusted. At any moment another lovesick woman would show up on the doorstep. But her heart refused to listen to such sage advice. She blurted out, "Why don't you stay for dinner? There's plenty."

The smile that accompanied her words accomplished little—Jason seemed completely impervious to it. She sighed in disappointment when he declined the invitation.

"Sorry, Alison, I can't. I've got another business dinner tonight. Let me take a rain check, though. I dropped by to pick up a seismic report I left in my bedroom. And to retrieve one of my suits, which you forgot to bring to the apartment." He glanced at his watch. "Damn! I'll never be able to make it to the apartment before dinner."

"Why do you have to go to the apartment first?"

"To shower and clean up," he replied absently. "Mr. Carlson always insists on discussing business in one of the city's most elegant French restaurants. I'm hardly dressed for it. I'd much rather relax with a nice cold beer."

Another business dinner, she thought wryly. But she had to admit this one did sound legitimate. "You can shower here, Jason," she volunteered. "I don't mind. After all you *are* half owner of the cottage."

His sharp gaze studied her intently. "Are you sure you don't mind? I wouldn't even bother with the meeting, but for the last two months, I've been trying to get Mr. Carlson to agree to an oil lease. He's as cagey as an old lion, but I think he's beginning to weaken."

"Really, I don't mind," she assured him. "Go on, and let me eat before my dinner gets cold."

Evidently convinced of her sincerity, he grinned boyishly. "Thanks, Alison. I owe you one."

"So much for being irresistible," she said sardonically as he disappeared from view. She had asked him to dinner only because she was lonely. She would have asked the same thing of John or anyone else who arrived on her doorstep at mealtime. *Sure, Alison,* her conscience taunted her. Jason's dark good looks and devastating charm didn't enter into it at all!

Rejecting the depression that was threatening to overtake her, she reached for another plate and filled it with food she really didn't want. As she sat down at the table, her glance hovered at the empty chair opposite her before returning to her plate. How could she eat? Her appetite had fled when Jason had turned her invitation down. Lethargically she picked up her fork and forced herself to eat. She tried to concentrate on her plans for the house, but to no avail. Two blue eyes, alight with mockery, kept getting in the way of her thoughts. The meat loaf, for all the enjoyment she received from it, might just as well have been mush. The potatoes she pushed from one side of the plate to the other.

The ringing of the telephone interrupted her lonely meal, and she welcomed the distraction. But when a husky, feminine voice asked to speak to Jason, she found herself gritting her teeth. "I'm sorry, Jason can't come to the phone right now. May I take a message?"

"Are you sure?" the caller asked suspiciously. "If you tell him Christina Carlson is on the line, I'm sure he'll take the call. We have a dinner date tonight, and it's imperative I speak with him."

Alison immediately took exception to the woman's haughty tone. It would serve her right if Jason told her to go jump in the lake. With an acquiescent murmur, however, she laid down the phone. Grudgingly she climbed the stairs and knocked at the bathroom door. "Jason, there's a telephone call for you," she called loudly over the running water she could hear through the closed door.

The sound of the water ceased abruptly. "Find out who it is."

"It's Christina Carlson." His order annoyed

her and she didn't attempt to inject any warmth into her voice.

"What does she want?" he asked through the still-closed door.

The panels of the bathroom door received the glaring look she wanted to give him. "How do I know what she wants?" she asked in exasperation. "She didn't say."

"Never mind. I'll ask her myself," he said.

Suddenly the paneled door was pulled open and Alison found herself face to face with Jason. He was only inches away, towering over her, the fresh, clean scent of him drifting toward her, assailing her senses. She felt the blood rush to her face as her eyes were drawn unresistingly down his tall body, but there was no cause for embarrassment. His navy blue terry robe, belted at the waist, amply covered his tanned physique.

His deep chuckle did nothing to lessen the heat in her cheeks as he knowingly followed the path her eyes had taken. Hurriedly she returned her gaze to his face, having to tilt her head back in order to meet his glance with flashing eyes. "Don't you ever wear any clothes?"

His dark brows rose at her tone and his lips twitched traitorously. His features were fixed in an expression of mild interest. His eyes, however, were dancing with laughter he made no effort to conceal. "Not when I take a shower—it's an odd quirk I have. I take it you don't care for my robe. No problem. I'll change." His hand at the belt, he made a movement to untie it.

With a muffled groan, Alison whirled away from him, her cheeks still flaming, and marched to her bedroom door. Her back was ramrod straight as she said without looking at him, "You'd better hurry. Your friend will wonder what's happened to you." Stepping into her room, she closed the door forcefully behind her and leaned weakly against it. Even through the door she could hear his laughter, the vibrant tones fanning her anger.

So he was having dinner with a cagey old lion! She sounded more like a purring cat to Alison! And if Jason wasn't careful, he just might be dessert. The woman's voice was irritatingly familiar....

Realization hit her like a Mack truck. She was the same woman who had lain in wait for Jason in his bedroom!

Clouds of confusion drifted through Alison's mind. What was wrong with her? She was depressed and angry, her thoughts centered on things that were none of her business. This constant state of turmoil was new to her. It wasn't like her to blow up over trivial things, but since meeting Jason Morgan she had done nothing but lose her temper. He seemed to delight in irritating her. In self-defense, she found herself snapping at Jason every time he came within her line of vision. He must think her some kind of a shrew. She'd have to start watching her tongue or he would start avoiding her, a thought that sent her spirits plummeting.

Squaring her shoulders, she walked to the dresser and ran a comb through her hair before returning to the hall. The sound of his low laughter drifted to her as she descended the stairs. Resolutely she pushed away the anger that was ready to spring into life, refusing to give in to the mixed feelings she wouldn't put a name to. Instead she proceeded to the kitchen, studiously ignoring his stance by the window where he was laughingly conversing with the sultry-voiced Christina Carlson. In her flight, Alison failed to see the speculative light in his eyes as he watched her retreat.

Squirting emerald green dishwashing detergent into the stainless steel sink, she watched the force of the water turn the soap into bubbles. Alison thankfully immersed her hands in the warm water, hoping the activity of washing dishes would chase away her disquieting thoughts. The sounds from the living room had ceased; she could only assume Jason had hung up and was getting dressed.

She could still hear the sensuous voice of the caller asking for Jason. Regardless of how he referred to their dinner date, the lady definitely didn't have business on her mind! Alison scowled at the pot she was attempting to wash. She was probably tall and leggy, with a voluptuous figure that had drawn more than its share of wolf whistles. And with a voice like that, she had to be a blonde with a beautiful tan. She certainly would not have freckles!

Glumly she swished the pans through the rinse water before banging them loudly onto the drainer to dry. The noise relieved her tension, bringing a smile to her lips as she reached behind her to untie her apron. Turning to hang it up, she halted in momentary surprise, her eyes widening at the sight of Jason standing in the doorway.

A white shirt and beige sports coat highlighted the deep bronze of his tan, and his chocolate brown tailored slacks matched the muted browns of his tie. Advancing into the room, he eyed her uneasily. "What are you smiling about?"

"I'm plotting a murder," she retorted sweetly. Her heartbeat had accelerated rapidly at his sudden appearance and was only just now returning to normal.

"Not mine, I hope." His eyes traveled the contours of her face searchingly, as if seeking a clue to her mood. When he could find none, he frowned slightly. "Look, Alison, I'm sorry about tonight. I know it must be lonely for you, being new in town and not knowing anyone. As soon as I get a chance, I'll introduce you around. But this meeting tonight is—"

"Don't worry about it, Jason," she interrupted. "I didn't expect you to stay and entertain me. I've got a lot to do tonight—it'll probably be midnight before I get to bed. I want to start reading grandmother's diaries, and I haven't written anything since I left New York. Once I get involved in that, I won't have time to be lonely."

Through the screen of her thick lashes she watched his face, waiting to see if he believed the brave words spoken entirely for his benefit. She hadn't lied. She planned to do just exactly what she claimed. If, however, he had changed his mind and decided to stay, she would have tossed her plans right out the window. But she had no desire to be an obligation to him, honored by his company simply because he felt sorry for her. She had more pride than that. Nothing would induce her to reveal just how much she would have liked him to stay or how she dreaded the thought of a solitary evening.

As he looked at her thoughtfully, his expression lightened only slightly. It was obvious he was not thoroughly convinced. "I still feel like a heel for deserting you this way. But if you're sure you want to write, I guess you don't want company." Glancing at his watch, he pulled himself away from the doorjamb. "I'd better be leaving. Don't work too hard."

"I won't. Good night." Her words were spoken to an empty room, however, for his long legs had quickly covered the distance to the door.

With his leaving, the house seemed to grow cold and empty, its vital life-force having deserted it in favor of a business meeting. Dispirited, Alison wandered into the silence of the living room, her idle hands reaching out to straighten the painting hanging over the fireplace. With one slim finger she traced the curve of a crystal vase that she had earlier filled with honeysuckle, its sweet scent filling the room with the essence of spring. A sigh escaped her; she couldn't seem to shake the despondency that gripped her. Her dull eyes lingered on the doorway to her tiny office. She had told Jason she was going to spend the evening writing, but her words had mainly been to save her injured pride and relieve the guilt that she felt was nagging him....

But eventually the desire to surround herself with fictional characters and become engrossed in a world of her own imaginings drew her to the typewriter. Taking off the gray plastic cover, she inserted a sheet of white paper, only to stare at it blankly. For several minutes she was unable to think of one single word. What a time to get writer's block!

The oppressive silence of the cottage hovered over her, mocking her inability to write. In self-defense she turned on the radio, but the country and western tunes did nothing to dispel her mood, so she snapped it off again. Writing was out, so that left reading. She ran upstairs.

Moments later she was curled up on the couch with her grandmother's first diary. The leather-bound volume retained a faint, musty scent that seemed to draw Alison back to a distant era. With a sense of mounting excitement, she opened the book carefully to reveal the first entry.

The flowing script was that of a young girl, and the passages were at first haphazard, often skipping weeks at a time. The main topic of interest seemed to be school; little had been written about her home life. But when Alison Ford Morgan was seventeen, her mother had died and everything had changed. She had obviously been shattered by the loss. Her father, too, had been devastated, unable to pull out of the depression he had sunk into as a result of his wife's death. He'd lost his job, thus forcing his daughter to quit school and seek employment. She'd been hired as a seamstress and maid to the mansion's mistress, and her father had been employed as head gardener.

Alison was astounded by the depth of emotion revealed in her grandmother's entries. The people she wrote about were real, with real joys and heartaches. Without even realizing it, Alison found herself spirited into the pages of the diary, encouraging her sensitive, heart-broken great-grandfather, sharing her grand-mother's joy when he'd gradually returned to the business of living. Their struggle together had been a difficult one, their daily existence hard. She marveled at her grandmother's energy and determination. Alison Ford Morgan had adored her father, and the diary's warmest passages were those delighting in their com-radery and support for each other. Despite the excessive demands of their employers, their life together had had its bright spots.

Alison absently closed the diary at the conclu-sion of the first year and stared thoughtfully into space. With astonishing ease, she had been drawn into her grandmother's memoirs, exper-iencing for herself her grandmother's emotions. She found herself liking and disliking the same people, laughing at or cursing the tricks of fate that happened to her. Why couldn't she herself write like that?

She walked into the office, picked up the first chapter of her manuscript and began to read. After several minutes she dropped it in disgust. The first ten pages were lifeless, that was the problem! Even her grandmother's diary had more life than this manuscript.

Again she rolled a sheet of paper into the typewriter, her writer's block forgotten. Arabella Clayton, the heroine of her novel, was too insipid; she lacked the fire necessary to attract anyone, let alone the hero. And since the focus of the manuscript was on her, it was with her the changes had to begin.

With a brutality she almost found amusing, Alison replaced her sweet Southern belle with a sometimes defiant and never conventional tomboy, the despair of her genteel mother. Despite her rough exterior, the new Arabella was vivacious and stubborn, with an unwavering faith in her family. To make such drastic changes in a character's personality, especially the heroine's, Alison knew she would have to do extensive rewriting. But as she read over the changes she had made in the first chapter, she laughed. Now this girl she liked! No one would ever call her insipid.

The sudden ringing of the telephone grated on her nerves, effectively drawing her out of the private world she had been encased in for the past two hours. Irritated by the interruption, she hurried into the living room to answer it. Her abrupt hello was met by silence. She was on the point of hanging up when she heard a familiar voice.

"Alison, is that you?" John Peters asked in a stunned voice.

Smiling at his surprise, she replied, "Yes, John, it's me. How are you?"

"Fine. I. . .actually, I'm a little surprised. I called to discuss some business with Jason. You're the last person I expected to answer the phone."

"I'm sorry, John, but he's not here. He's having dinner with a client."

"And he left you there alone?" The surprise in his voice quickly bristled into anger. "What the devil's the matter with him? I know you two were at each other's throats the first time you met. But that's no reason to invite you to the cottage and then desert you while he has dinner with a client. It's downright rude! Just wait till I see him!"

With cheeks faintly flushed, Alison sought to stem his rising irritation. "Actually, John, it wasn't quite the way you think. Jason didn't invite me to the cottage. I more or less invited myself. You see, I'm living here."

"You're what? But what. . .when did all this happen?"

"The night of my arrival. I moved into the cottage, and Jason volunteered to stay at the apartment behind his office."

Wearily she raked her fingers through her short curls and arched her back in an effort to relieve its sudden aching. "Look, John, I'm kind of tired. And I'd really rather not discuss this over the phone, if you don't mind."

"Of course." Immediately solicitous, he asked, "Are you settling in all right? Do you need any help?"

"Thanks for the offer, but everything's fine. Your sister came over this morning and helped me clean out the kitchen cupboards. And I unpacked the rest of my things after lunch."

"Nancy was there?" he exclaimed in surprise. "My sister Nancy?"

Alison laughed. "She said she was your sister, and I didn't have any reason to doubt her. She stayed about two hours. I really like her."

"Good. So you're all settled in?"

"For now. The rest of my things still have to be shipped from New York, though there'll be a few things I won't be needing—like my ice skates and winter coat."

He chuckled softly. "So the heat's getting to you, is it? Well, don't let it fool you; it does get cold enough for a winter coat, especially when a blue norther blows in."

"Blue norther? What in the world is that?" she asked, intrigued.

"That's a cold front to you Yankees." When their joint laughter died down, he asked, "Did you and Jason get everything worked out about the mansion?"

Laughingly she exclaimed, "Yes, but only after a lot of fast talking on my part. I'm sorry about the scene in your office. I don't know what got into me."

"I do," he retorted in mock disgust. "Jason Morgan. I've watched it happen since our days in college together, and I still don't understand it. Love him or hate him, I've yet to meet a woman who can remain indifferent to Jason."

"Oh, but I—"

"Don't bother denying it, Alison," he interrupted. "Remember, I was there. The sparks flew when you first laid eyes on him." He laughed softly at her silence. "See, you should have had dinner with me that first night instead of with Jason. He's been chased by countless women, the lucky bum! I don't know how he does it. It must be the dark hair." At Alison's giggle, he chuckled, "Don't laugh—it's not funny! And it's not as if he goes around chasing women. They chase him! Somehow he always manages to elude them. If you really want to get his attention, don't fall down at his feet like those other airheads. Most women are so anxious to get him to the altar, they wouldn't dream of telling him no."

"But, John, I wasn't trying to get his attention. I really do want to keep the mansion."

"I know, and you just may be the one to make him change his mind. You've got more of your grandmother in you than you think. She wouldn't let him get away with anything. And you shouldn't either. That's why you need to go out with me. You don't want Jason to think you're sitting at home waiting for him to call."

Alison smiled into the phone. John was so open and predictable, so refreshing after Jason's moodiness. "What did you have in mind?"

"Nancy's having a barbecue tomorrow night. Would you like to go? It would give you a chance to meet people and make new friends."

The thought of spending another evening alone was more than she could stand; eagerly she accepted his invitation. "I'd love to, John. It sounds like fun. What time?"

"I'll pick you up at seven. Oh, and bring your bathing suit. There'll be swimming, too."

"Sounds better and better. I'll see you then." Hanging up the receiver, Alison climbed the stairs with a light heart. As she prepared for bed, her eyes glowed with quiet excitement. Meeting other people would, she hoped, get her mind off Jason. Then, just maybe, she would be able to get over this stupid, schoolgirl infatuation she seemed to have for him!

CHAPTER SIX

WEARILY ALISON PUSHED the clinging tendrils of hair away from her face, wishing in vain for a cooling breeze. Lord, it was hot! Not a breath of air stirred, the cloudless azure sky offering no respite from the piercing heat of the sun's rays. Only the cicadas seemed to be enjoying the oppressive heat; their shrill singing droned on incessantly. Licking her lips to ease their dryness, she shaded her eyes from the bright glare, trying to make out the city skyline in the distance. Waves of heat blurred the silhouette of old and new buildings, causing it to waver before her eyes. With a sigh, she stepped back into the large bedroom located on the second floor of the mansion. What she wouldn't give for an icy drink and a dip in a cold swimming pool! But in this heat the water would probably be tepid, she thought wryly. A noise in the hall distracted her thoughts from the heat. Turning around, she smiled at the gray-haired man who stepped into the room, at the look of disgust on his weathered face as he noted the state of the room.

"Don't blame me, Mr. Halston," she said. "I had nothing to do with the condition of the house. I only hope it hasn't gone so far that it can't be saved. I would hate to see it torn down."

"Don't be worrying about that," he replied reassuringly. "Back in the days when this house was built, they built 'em to last. I just hate to see a place like this neglected. Whoever allowed this to happen ought to be horsewhipped!"

"I agree, but I'm afraid I have no idea who the culprit is." Shoving her hands into the pockets of her jeans, she asked hesitantly, "Have...have you made a decision about the plumbing? Does it all have to be replaced?" The thought of having to replace the fixtures of eight bathrooms was a daunting one. She almost cringed as she awaited his answer.

"Now, Miss Bennet, don't be so pessimistic!" he admonished kindly. A twinkle lighted his dark eyes as she heaved a sigh of relief.

"Surprisingly, the second-floor bathrooms seem to have survived in much better shape than the ground-level ones. Even the shower doors are still intact. Of course, if you want to modernize up here, you can. But there's nothing wrong with any of the pipes or the fixtures. You might want to change the tile, though. I don't know who picked out the colors. Maroon and gray aren't bad, but that shade of green is absolutely hideous! Of course, it's your decision."

Laughing at his humorous expression, Alison declined the offer. "If there's nothing wrong except the colors, I'd rather leave them. They can always be changed later. What about the downstairs?"

Taking out a small pad of paper, the man shook his head. "Now that's another story. You probably noticed that the kitchen has been stripped of everything, including the sinks. The hot-water heater is ancient; it definitely has to go. And the four remaining bathrooms have really been abused—everything will have to be replaced."

With a sigh, Alison sat down on the wide window ledge. "How about the heating and air conditioning?"

Grinning, the plumber replaced his note pad in his shirt pocket. "I don't know how to tell you this, but there isn't any air conditioning." At her gasp of dismay, he chuckled. "You must remember, this house was built before the days of such modern luxuries. There are, however, two large attic fans. I know that's little consolation, but at least they draw the heat from the house. As for the heating system, it's located in the basement and it's very old. I doubt if you could get parts for it. For the moment, it works, although it needs a good cleaning, as does everything else. I recommend you replace it."

Rising to her feet, Alison paced up and down indecisively. This was all so new to her. There were so many things to consider. The repairs Mr. Halston was suggesting would take a third of her money. What if the other renovations cost more than she anticipated? She simply couldn't afford to chance it. "Only replace the fixtures that are absolutely necessary, Mr. Halston. As for the furnace, as long as it's working, it will have to do. I may be able to replace it at a later date, but not now."

"Whatever you say. I'll call you sometime in the next few days to let you know when I'll be able to start work."

Shaking hands with him, she escorted him to the front drive where he had parked his truck. "Thank you so much, Mr. Halston I'm going to try to clean up most of the house before you come out to work. I'll be waiting for your call." Waving goodbye, she watched his truck depart before walking slowly back to the cottage. So far, she was pleased with the reports different professionals had made to her. The roof was slate and required no repairs whatsoever. In fact, she had been assured it would last for years. The wiring was adequate, although there were a few rooms where wall sockets had to be replaced. And every room would need light fixtures. . . .

The sun was on its downward path, casting long shadows on the lawn, when she finally dressed for her date with John. Her maillot swimsuit clung to her sinuous figure, nicely displaying her curves. The honey color of her tan was highlighted by the terra-cotta color as well as by the black-and-white stripes that ran from the scooped neckline, down the sides of her breasts and waist to meet at the center of the deep U-shaped back. Reaching for the matching wraparound skirt, she pulled the waistband snugly around her and tied it at the side, allowing the skirt's full folds to fall around her.

She was already applying mascara to her dark lashes when a pounding at the front door startled her. She frowned. Who could that be? She didn't have time for visitors before John arrived.

"Alison? Where are you?"

The deep timbre of Jason's voice froze her in her tracks before the wild beating of her heart pumped color into her cheeks. What was he doing here? She swallowed, forcing her voice to an even keel as she called, "I'm upstairs, Jason. I'll be right down."

The sound of his feet on the stairs told her he had ignored her call, and his cursory knock gave her little notice before he stepped into her room.

Alison caught her breath, unprepared for the sight of him. He was dressed casually in jeans and a cream-colored cowboy shirt, the open collar revealing the strong column of his neck. His impatient fingers had raked his hair into wild disarray. His blue eyes danced with a devilish light as the searing scrutiny of his gaze swept over her.

Alison's heart tripped over itself. As his piercing look reached across the room to caress her, her skin burned from the almost physical touch of his eyes. Feeling herself mesmerized by him, she fought against it, trying to tear her gaze away. Her slightly dazed eyes returned to the mirror, where she studiously avoided his reflection and continued applying her mascara. It smeared, and with a disgusted exclamation she reached for a tissue.

"You haven't started cooking dinner, have you?"

The unexpectedness of his question took Alison by surprise. She shook her head.

"Good. Then I can collect on that rain check you gave out last night. Is there anywhere special you'd like to go?"

Conflicting emotions warred within her—disappointment, anger, excitement. She was shocked to discover she wanted nothing more than to go with him. Yesterday she would have been walking on air if he had asked her to dinner. Much as she had fought it, she'd been attracted to him from the moment they'd met.... Just like half the women in San Antonio; she forced herself to remember that. But it was hard, terribly hard. She picked up the mascara again, the calmness of her features revealing little of her racing thoughts. "I'm sorry, Jason. I've already got a date for tonight."

His eyes narrowed at her words; he walked into the room with the quiet tread of a panther and came to a halt directly behind her. Lazily, as if waiting to pounce, he watched her every movement. "Oh, really? With whom?" he finally asked after the silence had stretched unbearably.

Alison bristled at his tone of surprise, and she whirled around to face him. "Yes, really!" she said sarcastically. "Why is it every time we talk I get the impression you're questioning my competence? First you ridiculed my ability to have the mansion repaired without your expert guidance, and now you're deriding my ability to get a date! There really is no bounds to your audacity! Well, let me tell you something that may surprise you, Jason Morgan. I don't need you to hold my hand and show me the way. I don't need you to—"

In one fluid motion his hands grabbed her shoulders and hauled her against his chest, cutting off her tirade in a gasp. His blue eyes had darkened alarmingly and a tightly clenched muscle ticked warningly along his jaw. "Watch it, Alison! You're pushing your luck," he growled. "I'm getting damn tired of your always jumping to the wrong conclusion about me. I came in here to see if you'd like to go out. I know how hard you've been working; I thought you'd like a break. But you throw my suggestion back in my face. If you don't want to go, all you have to do is say no. I've heard the word before. And I wasn't questioning your ability to get a date. I was just surprised. I didn't know you knew anyone else in town."

Appalled that she had again made a mistake, she felt a painful blush burn her cheeks. She tilted her head back to look into his eyes, angry eyes that were inches away from her own. "I... I'm sorry, Jason. I didn't mean to snap at you. John Peters called last night and asked me to his sister's barbecue. If I had known you wanted to—"

"Forget it. I should have asked you sooner. But I got tied up in meetings and lost track of time. It seems that John didn't, though. He knows a pretty girl when he sees one."

Again his eyes swept over her figure; this time the anger was replaced by a glowing appreciation that sent the blood pumping through her veins. His hands tightened on her bare shoulders to draw her even closer to his powerful frame.

Spellbound by the unspoken message his eyes were transmitting, Alison was unable to tear her gaze away. She was sure he could feel the frantic beating of her heart, so closely was she wrapped in his arms. His eyes left hers to focus on the trembling softness of her lips. When he traced the sensitive outline of her mouth with his finger, a sensuous smile played on his own lips. "Do you have any idea how sexy you look in that outfit?" he murmured. "If I had any sense, I wouldn't let you go near John Peters dressed like that."

"You couldn't stop me." Alison hardly recognized her own voice, which was husky with strange emotions.

"Oh, no?" he asked mockingly. His hand brushed her cheek and came to rest just below her ear. His thumb lifted her chin as his head began its descent toward her softly parted lips.

The pealing of the door bell shattered the spell, destroying the moment. Alison stiffened in his arms, her hands fluttering to the hard muscles of his chest. "That's probably... J-John," she said breathlessly. She avoided meeting his gaze lest he should see how moved she was by what had nearly happened. "I have to go."

Smiling sardonically, he stepped away and motioned toward the door. "You don't want to keep John waiting. He might start to wonder what's keeping you. Or should I say who?"

As he walked from the room, she caught the flicker of annoyance in the depths of his eyes, and she stared at his retreating back quizzically. She longed to call after him, to question his sudden ill temper, but instead she held her tongue.

THE PARTY WAS IN FULL SWING when they arrived, the crowd and the noise spilling onto the spacious lawns that surrounded the single-story ranch-style house. Chinese lanterns, bright and cheerful, were strung between the clustering oak trees to provide colored light even though it was not yet dark. Occasional bursts of laughter mingled with the sounds of the country music being produced by a small group. With a sigh of anticipation, Alison watched the couples near the pool twirling and swaying to the music.

Catching sight of her expression, John grinned. "We'll dance later. First let's go find Nancy and Tony."

Nodding agreement, she followed him through the house in search of his sister. When they stopped for a moment, Alison's eyes drifted to the small group, then back to John. "Does Nancy always hire a group for a backyard barbecue?" she asked in amazement.

Chuckling, he shook his head. "No, but this

isn't your everyday-garden-variety-flies-and-mosquito barbecue! They're celebrating their tenth anniversary. And that's something to celebrate! I wouldn't have given them six months together, let alone ten years."

"You never did appreciate me, brother dear," a musical voice replied.

John turned to the blond-haired woman who had come up behind him, her pale green dress shimmering with every movement she made. With a growl of approval he enveloped her in a bear hug.

Nancy laughed gaily, the happiness in her eyes rivaling the sparkle of the diamond clips that held back her hair. "It took a man of superior worth to recognize my value. Tony knew what a jewel I was the first time he met me!"

Releasing her, John stepped back to gaze down at his sister, his affection evident in his eyes. "Talk about gratitude! And who introduced you to old Tony?"

"Who are you calling old?" an affronted voice asked. A slightly heavyset man, with wings of premature gray at his temples, appeared behind Nancy. His gray eyes twinkled at John's sheepish grin.

"Just kidding, Tony."

"Alison!" Nancy exclaimed, suddenly catching sight of her. "I'm so glad you could come. I really did mean to invite you yesterday, but it completely slipped my mind when I realized how late it was."

The man at her side grinned indulgently at her before turning to Alison. "One of the first things you should know about my wife is she's a trifle scatterbrained. Pay her mental lapses no attention." He offered his hand. "I'm Anthony Sommers."

"Alison Bennet," she replied, instantly liking his calm friendliness, which was so at odds with his wife's restless energy. "John didn't tell me it was a special occasion. Congratulations."

"Thank you. You've just arrived from New York, haven't you? How do you like Texas?"

"It's not at all what I expected," Alison confided. "Where are all the oil wells?"

"On someone else's property," Nancy laughed. "Don't worry, though. Texas tea is not a myth." She grinned impishly. "You boys go get us something cool to drink. I'm sure this heat is killing Alison." Without waiting to see if they obeyed her dictate, she turned back to her guest. "Did you finish your unpacking?"

"Yes, thank God!"

Nancy eyed Alison speculatively, a mischievous smile on her mouth. "Are you some kind of magician? You haven't even been here a week, and you've already convinced Jason to move out of the cottage into that tiny apartment of his. How'd you do it? With mirrors? Witchcraft? Voodoo dolls?"

"No," Alison laughed. "Nothing quite so mystical. I just convinced him my moving into the cottage was the right thing for me to do. He didn't agree at first, but eventually he came around to my way of thinking."

There was a knowing look on Nancy's face. "You're definitely related to your grandmother. She was a sweet old lady, but stubborn as they come. Without half trying she could drive Jason and John into fits. Once she got an idea in her head, there was no stopping her. The end result was always the same—the boys would throw up their hands in disgust and go along with whatever she wanted." Chuckling in remembrance, Nancy shook her head. "It's a shame you never had the chance to know her. She was a remarkable lady."

"Jason has told me a little bit about her—a very little bit." Words hesitated on her lips; searchingly she studied the older woman. "I didn't realize Jason and John had known each other that long."

"Lord, yes. Our families used to be neighbors. I'll never forget the day Jason came to live with Mr. and Mrs. Morgan. He was ten. His parents just dropped him off like he was a burdensome piece of baggage. No wonder he has no use for them today. The Morgans were his real family—they were always there for him. I doubt if his mother even remembers his birthday.''

She blinked, her quick smile lightening the mood. ''John was at your grandmother's house more than he was at home. He and Jason went through school together; in fact, they shared an apartment in their undergraduate days. For a time it seemed like they were always interested in the same girl, and they'd do almost anything to beat each other out. Of course, as soon as she showed either one of them the slightest bit of interest, they'd back off.''

The two of them were laughing when John returned with the punch. Nancy and her husband excused themselves to see to their other guests, and Alison grinned impishly at her escort. ''Your sister's been telling me about your college days. How many girls did you steal away from Jason?''

He laughed at her teasing. ''She shouldn't have dragged that up; it's ancient history!'' But when Alison kept looking at him, he shrugged good-naturedly. ''You know how it is when you're in college. We did a lot of crazy things—like trying to steal each other's girls. Four of us guys played the field, rushing whomever the next one had his eye on. After a while, of course, the girls found out about it, and they made the game that much harder. I think they enjoyed it more than we did. Except for one. Bonnie Jean Steadman became deadly serious when she saw Jason. That girl had marriage on her mind, and old Jason had to do some pretty fast running to escape her clutches!'' Shaking his blond head ruefully, he took her now empty glass and set it on a nearby table. ''C'mon. Let's dance.''

As they neared the dance area, Alison gazed at the whirling couples in delight. ''It's just like *Urban Cowboy*!''

''Not quite,'' John laughed. ''But that movie sure did a lot for country and western dancing. If you don't know the steps, don't worry, I'll teach you. It's easy.''

Before she could say a word, she found herself being propelled into the middle of the dancers, John's hands there to guide her faltering steps. Her feet caught the rhythm, and her confidence soared when she successfully completed a series of turns. Laughingly she gazed up at John, her lips parted and the sparkle of triumph lighting her eyes. ''I love it, John!''

''See, I told you. There's nothing to it.'' His hand tightened to draw her closer. ''We're made for each other, just like Fred and Ginger, Gable and Lombard—''

''Abbott and Costello?'' Alison laughed at his chagrined expression. ''Nice try, John. Did you use that line on your girl friends in college?''

His wide grin was all the answer she needed. ''You ought to be ashamed of yourself. You might have broken some poor unsuspecting girls' heart—or better yet, had yours broken! It would have been poetic justice. I'm surprised one of those girls wasn't crafty enough to catch you or Jason.''

''It will take more than craftiness to get Jason to pop the question,'' John confided. ''His parents' marriage is a joke—they've been going separate ways for years. When Jason was a kid, they used to fight over which one of them would take care of him. He was shipped back and forth across the country like a ball in a tennis match. It's no wonder he doesn't have much to do with them. And marriage! His childhood left a bad taste in his mouth. He's been avoiding commitments ever since—they're too painful.'' Shrugging off his solemn mood, he looked down at her with mischief in his green eyes. ''My reasons for avoiding matrimony are completely different from Jason's. All these years I've been looking for an angel with just the right touch of devilry to keep life interesting. I was beginning to think she didn't exist. Has anyone ever told you you dance like an angel?''

Alison laughed. ''No, but I've got a feeling you're about to. You're wasting your talents as a lawyer, John. With the line of blarney you hand out, you'd make a terrific writer.'' The lightness of her tone effectively concealed the uneasiness created by his playful banter. She liked John—he was easygoing and fun to be with. But he didn't raise her pulse in the least.

Her glance slid from his to rove over the other guests. Almost immediately a pair of blue eyes ensnared hers. She stumbled; John's arms tightened, and he noted her surprised face in concern. ''Alison, what is it? What's the matter?''

''I. . .I didn't realize Jason would be here.'' Her voice was so low he had to bend his head to catch her words. ''Who's that w-with him?''

John turned to survey the crowd, his eyes narrowing at the sight of the statuesque blonde draped on Jason's arm, her hands clinging to him as if afraid he would slip away. A sensuous smile revealed her lustrous white teeth, as she leaned against Jason. Her black dress contrasted beautifully with her hair and honeyed tan, the simple cut of the garment proclaiming a sophistication that made the other women at the party seem overdressed in comparison.

''That's Christina Carlson,'' John muttered. ''Damn! I hate to see her get her clutches into Jason. I warned him about her, but he just won't listen to reason.''

Alison hardly heard his words after he identified the woman. She should have known.

Christina Carlson: the sultry-voiced woman on the phone, the woman who had greeted him at her door with a kiss, the woman who had surprised him in his bedroom—they were all one and the same. Jason appeared entranced as he laughed with her, his arm around her waist holding her close to his side. It hadn't taken him long to find another date, Alison thought bitterly. Her eyes turned to the blonde, whose fair coloring was such a contrast to Jason's darkness. They made a stunning couple.

"I don't know how real her curves are, but that blond hair came straight out of a bottle." She hadn't realized she'd spoken aloud until she heard John's hoot of laughter. Looking up into his grinning face, she smiled sheepishly. "That was catty, wasn't it?"

"But true." Still chuckling, he continued, "I don't know what it is about her that irritates me. I guess I resent the way she throws her father's power and money around. She's always been a spoiled brat—Jason and I have known her for years. We used to laugh about the poor guys she dated, leading them around by the nose until they finally got fed up with it. She's one bossy lady, and it will take a strong man to control her. She's decided Jason is that man. Thank God she didn't cast her eyes my way! Bonnie Jean was a kindergartener compared to Christina. She knows all the tricks and then some!"

Forcing herself to ignore the other couple, Alison reacted with surprise. "If she's so terrible, why does Jason have anything to do with her?"

"Don't mistake me, Christina can be a lot of fun. She has the knack of making a man feel he's the only one in the world. But I suspect part of her attraction for Jason is business. He believes her father's land is floating on oil. But Christina has Daddy wrapped around her little finger. One word from her could make or break any deal Jason makes with old man Carlson. So if he wants to drill on his land, he's got to squire the daughter around first. Personally, I think he's crazy! She may be beautiful, but she's too spoiled for my taste."

Silently agreeing with John's assessment of the blonde, Alison frowned in confusion. Was that really Jason's reason for dating the lovely Christina? She refused to believe he would lick anyone's boots, especially for business gains. He must be infatuated with her. Pain seared her heart and she quietly screamed denial, but she couldn't close out the sight of the woman in his arms. Turning her back on them, she flashed John a brave smile as her pride rushed to the rescue to buoy her sagging spirits.

They danced for a while longer, then swam and ate. Alison's efforts to force Jason from her thoughts only succeeded in keeping his image in her mind. Soon after they left the dance floor, she lost sight of the other couple for good, and spent the rest of the evening unconsciously searching the crowd. Finally, irritated with herself and with Jason, she welcomed John's suggestion that they leave.

The silence in the car was marked, although Alison, wrapped in her own thoughts, was totally unaware of the curious glances John occasionally shot her. They had nearly arrived at the cottage when he broke the silence. "How did you convince Jason to let you move into the cottage? I was never more surprised in my life than when you answered the phone. How did you do it?"

"I reminded him that the cottage was just as much mine as it was his, and I had as much right to live there as he did."

"And he accepted that? Just like that?" he asked incredulously with a snap of his fingers.

"Well, no." Toying with the tie of her skirt, Alison met his glance defiantly. "I told him I intended to stay at the cottage, with or without his permission. If he wouldn't let me, I would go to you and get a duplicate key."

John whistled softly. "He must have been furious! You know how independent he is... he's not used to having ultimatums thrown at him. Sometimes your grandmother could charm him around to her way of thinking, but that was a rarity. He can be awfully stubborn."

"Tell me about it," she retorted wryly. "This time, though, he didn't have any choice. He knew I was right."

"I know. It's just that I've never known him to give in graciously without a struggle. He must be mellowing with age."

"Hardly." A sudden laugh escaped her as she remembered Jason's frustration. "I didn't say he was gracious about it, in fact, quite the opposite. We're now in the middle of an armed truce, but renewed hostilities could flare up at any moment. It's like walking through a mine field—one false step and it's all over!"

Their arrival at the estate temporarily halted conversation as John maneuvered through the open gates of the property. Pulling up in front of the cottage, he switched off the engine before turning to face her, his arm stretched out across the back of the seat. His eyes were teasing as he scanned her face in the darkness. "Then you should make a point of avoiding Jason. And I'm just the man to help you do it. Why don't we go to a movie tomorrow night?"

Despite the lightness of his words, Alison was not deceived. If she wasn't careful, she could very easily become a pawn in another one of their dating games. They had both asked her for a date tonight, and even though Jason had quickly substituted Christina, she had no intention of encouraging either of them. "I'm sorry, John. The rest of the week is going to be pretty hectic, especially when the renovation work starts. Why don't you call me next week? I'll need a break by then."

"It's because of Jason, isn't it?" Before she could deny it, he shook his head. "Don't answer that, I retract the question. It's really none of my business." At her relieved expression, he grinned. "Now tell me all about the mansion and your plans for it."

"Jason agreed to let me try renovating it. I'm in the middle of getting estimates on the various jobs. I've only got two months to complete the project, and if I can't get the work done for the price Jason and I agreed on, I'll have no choice but to sell it. I spent hours on the phone this afternoon trying to find contractors who would do the repairs for a reasonable price. Staying within my budget isn't going to be easy. But don't tell Jason that."

"Don't worry, your secret's safe with me." He frowned thoughtfully. "When I had my office redecorated, I was able to buy the wallpaper at wholesale prices. You should do the same thing—it could save you a lot of money." He closed his eyes in an effort to remember, but finally shook his head in defeat. "It's no use. I can't remember the name of the place, but if you call my office tomorrow, I'm sure my secretary will be able to tell you. You also need someone to hang the paper. You might try the medical school."

At her look of surprise, he laughed. "I'm not kidding. Some of the medical students take odd jobs to supplement their income."

"That's a good idea. I'll have to check it out." With her hand on the door handle, she turned back to him. "Thank you, John. I really had fun tonight. And thanks for the advice about the mansion. I know it'll be a great help to me." Impulsively she leaned over to kiss his cheek. "Good night."

"Good night." His soft words drifted to her on the night air as she climbed onto the porch. Unlocking the door, she turned on the threshold to wave. The bright red taillights of his car were lost to sight before she stepped inside and closed the door, a soft smile on her lips.

"That was a touching scene."

Alison screamed, her heart jumping into her throat. Her eyes were wide with fright as she tried to see into the darkness that shrouded the living room. With a trembling hand she groped for the light switch. When she found it bright, blinding light flooded the room; her eyes blinked in protest.

There, standing by the window, stood Jason, and from the mocking lift of his mouth, she knew he had observed her leave-taking of John. Color washed her face, accompanied by a jet of anger. Her eyes flashed with fire as she threw her purse on the couch before storming across the room. She stopped within two feet of him, her hand outstretched. "I want your key! Right now! This is the last time you're going to slip in here and scare me to death."

His lopsided grin mocked her rage. "I wasn't trying to scare you. I was just making sure you got home safely. Someone has to watch over you, especially when you walk around half dressed."

"That's a laugh, coming from you!" she almost yelled.

His eyes were roaming over her figure, caressing every curve revealed by the clinging material of her swimsuit, before returning to her face. There they lingered with burning intensity on her mouth. He was doing it again, raising her blood pressure without half trying! "Stop looking at me like that," she snapped. "And don't try to change the subject. I want your key."

"Whatever you say," he chuckled. With one step he eliminated the distance between them. His sapphire eyes entrapped hers, the devilry there daring her to back away. With deliberate, unhurried movements, he slipped the cool metal of the key between her breasts. His fingers lingered there to burn her sensitive skin. "I can always go to John and get a duplicate," he mimicked her softly.

Alison gasped, her heart knocking against her ribs. She was frozen, unable to move even when he freed her of his touch. His closeness was doing crazy things to her breathing, the glint in his eyes threatening to buckle her knees. She swallowed, her tongue unconsciously provoking as it ran over her suddenly dry lips. In desperation she sought to return to sanity. "Did you enjoy the party? I didn't see you leave." *You idiot,* she chided herself, *you might as well tell him you couldn't tear your eyes away from him all evening!*

"It was all right, though I don't care for crowds. I left after about an hour." His hand reached out to brush her hair back from her facc. Her involuntary shudder did not escape his notice. His eyes narrowed fractionally. "How's your writing coming? Has living on the estate really helped that much?"

With her pulse pounding in her ears and the touch of his hands bringing her nerves to awareness, it was incredibly difficult to reply coherently. The spicy male scent of him engulfed her. Urgently her common sense reminded her of the many women who were chasing him. She didn't want to be another in a long string of conquests. She stiffened, forcing herself to say lightly,

"The mansion has been a big help. I told you it would be. And reading grandmother's diaries has helped me make a lot of changes in my heroine. She's more realistic now."

"So the mansion has improved your setting, and grandmother's journal helped your characterization. What about the love scenes? Do those need work, too?"

She answered cautiously. "A little. Why?"

He shrugged, his feigned innocence doing nothing to alleviate her suspicions. "No reason. I was just wondering." His hand settled on her shoulder, its momentary tightening her only warning before he asked abruptly, "Are you a virgin, Alison?"

"What?" she screeched, totally unprepared for his question. Color flooded her face all the way to the roots of her hair. "That's none of your damn business!"

"That's what I thought," he laughed, enjoying her discomfort. His bold eyes swept down her body teasingly. "How can you write romances when you haven't any experience? Aren't the love scenes difficult to write?"

"I didn't say I was inexperienced," she denied hotly. How had they settled on this topic? She lifted her chin, refusing to back down from the laughter in his eyes. "I've got a good imagination. I just picture you with Christina or Lana, and I've got a love scene."

"Lana!" he exclaimed, genuinely shocked. "Good God, she's a teenager! Her boyfriend's a football player—he'd kill me if I laid a hand on her. Which I wouldn't, since she's just a kid. Her brother works for me."

"Oh." Alison's heart lightened illogically. She was a fool to care about the women in his life. She may have been mistaken about Lana, but his interest in Christina was obvious. She frowned in irritation. "This is a stupid subject, and I don't know why I'm standing here discussing it with you."

"Because you know I'm right," he retorted promptly. "You need firsthand experience to improve your love scenes. And I'm perfectly willing to further your education. In fact I feel it's my duty."

"You're out of your mind if you think I'm going to jump into bed with you just to improve my writing!" Alison exclaimed indignantly. "Your conceit is unreal!"

"Who said anything about going to bed?" Jason asked innocently, his eyes brimming with laughter. "You don't jump in over your head without even knowing how to swim. I'm talking about step-by-step instruction in the art of making love."

Alison eyed him warily. If anyone was a master at making love, she suspected Jason was. She couldn't deny that the love scenes in her manuscript desperately needed help, but could she trust Jason? It wasn't as if she'd never been kissed. But few of the men she had dated had inspired real passion. And, indeed, how could she write about something she'd never experienced?

"What's the first lesson?" The question popped out before she could stop it, and she wanted to kick herself for her impulsiveness.

The warmth of Jason's grin enveloped her. Suddenly only a few inches separated them. His hand lightly trailed up and down her bare arm, setting her nerves atingle. "First, you, or rather your hero, has to remember not to rush in like a bull in a china shop. Virgins are skittish—they can't be rushed."

The laughter in his voice was more than she could bear. She stepped back, cringing from his touch. "Jason, it isn't going to work. This is all just a joke to you, and I don't especially like being the punch line," she protested resentfully.

"Hey, come back." His hands settled on her shoulders to halt her retreat, his amusement quickly turning to contrition. "I'm not laughing at you, Alison. I promise I'm not. You've got to remember this is a little unusual for me, too. I don't know many virgins. Did your aunt lock you away from the world or something? Surely you've been kissed before."

"Of course I have. Being a virgin isn't a

crime, you know,'' she said stiffly. ''I'm not in the habit of throwing myself at men. Anyway, I haven't had much time for a busy social life. Aunt Gwen's illness and my writing didn't leave room for much else.''

''Well, it's time you joined the human race.'' He lifted her chin, forcing her to meet his gaze. ''Stop looking like a scared rabbit; I'm not going to hurt you. You might even find you like it.'' The hands that had been absently kneading her shoulders moved up to frame her face. His eyes lingered on her mouth. ''All I'm going to do is kiss you. Relax.''

That was easy for him to say! He was standing so close she could see the laugh lines around his eyes, and to relax with him in such proximity was impossible. Her stomach knotted with tension. She stood stiffly in his grasp as his head lowered to block out the light.

Then his mouth settled on hers with butterfly softness, demanding only that she let him enjoy the sweetness of her mouth. His lips played with hers, teasing and tasting. His arms soon joined the sensuous assault, moving around her to weld her to his lean strength.

Alison was devastated. The romantic encounters she had experienced in the past had not prepared her for this attack on her senses. Jason's hands, not content with just holding her, began a subtle exploration that fanned the flames ignited by the sweet possession of his mouth. She felt the world slipping away, spinning out of control. When his tongue traced the outline of her lips, wild, totally foreign emotions threatened to inflame her. All thought of resistance fled.

It was an unwelcome shock when Jason tore his mouth from hers, his hands holding her at arm's length. The burning light in the depth of his eyes gradually gave way to a glimmer of satisfaction. "End of lesson one," he said, the husky note in his voice belying his sudden detachment. "I keep forgetting you're a beginner. With a little more practice, you'll be ready for the advanced course."

His words effectively doused the heat licking her veins and painfully pulled her back to earth. "I'll have to make sure I get plenty of practice before our next lesson," she retorted, her pride coming to the fore.

But her emotions were in turmoil, with tears only seconds away. Hastily she bade Jason good-night and ran upstairs. By the time she reached her room, her cheeks were wet and sobs were rising in her throat.

How could she have been so stupid! This was all just a game to him. His kiss, the touch of his hands, the burning light in his eyes—they had all been calculated to destroy her resistance. Her inexperience was a novelty, a challenge to his sexual prowess. Once the uniqueness of tutoring her in the art of love wore off, she would see the back of his head in retreat. And if he thought she was going to let him continue with these ridiculous "lessons," he was crazy! My God, she thought wildly, what does the advanced course include?

CHAPTER SEVEN

ALISON FOUND HER WAY DOWNSTAIRS, lethargy weighting her limbs so that every movement was an effort. The night had seemed unending, the seconds passing with painful reluctance. For Alison the long hours between midnight and dawn had been filled with doubts and self-reproach. Had she taken leave of her senses? Her every thought was centered on a man who last week she hadn't known existed.

As if on a movie reel, the scene that had happened between Jason and herself flashed again and again in her mind. She could feel his arms go around her to press her close, while his lips coaxed her to a response she could not deny....

From their first meeting she had tried to fight the attraction she felt for him. During the night even deliberate reminders of Christina Carlson hadn't helped. And now he had decided to instruct her in the finer art of making love. How was she going to resist him? Her meager defenses crumbled at the very sight of him. There was no contest; the battle was won before it had begun, with his emotions intact and hers shattered. How had she let herself get into this mess?

Somehow she had to convince Jason she was not interested in gaining sexual experience for her writing. If only he wasn't so very persuasive!

Exhausted slumber overtook her near dawn, but she had had only a few hours of sleep before she dragged herself awake. She couldn't stay in bed all day; she had too much to do. With a groan she climbed out, dressed and stumbled downstairs to the kitchen. She measured coffee into the coffeemaker in hopes that caffeine would dispel the cloudiness from her mind. Today she doubted that anything would help.

The blare of a car horn startled her; it seemed to come from just outside. Curiosity led her to the front door, and she halted in surprise at the sight of a florist truck parked outside the locked gates. When the driver deliberately leaned on the horn again, she snatched up the key and hurried outside. "All right, all right, I'm coming!"

She quickly unlocked the gates, allowing the delivery man to thrust a large arrangement of flowers covered with tissue paper into her hands. Alison stammered a thank-you and walked back to the cottage, curiosity hurrying her steps. She set the flowers on the coffee table, then stripped off the covering. It was an exquisite arrangement of daisies. Her hand automatically reached for the tiny card tucked among the blooms. Her name was printed in bold letters across the envelope. With trembling fingers she withdrew the card, sinking to the couch as the words fairly leaped at her.

> Alison, I was called out of town unexpectedly and will be gone for at least a week. If you have any problems, contact John.
>
> Jason

A postscript at the bottom of the short note caught her eye, the mocking words doing nothing to alleviate her distress. "Lady, you get an A+ for last night. Our next lesson should be very interesting."

What was she to think of such a note? A sudden laugh escaped her as she reread the postscript. He was incorrigible. And totally impossible. John was right. For her own peace of mind, it was imperative that she avoid Jason at all cost. He was too experienced. He already dominated her thoughts; she had no intention of letting him break her heart. And break her heart he would if she was ever foolish enough to let down her guard. There was no room in his life for commitments. She had little reason to think he would change because she might want more from him. But how was she going to keep him at arm's length?

Breakfast did much to raise Alison's flagging spirits and to strengthen her resolve to put Jason out of her mind. Determinedly, she returned upstairs to change into coveralls and tie a bandanna around her short curls. Then, armed with broom, dustpan and giant garbage bags, she made her way to the mansion, bent on making progress in her cleanup campaign. Sweeping out the debris was a huge undertaking, one that would easily take several days. And the most logical place to start was in the attic, from which she could work her way down.

Diffused light filtered through the dust-covered windows, casting shadows in the corners while bringing the heaps of cluttered debris into sharp relief. Situated directly under the roof, the attic was a stifling sweatbox. Hurriedly Alison pushed the windows open to allow the breeze to cool her hot cheeks.

Her eyes revealed her disgust at the rubble-filled room, but she didn't allow it to deter her from the task at hand. Dust swirled around the room as she attacked the mess, but as soon as it settled it was caught up in her dustpan and deposited in a garbage bag.

The light had dimmed drastically and the ache in Alison's lower back was nagging her to stop when her broom finally reached into the last untouched corner of the attic. There, too, she made short work of the chaos as dirt and old papers found their way into her garbage bags. At one point Alison stooped to pick up an envelope, squinting in the darkness to read the name written there. Then she gasped, dropping the broom to snatch up the few other letters scattered on the floor. They were from her grandmother, addressed to Edward. After poring over the diary, she'd recognize that handwriting anywhere. Now maybe she'd get some answers!

She started to open the letter, but in the ill-lit room it was almost impossible to read the faded ink. For the first time she noted that the sun was no longer shining through the windows but had passed over the house and was quickly making its descent toward the horizon. She had been cleaning all day! Eight green plastic bags, stuffed to their limits, sat in the middle of the room, with one left to be filled. She glanced back at the letters and knew she simply could not put off reading them.

Her footsteps echoed loudly as she ran downstairs, the precious letters clutched in her hand. She had never dared to hope that the mysterious Edward Smythe would have kept any correspondence from her grandmother. How many years had the letters been in the attic collecting dust? Would they reveal anything more than

Edward's had? Her eyes shining with excitement, Alison bounded across the grounds to her honeysuckle-draped porch and rushed into the living room to collapse on the couch.

Without bothering to put them in any kind of order, she reached for the closest envelope. Quickly she extracted the letter and began to read. The missive held none of the eloquent confessions of love that Edward had written in his own letters. Instead, it was a condemnation of him for so readily believing what was obviously an outright lie. Her grandmother claimed to be innocent of any wrongdoing, but if he had so little faith in her or her love for him, it was better that they part now instead of prolonging the agony....

What wrongdoing? Alison wanted to scream in frustration. Why did everyone talk in riddles? Quickly she scanned the remaining letters, but when they, too, failed to explain the sudden rift between the lovers, she reached for the diaries. Her grandmother had consistently poured out her feelings in the leather-bound volumes. There had to be an explanation of her breakup with Edward.

The pages soon revealed that Alison Ford Morgan had met Edward Smythe when he'd come home from college for summer vacation. He'd been twenty-one, she had just turned eighteen. They had both been living on the estate, but because of her duties as maid and seamstress, her grandmother had come into little contact with her employer's only heir. He, however, often had the chance to observe her unawares, and it wasn't long before he'd begun to seek her out.

Alison laughed at her grandmother's chagrin when he'd deliberately waylaid her in the hall. Fearful of being discovered flirting, she'd reluctantly agreed to meet him near the fountain after dark. She had been taking a tremendous chance. If anyone had happened upon them, she and her father might both have lost their jobs. A housemaid did not presume to fall in love with the heir to a large estate. Especially when that heir was engaged to marry someone else!

The unexpected ringing of the telephone startled Alison. She swore silently. Just when it was getting interesting! Carefully she marked her place in the book before grudgingly reaching for the phone. "Hello?"

"Alison? Hi. This is Nancy. How are you?"

"Oh, Nancy... I... I'm fine." Deliberately she pushed the diary she'd been reading out of reach, saving it for another quiet moment. "I'm so glad you called. How are you? I was just sitting here relaxing after working at the mansion all day."

"I suspected as much," Nancy replied. "John told me about Jason's and Christina's trip to

New Orleans. He had a feeling you'd bury yourself in work this week with no one to rescue you from the drudgery. I see he was right. So I promised him I would call you, and maybe we'd go shopping or something."

"That sounds like fun. Are you still interested in inspecting the property with me?" She was already rushing merrily on when sudden realization swept over her, leaving her stunned. Jason and Christina! In New Orleans together!

Shadows clouded her eyes, until the only shine was that of threatening tears. She was staggered by the agonizing constriction of her heart, the sudden sharpness of it all the more painful because of its total unexpectedness. She didn't care, she told herself fiercely, angrily, but the trembling of her voice belied her denial. "D-did you say...Chris-Christina went with Jason?"

"Why, yes," Nancy said in surprise. "Didn't Jason tell you? Obviously he didn't or you wouldn't be asking." The silence in the wires was heavy as she hesitated, puzzled over the other woman's obvious distress. "Alison, you're not—look, this is none of my business, so if you don't want to answer, just say so. Are you...falling in love with Jason?"

The hysterical laughter that bubbled up in Alison's throat quickly changed to a sob. Suddenly she couldn't pretend anymore—to Nancy or to herself. And she had to talk to *someone*. Nancy had offered her friendship from the first. Instinctively she knew she would respect her confidences.

"Doesn't everyone fall in love with Jason?" she sniffed. "At least for a little while? Oh, I know I'm wasting my time. John has told me all about Jason's parents' marriage and how he's leery of commitments. But it doesn't seem to matter. I can't get him out of my mind!"

Encouraged by Nancy's murmur of understanding, she poured out her heart to her; and like a dam that had burst, once she'd started she couldn't stop. "Oh, Nancy, am I a fool? I can't eat or sleep without thinking of him. And when he comes anywhere near me, we immediately start arguing. I've never felt this way about anyone before, and it's driving me crazy! It's probably a good case of infatuation—like the measles, frustrating when you have them but not terminal. I don't see how I could fall in love with someone I've known less than a week. But if it isn't love, then what is it?"

"Whatever it is, it sounds like you've got a pretty serious case," Nancy replied. "Look, Alison, I can't tell you whether or not you love Jason. That's something you have to work out for yourself. I don't have to warn you he's a pretty potent package. It's obvious you've already discovered that. Even the most experienced female would be susceptible to his charm. But what about Jason? Has he given you any clue to his feelings?"

"Only that he'd like to take me to bed," Alison retorted bluntly.

"At least he's not indifferent," Nancy chuckled. "If he's given you the slightest bit of encouragement, then you're luckier than most. I know it looks as though he's got a dozen women on a string, but don't let him fool you. Usually *they* are chasing him. And, of course, if a woman insists on throwing herself at him, he's not going to turn her down. But I'm pretty sure his feelings aren't that involved—or at least they never have been before. I'd guess that casual relationships are his means of protection. He shies away from any woman who threatens emotional entanglement."

"Thanks a lot, Nancy. I really needed to hear that," Alison said dryly.

"I didn't mean to sound discouraging," the older woman objected. "I just wanted to warn you that if you want a deeper relationship with him, you won't have an easy time of it. You're going up against some pretty painful memories. He doesn't give his love easily. Ask Christina. She's been trying for years and it's never got her anywhere."

"I don't know what I want," Alison wailed miserably. Her fingers raked her tousled curls.

"I'm so confused. I can't think straight when he's around. Maybe it's a good thing he'll be gone all week. His absence will give me time to do some soul searching."

"Well, don't spend all your time thinking about Jason Morgan! You'll be climbing the walls before the week is over. Why don't we inspect the property tomorrow? I'm really anxious to see it. I don't think your grandmother ever went near the place. And I want to hear some more about your book. We can go shopping later in the week. That should keep you busy enough to forget about Jason, at least for a while."

"At this rate, I'll never get any work done," Alison protested laughingly. In the end, however, she agreed to all of Nancy's suggestions.

When she hung up she stared thoughtfully at the phone, trying to ward off the depression that still wouldn't be dismissed. Deciding not to bother with supper, she slowly climbed the stairs to her room, refusing to give in to the oppressive sadness that hung over the house. Not bothering to turn on the light, she walked across the room to the window.

The glow of moonlight turned the trees near the cottage to silver, creating dark shadows across the grass below. Only the leaves stirred from the faint breeze that whispered through them; everything else in the enveloping night was still, quiet, except for the faint barking of a distant dog. A shiver danced over her skin; she crossed her arms in front of her, wishing Jason was there to hold her close and dispel her doubts.

Was the moon shining in New Orleans as brightly as it shone on her? And somewhere in that city of romance, was a couple standing on a balcony locked in each other's arms, the woman's platinum strands contrasting vividly with ebony hair that challenged the night for darkness? And did his indigo eyes darken with passion as they had with Alison?

A muffled cry escaped her at the tortured thought. Flinging herself on the bed, Alison clutched a pillow to her, trying desperately to dismiss such agonizing conjectures from her mind. An entire week in New Orleans with Jason. Would Christina be able to pierce the protective shell that encased his heart? Or perhaps she already had, and that was why she had gone with him....

Why did she care, Alison asked herself numbly. She had never liked standing in line, and doing so for a man was a definite blow to her feminine pride. But she had a sinking feeling she'd do it for Jason. He was different from any man she had ever met, and she couldn't pretend indifference. His wicked grin sparked a response deep within her. If only she knew how he really felt! He'd made no secret of the fact that he found her attractive. She wouldn't have to fight to get into his bed—he'd made that patently clear. Conversely she doubted if she'd have to struggle to get out of his bed, either. He'd probably let her go without a backward glance. Jason preferred casual relationships and she had always avoided them. Who was going to change?

In a turmoil, Alison dressed for bed and climbed under the covers. For hours she lay staring into the darkness, courting a sleep that would not come.

THE NEXT MORNING seemed a bit brighter to Alison. She took Nancy up to the mansion, their footsteps echoing loudly in the empty house. At the sight of the vandalism the first floor had been subjected to, Nancy wrinkled her nose in distaste. "This is terrible! Does the whole house look like this?"

"Just about," Alison retorted dryly. "Some of the rooms are worse than others, but it's all pretty bad."

"I can understand that someone might come in to get warm on a cold night, but did they have to throw a beer party, too?" In disgust Nancy kicked an empty can into the already full grate of a fireplace. "They could have at least cleaned up their mess."

"And saved me all this work? Alas, no such luck!"

Upstairs they went from one bedroom to the next, trying to overlook the debris left by vagrants in order to picture the house as it once must have been. At the foot of the attic stairs, Nancy could no longer contain her enthusiasm. "You know, Alison, aside from all the dirt, this place isn't half bad. Once you get it restored, it's going to be beautiful. Do you have any idea what it would cost to build this house today?"

"A fortune," Alison laughed. "That's why I'm determined to hang onto it. I never thought I'd own a house like this. How could I sell it?"

Nancy started up the attic steps. "Have you given any thought to decorating? Of course, you've still got a long way to go before you start picking out furniture, but you must have a few ideas."

"Chrome and glass is definitely out. I love wicker, but I can't put that in all the rooms. I still have to give it a lot of thought. I don't want anything that would clash with the plantation style of the house." She pushed open the door to the attic and abruptly stopped dead in her tracks. "Oh, no!"

"What's the matter?" Nancy looked from Alison's stricken face to the debris-filled attic, but could find nothing to explain her friend's distress. "This isn't any dirtier than the rest of the house."

"You don't understand," Alison cried. "I spent all day yesterday cleaning this room! Now look at it. It's almost as bad as before. They must've ripped open some of the garbage bags."

"But who—"

"Vandals!" Alison retorted succinctly. "Damn them! They must have sneaked in here last night after I went to bed. Jason warned me about prowlers, but I really didn't take him seriously." She slumped against the wall. "This just wrecks everything. How can I possibly restore the house when I have to fight intruders all the time? I'll never get anything accomplished."

"You need a security system," Nancy informed her promptly.

"Sure I do. But I can't afford it. The repairs for the estate are on a strict budget already. There's no way I can stretch it to include electronic security."

"It doesn't have to be electronic. There's probably neighborhood patrol in this area." At Alison's blank look, Nancy explained, "All the neighbors chip in and hire a security company to make hourly rounds. Signs are posted and the men patrol in marked cars, so burglars know there's a good chance they'll get caught."

"Is it expensive?" Alison asked doubtfully.

"Not as expensive as having vandals destroy all your repairs. It's really the only sensible thing to do."

Alison agreed with her, but later that day she again had doubts. She frowned again at the papers spread out before her. There was no way she could afford all of the repairs *and* the neighborhood patrol, too. And since she had signed up that afternoon for the security system, the money would have to come from somewhere. She sighed heavily. How had she ever got talked into it? Largely because of her own fears, she knew. At night she was alone on the estate, and the cottage, despite its locked doors, was just as vulnerable to intruders as the mansion was. Even an hourly appearance by a watchman would make her position much less defenseless. She would definitely sleep better—if she could only stop thinking of Jason. But where was the money going to come from?

SEVERAL DAYS LATER she still didn't know where she was going to get the money, but she'd resolved to get it somewhere. The new security check was worth every penny. She didn't sleep any better, but at least her restlessness wasn't due to fear.

The days had settled into an exhausting routine; each morning found her dressed in work clothes, sweeping years of accumulated litter from the mansion. There had been no more intruders to disturb her, so the work went smoothly. Mr. Halston and his workers had begun the extensive repairs to the plumbing, and the sounds of their banging helped dispel the silent gloom from the old building.

As Alison had promised, she went shopping with Nancy one afternoon and returned home in better spirits, buoyed by the other woman's bright chatter and laughing comments. By mutual agreement they had avoided mention of Jason, although he was never far from Alison's thoughts.

The activity of the days helped to keep her preoccupation with him at bay, but the lonely nights assaulted her resolve. Each morning when she awoke from a troubled sleep, she vowed to work twice as hard as the previous day in hopes that she would stumble into a senseless slumber when bedtime finally came.

On the fifth day she spent hours stripping the torn and faded wallpaper from the walls. Unable to reach it all, she climbed up and down a ladder innumerable times in order to bare the walls. Her back ached from the strain when she finally quit, and she rubbed it wearily in an effort to relieve the pain. Walking to the cottage just before darkness descended, she silently cursed Jason for forcing her to go to such lengths to forget him. It just wasn't fair! He probably hadn't given her a thought since he had kissed her so many nights ago.

The soothing water of a hot bath relaxed her muscles, bringing an onslaught of sleepiness. But literary urgings pushed the lassitude away, and with languid movements she pulled on a pair of lace and cotton babydoll pajamas before heading for her typewriter in the small office. A passing thought of food brought a fleeting feeling of guilt—she had skipped several meals recently. Carelessly she dismissed it. Her appetite had been absent all week; she refused to force down another mouthful of tasteless food.

Sitting down at her desk, she turned to her typewriter and read the few sentences she had typed the previous evening.

The gains she had made in the development of her characters were tremendous. Arabella was no longer a stiff and emotionless doll. She was packed with an energy and vitality that spilled over the whole manuscript. The flow of words was no longer sluggish, and even though Alison realized she probably wasn't completely objective, she thought the improvements were good.

And they were all due to her grandmother. Her diaries provided a veritable character study, an in-depth portrayal of the hopes and fears of Alison Ford Morgan. They told the story of a young woman struggling to hold on to her dreams, and Alison turned to them more and more for inspiration in the development of the fictional Arabella. Consequently their lives were very similar. Arabella, like Alison Ford Morgan, fought the attraction she felt for the stranger who suddenly appeared in her life. Miles Hayden was an arrogant, bold requisition officer visiting her father's plantation. He was also a Yankee spy. He deliberately set out to encourage Arabella to defy convention, and the surrounding countryside was soon agog with their exploits.

Anyone familiar with the mansion would have recognized the fictional Claymore, the plantation home of the Clayton family. The columned porticoes were the same, the long drives up to both the real and the fictional house shaded by ancient oaks. With the magic of her typewriter, Alison miraculously repaired the mansion and even furnished it. And it didn't cost her a penny!

A yawn escaped her. She had been working on this chapter all week. She knew she should go to bed. She was exhausted, and she couldn't remember the last time she'd slept the night through. But she had to finish the chapter. Arabella was about to discover Miles was a spy....

She yawned again. Pillowing her head on her

arm, she leaned forward on the desk and closed her eyes. Only for a second, she thought. She would rest her eyes for just a moment and try to compose her next sentence. Her eyelids were suddenly heavy; she hadn't the strength nor the will to open them. With a sigh she let the resistance drain from her and gave herself up to the welcoming balm of sleep.

A frown knitted her brow, and the drowsiness that had overtaken her gradually slipped away, leaving her blinking in sudden wakefulness. Shaking her head to clear it of its grogginess, she looked at her watch and gasped in surprise. Two o'clock! And she had only intended to rest her eyes!

Wearily pushing her chair back, she rose to her feet, intent on going to bed. But an unexpected noise disturbed the quiet of the house. Frozen in her tracks, she held her breath, nearly choking with fright.

Stay calm, Alison, this is no time to have hysterics, she lectured herself. But her pulse refused to listen. Instead, she had a cowardly urge to run up the stairs and lock herself in the bathroom. *Don't be an idiot,* she chided herself. *It's probably just a mouse.*

But the muffled curse that followed the clang of a metal watering can rolling across the back porch was made by no mouse. The blood drained from her face. Where was the night watchman? Her worst fears were being realized, and her security force was nowhere to be found. She herself would be a puny match for even the weakest man. What was she going to do? Her nearest neighbors were not close, and were probably asleep, anyway. They wouldn't hear her even if she screamed her head off.

Furtive sounds at the kitchen door sent cold shivers of fear rushing down her spine. The intruder was persistent; it wouldn't be long before he gained access to the house. A moan of sheer terror escaped her as she glanced wildly about. Was she to be another statistic, another helpless victim of crime to be reported in tomorrow's papers? No! She wasn't going to sit here and patiently wait to be murdered.

John! Her eyes widened as his name suddenly came to her. Of course, why hadn't she thought of him earlier? He lived less than a mile away and would probably be here even before the police could make it. Dialing his number with nervous fingers, she waited impatiently for him to answer the phone, frantically praying all the while that he would answer before the maniac at the back door broke in and discovered her. When his sleepy voice finally answered, she was practically crying in relief. "Oh, John, thank God!" she whispered. "I was terrified you weren't home and. . . ."

"Alison?" His sharp tone broke into her

nearly hysterical rantings. "What's the matter? What's wrong?"

Her hushed voice quavered with her growing panic. "S-some-one is b-breaking in the back door... John, please help me. I'm p-petrified!"

"Hold on, I'll be right there! Stay calm, Alison. Go in the office and lock the door. Barricade it with the desk if you have to. And whatever you do, don't come out until I get there. Okay?"

Nodding agreement, she suddenly realized he couldn't see her. "Okay. But hurry!"

"I'm on my way!"

His reassuring tone soothed her jumpy nerves, and she was able to hang up with a sense of relief, confident that help was on the way. Quickly she locked the door into the living room, and she was on the point of pulling the desk in front of it when doubts began to undermine her confidence. If someone was crazy enough to break into the house, he wouldn't let a simple barricaded door stop him. If he broke it down, she'd be defenseless against him. Better to get the intruder before he got her.

Silently praying she was making the right decision, she switched off the lamp above her typewriter, casting the small room into total darkness. Softly, slowly, she opened the door into the living room and stood on the threshold, waiting for her eyes to adjust to the absence of light. Her heart beat a frantic protest in her ears, urging her to abandon such insanity and return to the comparative safety of the office. But stealthy, muted sounds from the kitchen interrupted her thoughts, and she knew she couldn't cower in the office and wait for John to rescue her.

Her shaking fingers closed around the smoothness of glass; she peered at the object in surprise before recognizing it. A leaded glass vase. It was probably a priceless family heirloom, but she couldn't be bothered with that right now. Sheer fright loosened her grip; she had to grab it with both hands to prevent herself from dropping it.

Her mouth was suddenly dry, the knocking of her knees so loud she was sure the person in the kitchen could hear it. Catching a breath and holding it, she tiptoed through the living room and into the kitchen, a wraithlike figure slipping like a soundless shadow through the dark house. The distant flicker of streetlights filtered through the windows to silhouette the man's large and powerful body as he stood with his back to her, unaware of her approach. Alison's fingers tightened on the cool glass of the vase before bringing it crashing down on his unsuspecting head, the force of the blow numbing her hands. A muffled groan, accompanied by the tinkling of shattering glass, was the only sound as the man crumpled to the floor.

Dazed by the results of her brutal action, Alison stared aghast at the still form, suddenly afraid she had killed him. Hurrying to the light switch by the door, she turned it on and flooded the room with light. In the sudden glare she blinked a few times before her eyes could focus on the intruder. Then she gasped in horror, "Oh, no!" Terror gripped her heart as she ran to the man lying on the floor. Impatiently sweeping several large pieces of glass aside, she babbled, "Jason, Jason! Dear God, open your eyes!" as she knelt down next to him. Lifting his head into her lap, her caressing hands swept the black hair back from his strong forehead, unconscious tears rolling down her pale cheeks to fall on his seemingly lifeless face. "Jason, I didn't know it was you.... Please, Jason, wake up and say you forgive me!"

"I forgive you, I forgive you! For God's sake, stop crying all over me!" he growled suddenly. One blue eye opened to glare up at her impatiently. "What the hell is going on? If you're upset about something, just tell me. You don't have to hit me over the head to convey your message." As he tried to lift his head he groaned.

Under his malevolent gaze, she sputtered awkwardly, "There was a...a noise and...and

I remembered you'd mentioned prowlers...." Her hands twisted in agitation as her words trailed off.

"Alison!" John's voice called frantically. The sound of his pounding footsteps preceded him as he sprinted into the kitchen, worry etched across his handsome face. His gaze swept the room to stop dead at the sight of the couple still on the floor, splinters of glass all around them. Then his eyes began to dance. A muscle twitched traitorously at the corner of his mouth, but there was only a slight shaking of his voice to indicate his amusement. "Thanks, Alison," he said dryly. "My one chance to come charging to the rescue and you ruin it. Thanks a lot!"

Pushing himself to a sitting position, Jason grabbed his head in pain for a moment before snapping, "What are you doing here? Have you both taken leave of your senses?" His eyes narrowed as they moved from John's sardonic look to Alison's guilty expression. "I had a feeling you were a fast learner," he added softly. "Has John been tutoring you?" Suspicion glinted from his darkening eyes.

A bright blush fired Alison's cheeks. "Of course not, Jason. I...I called John because I thought you were a burglar."

His skeptical look sent a wave of righteous indignation coursing through her. Angrily she jumped to her feet, her eyes snapping with outrage. "What were you doing at the back door, anyway? Sneaking around like a thief! I was scared out of my wits!"

"In case you've forgotten," he reminded her coldly, "I have just as much right to be here as you do."

"Not any more you don't. You moved out, remember?"

"I was only thinking of you. If I'd known you were expecting late-night callers, I'd have saved myself the trouble."

Alison gasped. "Don't you dare question my morals," she protested indignantly. "This is not the Victorian age. Anyway, you can't even lift an eyebrow at my activities this past week. Why, compared to you and Chris—"

Just in time she realized what she was saying, and she clamped her teeth tightly together. She could have cheerfully bitten off her tongue. Swiftly she counted to ten, then added five more just for good measure. Squaring her shoulders, she met his suspicious glance huffily. "Believe what you like, but I did think someone was breaking into the house. That is the only reason I called John."

"That's right, Jason," the attorney concurred. "And let me tell you, I broke every speed limit in the book getting here. I didn't know what I'd find, but I certainly didn't expect to find you on the floor with Alison crying all over you. What happened?''

''I came in the back way so I wouldn't wake her up, and she whacked me on the back of the head. Damn, it hurts!'' Rubbing the injured spot tenderly, he looked around at the pieces of glass sparkling on the tile. ''What did you hit me with, anyway?''

''A vase. It was the first thing I could find to use as a weapon. I almost grabbed a poker, but I didn't want to cause that much injury,'' she replied sheepishly.

''Didn't want to injure me!'' he exclaimed. Suddenly his broad shoulders were shaking with laughter. The deep rumble of amusement in his chest brought an answering grin to Alison's face. ''Next time you don't want to hurt someone, try using something a little softer, like a pillow.''

''Next time, don't come sneaking in the back door without warning me first,'' she advised. ''What are you doing here anyway?''

''My flight was delayed in Dallas because of mechanical problems, so I was late getting in. It's over thirty miles to the apartment. I'm tired, and I sure as hell don't want to drive all that way tonight. So I thought I'd sneak in and go up to my room. I figured I'd be gone before you woke up in the morning and you'd be none the wiser. I didn't expect you to waylay me in the kitchen...though being taken by surprise does have its advantages." His gaze moved down from her face to caress her pajama-clad figure. His burning look swept from the silken length of her legs to linger at the gentle rise and fall of her breasts.

Heat coursed into Alison's cheeks. The eyes devouring her could easily pierce the lacy bodice of her skimpy pajamas. He was stripping her naked, and she was standing there like a dummy! "Excuse me," she murmured. "I'll run upstairs and get my shoes, then I'll sweep up this mess."

Stepping gingerly through the shattered glass, she avoided the knowing glances of the two men and hurried from the room. On winged feet she reached the privacy of her room; quickly she dragged a comb through her tumbled locks and stepped into her mules. Minutes later, her pajamas respectably covered by a full-skirted pink robe that matched the blush in her cheeks, she stepped into the kitchen to find Jason and John sitting at the small maple table. They glanced up at her entrance, each running an appraising eye over her before returning to their conversation. She blushed anew at the appreciative light reflected in both pairs of eyes before looking for the broom and dustpan. But the scattered remnants of the vase had already been swept up.

"How about some breakfast, guys?" Her

gnawing stomach pain had just reminded her that she'd skipped dinner. "Pancakes and bacon? It won't take long." Without waiting for their reply, she took the necessary items from the refrigerator.

Jason's eyes twinkled as he watched her swift, sure movements. "What if we don't want pancakes?"

"Tough!" Alison laughed as she started to mix the batter. "Don't look a gift horse in the mouth. You might not get anything."

"Who said we didn't want pancakes?" John protested. He shot Jason a scathing glance. "I, for one, never turn down breakfast with a lovely lady. Especially when she has irresistible brown eyes and looks delicious in pink."

Thanking him with a smile, Alison turned to her cooking. But her eyes drifted to Jason at every opportunity. Hungrily she took advantage of his turned back, enjoying the very sight of him as he spooned coffee into the automatic coffee maker. She told herself she was seven kinds of a fool for being so happy to see him, but when he turned and smiled that slow grin of his her heart couldn't help but respond.

In minutes the coffee was ready, and he turned with a questioning glance. "Coffee?"

"Yes, please." Alison's answer was quick and smiling before she turned back to the stove. "Pancakes are done, too. John, get the syrup, please. It's in the fridge." Deftly she served the cakes, slipping butter between each one before placing the plates in front of the two men, who had quickly seated themselves. When she returned to the small table with her own plate, Jason quickly stood up and, despite her protests, helped her with her chair.

After the first bite, John closed his eyes, a smile of pure bliss on his boyish face. "Mmm! This is heaven, sheer heaven! Where did you learn to cook like this?"

Laughter shone in Alison's brown eyes as she looked at him over the rim of her coffee cup. "You're just hungry, John. Pancakes aren't really that difficult to make. But they are from scratch. My aunt was a fabulous cook—she never used a mix in her life! I'm not as good a cook as she was, but I do all right. She made sure that if I ever caught a husband, he wouldn't starve to death."

"If this is a sample of what he's in for," he retorted, "the only thing he's going to have to worry about is how to lose all the weight he's going to gain."

"If she ever gets married," Jason reminded him mockingly. "So far, Aunt Gwen's lessons seem to have been in vain."

"I haven't gone hungry yet," Alison replied flippantly. Then her eyes grew wistful. "We had some good times together even though we were light-years apart in age. Her strict upbringing sometimes caused problems, but eventually I learned to deal with her. She was shocked by the sexual revolution, and she didn't hesitate to tell me her views on the subject. Gosh, the lectures I used to get!"

John pushed back his plate and patted his stomach. "Well, I don't know about the rest of you, but I think Aunt Gwen was one smart lady. Anyone who can cook this well would make a terrific wife."

"Why, John, is that a proposal?" Alison choked with laughter at his suddenly flustered look. "Don't worry, I won't hold you to it."

At his puzzled glance, she grinned. "Finding one's true love is like an enormous game of hide-and-seek. Mr. Right is out there somewhere, hiding. You've just got to find out where."

"That sounds like a fairy tale," John chided her. "I know you're a romantic, Alison, but surely you're not waiting for a knight in shining armor to sweep you off to paradise!"

"That does sound good, doesn't it?" she teased. She rose from the table to carry her empty plate to the sink. "I'll admit I am a romantic, but I'm not completely naive. Knights went out of style aeons ago, and paradise is of one's own making. I'll just have to keep hunting."

"Don't waste your time looking for the type of love found in fairy tales," Jason advised mockingly. "It doesn't exist, except in books. And the fair maidens were never in quite as much distress as they pretended."

In other words, he didn't believe her. Why did she let his cynicism hurt her? He had made it painfully clear where his interest lay, and it wasn't with her. So why couldn't she just shrug him off as she had the other men who had wanted no-strings-attached relationships?

Misery engulfed her as she watched him turn toward John, abruptly excluding her. "I'm glad you dropped by, old boy. Carlson is awfully hard to nail down about that lease. He hasn't sold it to anyone else, but he won't give it to me, either. He's holding out for a higher percentage. I brought some figures back from New Orleans, and I'd like you to take a look at them."

John nodded before glancing at Alison's still figure by the sink. His eyes met hers. "Don't say I didn't warn you," he said gently. "Thanks for breakfast. If you ever need me again, you know where to find me."

Alison's smile flashed, lighting her face. She knew he was referring to Jason's disillusionment with romance. And to his stubbornness. But she could be stubborn, too. He was going to learn he hadn't cornered the market on that commodity. "Thanks, John. I'll keep that in mind."

As the two men left the room, she turned back to the sink, plunging her hands into the warm suds. Automatically she washed the plates and silverware, her thoughts centered on Jason. What was she going to do about him?

This constant state of upheaval was playing havoc with her nervous system. Where he was concerned, she was a puppet, her emotions controlled by the pull of a string. Was he deliberately trying to antagonize her? He tormented her with his aloofness, snapped at innocent remarks she made. He flaunted his relationship with Christina before her, and then had the nerve to accuse her of having loose morals! What was it with him? He had no right to object to her life-style when his own was so questionable. Her love life was her own concern.

Love life—that was a laugh! But for a minute she chewed her lip thoughtfully. As much as she shied away from the thought, her feelings for Jason were too strong to be classified as mere liking. Despite his seemingly indifferent attitude, despite his other women, there was a sensuous awareness between them that could not be denied. His laughing eyes mocked her inhibitions while his spontaneous thoughtfulness—giving her the family album, for example—undermined her defenses. And the warm, languorous caress of his mouth on hers completely devastated her. He touched her in a way no man had before; her heart no longer accepted the reasoning of her head. She was perilously close to being completely, irrevocably, head over heels in love.

A tanned hand reached into the rinse water to extract a plate. Startled, Alison jumped nervously. Her widened eyes flew to Jason's before shying away, hesitant to encounter his scrutiny. Awareness of her feelings was too new, too vulnerable. She would not embarrass him or herself by revealing emotions that were better left unexpressed. Instead she said, "I'm sorry about tonight, Jason. You know I would never knowingly hit you."

"I think sometimes you'd like to try, especially when we're having one of our many arguments," he said softly, his voice a teasing caress. Puzzlement clouded his eyes, however, as his gaze lingered on Alison's face. Her lack of sleep and the long endless days of work had left dark circles under her eyes. Her cheeks were hollowed out, her skin translucent across her high cheekbones, giving her an air of fragility.

When he lifted his hand to caress her pale cheek, she flinched, not wanting his touch, afraid that in her vulnerable state she would give in to any of his demands. His jaw tightened visibly at her reaction, but he didn't force her to accept his caress. Instead he almost snapped, "What in the sweet hell have you done to yourself while I've been gone? A light wind would blow you away!"

Stung by his criticism, she retorted, "Don't expect all women to be as voluptuous as the ones you date. I may not be as full-figured as Christina, but as they say, more than a handful's a waste!"

Throwing his head back, Jason roared with laughter. The corners of his eyes crinkled in lines of unsuppressed humor as he clasped her around the waist and pulled her against his side. "You never cease to amaze me!" he chuckled. "All prim and proper on the outside, and frustrated passion on the inside."

"I am not frustrated!" she denied hotly.

"No?" he asked, a glint in his blue eyes sending the blood rushing through her veins. His hands moved from her waist to encircle her shoulders, effectively turning her into his arms. "Then let's just see how passionate you are."

The words were spoken softly against her lips before his mouth covered hers. He teased her then, his lips moving playfully over hers in light kisses that left her wanting more. His tongue taunted her, savoring the sensuous curve of her lips before gliding away.

Alison moaned in frustration. He was driving her wild, and he knew it! When his mouth settled at the corner of her mouth, the aching need inside her completely obliterated her pride. Her hands reached out for him. "Jason," she murmured.

As if waiting for a word from her, he abandoned the sensuous teasing, gathering her against him to take possession of her mouth in a hot, searing kiss. Possessively he explored the sweet recesses of her mouth. His hands stroked the flames of her desire, and it spread like wildfire. With a moan, Alison melted against him, her fingers caressing his shoulders and neck, gliding up to tangle in his thick hair. When his hands pushed her robe back to allow his wandering lips greater access to her silken skin, she shrugged her shoulders, allowing the offending garment to fall unheeded to the floor. His eyes lingered for a second on the tanned length of her legs and the rapid rise and fall of her breasts so tantalizingly covered by the lacy top of her pajamas. Then he bent his head to inhale the fragrance of her skin, his warm breath tickling the sensitive area below her ear as he said gruffly, "That little bit of nothing you're wearing is very tempting. Do you look as delicious out of it as you do in it?"

Alison wondered if he had caressed Christina so intimately while they were in New Orleans. The thought was so suddenly painful that she felt tears gather in her eyes. She began to struggle wildly against the arms that held her. "That's something you'll never know, Jason Morgan! Let me go!" she choked tearfully as her efforts served only to weaken her rather than to achieve her release. She glared up at him. "Have you decided I'm ready for the advanced course? Or is this just more practice?"

He laughed shortly, his arms gradually relaxing to hold her in a loose embrace. "Let's just call it a refresher course. C'mon, you're going to bed. You're dead on your feet." With a quick, lithe movement, he leaned down and caught her behind the knees, sweeping her up into his arms. With easy strides he quickly crossed the living room. At the foot of the stairs he frowned at her struggling body in irritation. "Dammit, Alison, will you be still! Anyone would think I was carrying you off to my bed to ravish you."

"Aren't you?" she asked tremulously.

"No, I'm not. You're exhausted. I doubt if you could make it up the stairs if I didn't help you."

Her relieved expression caused him to chuckle wryly. "You're great for a man's ego, you know. Just to set the record straight, I'm not in the habit of forcing myself on unwilling virgins. I like my women to want me as much as I want them. At the moment you don't. So I'm willing to wait."

Grinning at her indignant gasp, he let his eyes roam her body freely, bringing a hot, flustered look to her face.

Huffily she crossed her arms over her breasts, bristling with anger when he only laughed at her defensive action. She shot him a murderous look. "People in hell want ice water, too, but they'll never get it!"

Laughing, he pushed her bedroom door open with his foot. "Is that another of Aunt Gwen's little sayings or one of your own?" Without waiting for her answer, he carried her over to the bed before releasing her legs. Both arms were around her now, letting her slide down his body until her toes touched the floor. The intimate contact burned her skin, but she stood rigidly within his embrace, obstinately denying him the reaction he sought.

Crushing her to him, he forced her chin up to study her mutinous expression. "Okay, Alison," he said quietly. "I want an explanation, and I want it tonight! You must have lost ten pounds while I was gone, and it was ten you could ill afford to spare. You're all washed out. Why? What have you been doing to yourself all week?"

The sleep she had missed since his absence abruptly caught up with her. She yawned, her body swaying slightly until her head came to rest against his chest. When she tried to stand erect again, his arms tightened, his hand forced her head back down. Her words were mumbled against his chest, so he had to bend his head to catch them. "I worked on the mansion during the day and wrote at night. *And* read grandmother's diaries." Another yawn caught her, her words ending on a soft sigh as she leaned tiredly against Jason, allowing him to support her weary body.

"Now I know you're tired. This is the first time you've brought up the subject of those diaries without asking me questions." His hand came up to feather lightly over her soft curves before pressing her closer to the hard muscles of his body.

He pressed a soft kiss to her temple, his warm breath stirring the soft curls there. "You must have had some time off. Didn't John take you out to dinner?"

Alison stirred herself from the pleasant dream that encased her, fighting enveloping webs of exhaustion to murmur, "No, he called a few times. Nancy came over for a tour of the mansion, and we went shopping one afternoon." Her arms went around his middle as an exhausted numbness robbed her legs of strength and her voice slipped to a whisper. "Lord, I'm . . . tired."

Jason's arms again lifted her off her feet to deposit her in her bed. The covers were tucked around her. Shadows were rapidly shrouding her mind when Jason's voice urged her back to consciousness. She frowned as she tried to catch his words. "Alison, you're not going to work on that damn mansion tomorrow. You're going to spend the entire day with me. Did you hear me? You're spending tomorrow with me!"

"Mmm hmm." Her dreams were heavenly, and Jason was a part of them. With a contented sigh, she snuggled into her pillow, a smile on her lips as she heard his soft, "Good night, brown eyes." She had to be dreaming!

CHAPTER EIGHT

THE BRIEF RAP on the bedroom door cut rudely through the morning quiet. "Rise and shine!"

Alison groaned, squeezing her eyes tightly shut at the sound of Jason's bright, cheerful voice. How could anyone be so disgustingly happy in the morning? How did he manage it on so little sleep?

The events of last night came flooding back. She had agreed to spend the day with him. She must have been out of her mind! He had only to look into her face to see how much she was attracted to him. An entire day in his company was going to be pure torture.

She burrowed deeper under the covers, muffling her ears with the pillow. "Go away!"

Even through the pillow his mocking laughter was louder. He must have opened the door. "Come on, sleepyhead, you're missing the best part of the day."

She still refused to move—until, without warning, he dropped down next to her on the bed and pulled the pillow from her unsuspecting fingers. His low laugh set the back of her neck tingling seconds before he ran his mouth down the side of her throat, nibbling on her sensitive skin.

His touch seared her, making her heart skip a beat. Alarm bells clanged loudly. With a muffled shriek Alison jerked away from him and slid to the edge of the bed. "What are you doing?" she cried.

"I thought my intentions were obvious." His eyes traveled slowly and thoroughly over the lacy bodice of her pajamas before lifting to her wide brown eyes. He laughed softly. "I was going to eat breakfast with you, but the sight of you in those pajamas is enough to make any man forget about food."

Alison snatched up a robe, silently cursing the hot color that burned her cheeks. Her eyes avoided his, and for the first time she noticed the tray on the dresser. The tantalizing sight of crisp bacon nestled next to scrambled eggs, along with a small stack of golden toast, stirred her hunger. Steam rose from a carafe of coffee, and a small glass of freshly squeezed orange juice completed the tray. Her eyes locked with his. "Why...."

"You can wipe that suspicious look off your face, brown eyes, there's no ulterior motive. Except to fatten you up some." His eyes roamed over her slim figure, anger flaring in them briefly. "My God, girl, what are you trying to do to yourself? In less than a week you've wasted away to nothing."

"Hardly that, Jason," she retorted dryly. "All right, so I skipped a few meals. I was so busy working that it completely slipped my mind." Nothing would induce her to confess his absence had robbed her of her appetite.

"You need a keeper," he mumbled as he walked across to the dresser to retrieve the tray. "And I'm just the man for the job. I won't put up with any of your foolish arguments. Move over." At Alison's startled glance, he laughed. "You can save the maidenly outrage. I won't lay a hand on you. Unless you ask me to, of course."

"Don't hold your breath," she countered caustically, although her heart was pounding in her breast. She had never been exposed to this teasing, lighthearted side of his nature. Resisting him was going to be much more difficult than she had imagined. "I'm not in the market for a lover, Jason."

"Who said anything about a lover? I just want to eat breakfast. Are you going to let me sit down or not?" His teasing rejoinder produced the desired effect. She moved.

Seated side by side, propped up against the headboard, they ate the delicious meal. Alison studiously tried to ignore the accelerated beat of her heart. She thought she had succeeded until he grinned down at hcr, the devilish glint back in his eyes. "You know," he said conversationally, "perseverance really pays off. I knew I'd eventually get you in my bed."

Alison choked, her coffee cup clattering as she banged it down on the tray. The man had a one-track mind! She scrambled off the bed, heedless of the fact that she almost upset the dishes. From the safety of several feet away, she glared at Jason's lounging form. "This is not your bed; it's mine! And I wish you'd get out of it. I have no intention of going to bed with you, Jason. The sooner you accept that, the better."

Unperturbed by her sudden flare-up, Jason eased off the bed in turn, the breakfast tray in his hands. He sighed jokingly, his wide grin flashing. "Virgins! I must be crazy for getting mixed up with one." When he reached the door, he glanced over his shoulder and winked. "Wear something cool and comfortable, sweetheart. It's going to be hot today."

Alison stared at the panels of the closed door dumbly. Sweetheart...he had called her sweetheart! She staggered to the bed and collapsed. How could she withstand his seductive charm for so many hours? With just one simple word of endearment he'd robbed her knees of their strength! She could no longer lie to herself—her heart was hopelessly involved. She could summon no resistance to his touch, and that would surely lead to trouble. He had laughed his way into her heart with ridiculous ease. She was in love with a man who scoffed at love.

Despair weighted her shoulders. What a mess. Did he have any feelings for her other than simple, unadulterated lust? If only he wasn't so damn inscrutable! Considering his parents' marriage and his experience with conniving women like Christina, it was little wonder he avoided emotional entanglements. How was she going to convince him to make an exception in her case?

She wasn't going to chase him, that was for sure. There were more refined ways of cracking a man's resistance. Deliberately she went through her wardrobe with a critical eye. Today she would set him back on his heels! A smug smile parted her lips as she stood before the mirror moments later. A lace-trimmed camisole, in pale pink silk dotted with tiny roses, gave her an enchantingly feminine air. The delicate lace straps drew attention to the honeyed tan of her shoulders and back. A matching circular skirt hugged her waist and fell in soft whispering folds around her hips and legs. Her low-heeled white sandals contrasted beautifully with the tan of her legs and would be comfortable for walking. She brightened her cheeks with a pink blush, highlighting the delicate bone structure of her face. And even her large eyes looked extra wide and appealing, surrounded by the thick fringe of her lashes.

Grinning at her reflection, she dabbed perfume at her wrists and neck before deliberately scenting the creamy skin just above the neckline of her camisole. Her roommate in New York had always accused her of being too passive; that she'd never catch a man if she wasn't more assertive. What Susan had never understood was that Alison just hadn't met anyone she was truly interested in. But now that she had, she wasn't going to sit back and let Christina Carlson win hands down. Open aggression wasn't her way—subtlety would be much more effective with Jason. He had been chased by too many women to fall for the obvious.

Downstairs she found him in the kitchen adding a bottle of wine to an almost full basket. Her brows lifted in surprise, but she refrained from comment. Her lips parted enchantingly as she studied his tall, broad-shouldered frame, and her pulse did double time when his gaze traveled lingeringly over the length of her own body. As his eyes returned to her face, her blush deepened despite her frantic attempts to extinguish the revealing color. "You said to wear something cool," she said almost defensively.

Although she failed to meet the burning look of his eyes, she felt his gaze sweep over her again. "You call that cool?" he taunted softly. "That's just about one of the hottest little numbers I've ever seen."

She almost flinched at his words, suddenly doubtful of her chosen course of action. She had worn the dress with the intention of attracting Jason, but it seemed her success had exceeded all her expectations. Desire, not love, shone from his eyes. "Maybe I should change," she suggested.

"C'mon, Alison, where's your sense of adventure?" he teased. "You can't play it safe all the time. Don't worry, I can control my baser instincts, even if you do look good enough to eat!" Picking up the basket, he came to her side, placed his free hand at the back of her waist and gently pushed her into the living room. "Get a move on it, woman. We've got a lot of ground to cover today."

Before she had time to collect her thoughts, let alone voice an opinion, she found herself in his sports car, with Jason sitting so close that his thigh brushed hers. Warning bells rang loudly in her bemused head; halfheartedly she tried to quiet them. "I don't know why you're doing this, Jason. It's very thoughtful of you, but it's not—"

"Thoughtful be damned!" he exploded, casting her a scowling glance from beneath his craggy brows. "Did it ever occur to you that I might want to spend the day with you for the sheer pleasure of your company?''

His question momentarily robbed her of speech, and she stared at him in surprise. Her blatant honesty came rushing to the fore, however, as she exclaimed, ''Why, no! It never even entered my head. In fact, I didn't even think you liked me!''

His eyes were suddenly laughing. ''Fishing?''

''N-no, of course not,'' she stuttered. ''I—''

Placing his hand over hers, which were clenched in her lap, he said quietly, ''I suppose it's only natural we got off to a bad start. You came to Texas with dreams of setting up your career, and I more or less stood in your way. But it's nothing personal. I wanted to sell the mansion; you didn't. No wonder we snapped at each other. Don't you think it's time we put all that behind us and started over again? All this arguing is damn frustrating!'' At her continued silence his hand tightened on her fingers. ''What do you say? Do you think we can spend an entire day in each other's company without coming to blows?''

She lifted her eyes to his, a flash of mischief deep in the brown depths. ''I think it can be arranged. Especially if you've finally decided to quit picking on me. I've never met a man who likes to argue so much!''

''Me?'' he exclaimed incredulously. ''You've

done nothing but deliberately provoke me since the day we met! I—" The laughing glance she gave to her wristwatch abruptly stopped his words. An answering grin softened the harsh angles of his face. "There's another good idea shot to hell. How long did it last?"

"Thirty seconds," she choked. "So much for good intentions. I think we'd do better if we stuck to safe topics of conversation. Like the weather and. . . and. . . ."

Jason chuckled. "And the weather. You know what they say about Texas weather, don't you?" At the negative shake of her head, he said, "If you don't like it, stick around. It'll change. Of course, it could change to a tornado, or a hurricane, or a month of hundred-degree temperatures. Take your choice."

Alison shuddered. "I'll pass on the tornado, thank you. I have no desire to see if there really is a Wizard of Oz. Flying monkeys aren't high on my list of favorite animals."

He laughed softly, and they gradually slipped into a companionable silence, neither feeling the urge to break the peace. As they neared the varied collection of buildings that comprised downtown San Antonio, Alison looked around her with interest. The streets were crowded with Saturday shoppers and tourists, a conglomerate of nationalities, Jason explained, who would be speaking Spanish and English interchangeably.

Crossing a bridge allowed Alison a short glimpse of the River Walk, its green coolness beckoning like an oasis in the already hot morning.

Although the pedestrians seemed unconcerned with the rising temperature, Alison knew she would soon be wilting if she was long exposed to the heat. Warily she watched Jason as he maneuvered the car through the traffic. "Where are we going?"

"The Alamo. I don't know how much you know about Texas history, but the Battle of the Alamo is one part of our heritage we're intensely proud of. Every visitor to San Antonio should see it."

Alison stared at the weathered facade of the building, the large double doors still bearing the bayonet marks of an attacking army, the preserved walls covered with bullet holes. "It was a Spanish mission at one time, wasn't it?"

He nodded before turning the car into a parking space. "That's right, Mission San Antonio de Valero. The chapel served as church for the small mission. One hundred and eighty-two men defended it against a force of four thousand Mexicans in 1836. They knew they faced certain death but refused to give in to demands to abandon it. It was probably the most courageous battle ever fought. For thirteen days Jim Bowie, Davy Crockett and the others held off Santa

Anna and his men. They were all killed, but they gained the time needed for the Texan forces to win their fight for independence. About two months later, Santa Anna was captured."

Awed by Jason's words, Alison walked at his side into the crowded yet quiet chapel of the old Spanish mission. The interior, protected from the Texas sun by its thick walls, was cool, the dimmed lights and hushed voices of the visitors giving it an almost sacred atmosphere. Paintings hung on the walls, vivid scenes reflecting the agony and pain suffered by those men of long ago.

Enthralled by the place and by the obvious respect every tourist was showing for it, Alison wandered from the displays of weapons and other artifacts to the back wall, where a plaque listed the names and birthplaces of those killed. She turned widened eyes to Jason, who had followed her. "I thought all the men who fought here were Texans."

"Some of them were native Texans, but many had been born in other parts of the country and as far away as England and Scotland. Once the fighting started, nobody stopped to ask for credentials."

After Alison had seen the interior, Jason guided her outside, where spreading oaks shaded the grounds. Her eyes lingered on the aged stone of the building before turning to Jason.

"Would you have stayed and fought if you knew there was no chance of surviving?"

His eyes flickered toward the flags rippling in the breeze overhead. "I don't know. I like to think I would, for a good cause. But since the question is academic, we'll never know."

Shaking off their still-somber mood, he chuckled. "Several years ago an Arab sheikh tried to buy the Alamo for his son. You can't imagine the fury that caused. The whole state was up in arms!"

"Did they lynch the poor man?" she asked, following him leisurely back to the car.

"Nothing quite so drastic as that. But they let him know in no uncertain terms what he could do with his offer."

After they were seated in the car again Jason turned away from the city's center. "Now where?" Alison asked.

"Considering your tender Yankee skin, I thought we should stick to the cooler areas of town. You're probably not acclimatized yet."

His ribbing tone had her quickly defending herself. "I can take the heat as well as you can. It's much easier to adjust to it than it is to the bitter cold of winter. You'd probably freeze to death if you had to withstand a New York winter."

His hand reached for the air conditioner controls. "Since you feel that way, we won't need this."

Before she could stop herself, her hand stopped his, and she laughed at his knowing grin. "There's no need to prove your point; I concede. If you're a gracious winner, you won't refer to the matter again."

"I never said I was a gracious winner. What's the use of winning if you can't rub it in?" At her outraged look, he chuckled. "I'm only teasing. You make it so easy, I can't resist. C'mon," he said as he pulled into another parking lot and turned off the motor.

She quickly got out of the car and joined Jason as he came around to meet her. The unexpected sight of oriental architecture drew her gaze, and for the first time she noted the vast array of flowers that bloomed in well-tended beds not far from where they stood. Red, yellow and orange blossoms blended together to create an artist's palette of color. Alison's appreciative eyes turned to Jason. "It's beautiful! What is it?"

"It's called Sunken Gardens." Heading toward the concrete steps before them, he led her to the top and motioned to the rock walls, which were covered with clinging vines and overhanging branches. "At one time this was a rock quarry. That's why it has such steep sides. When the quarry business moved farther out of town, the city had the problem of what to do with this ugly hole in the ground. As you can see, they found a solution."

Growing vegetation and years of exposure to the weather had altered the harsh cliffs, softening the angles and the unsightly cuts made by men. Ponds of water had collected at the bottom, like mirrors reflecting the shine of the sun and many flowers lining the walls. Small islands dotted the bottom of the quarry, linked together by narrow walkways and ivy-covered arched bridges. At the far end of the gardens a waterfall cascaded from the top of the sheer rock cliff to the ponds below, dark green moss marking the water's trail. Watermelon-red crepe myrtle and feathery pink blossoms of mimosa trees shaded the paths, their flowers delicate and fragrant.

"It looks so cool and inviting, even in this heat," Alison stated quietly. "The goldfish have it made."

The flowers were even lovelier up close. Indulgently Jason followed her along the paths, allowing her to look to her heart's desire. When she voiced a wish to take the walkway that had been cut out of the side of the cliff, he warned, "That leads to the top of the waterfall. That path's not steep, but it's pretty hot going in this weather. Sure you want to try it?"

Placing her hands on her hips, she said saucily, "There you go again, doubting my abilities! One of these days you're going to have to admit you're wrong about me, and today just might be the day." Like a gazelle she turned and sprinted up the path, hardly giving him a chance to object. She glanced over her shoulder once, but the path had curved, and he was lost to sight.

The calves of Alison's legs were soon protesting fiercely at the pace she had set, and her brow was beaded with perspiration. A tiny pain in her side quickly grew to a stitch she couldn't ignore. Leaning against a convenient tree, she gasped for breath and felt the pain easing. A frown knitted her brow as she again glanced over her shoulder. But Jason was nowhere in sight. Where was he? With a sigh she pushed herself away from the tree and started off again. From the glimpse she caught of the garden below, she knew she was nearing the top.

When she turned her head back to the path she gasped in chagrin. "How did you get ahead of me?"

Sitting casually on a bench shaded by a mesquite tree, Jason grinned at her triumphantly. Not a hair of his was out of place. Rising to his feet, he sauntered over to her and flicked a damp curl away from her forehead. "I took the other path; it's easier than this one." His eyes took in her flushed appearance, her beaded brow, the damp tendrils of hair clinging to her neck, her shortness of breath. "From the looks of it, you should have taken it, too."

"Ohhh...!" She struggled valiantly to swallow the hot words that were bubbling for release. Her eyes swept him with irritation, but the sight of the wide smile on his bronze face and the twinkle in his eyes destroyed her anger more effectively than any words. Stubbornly she refused to let him see how easily he could get around her; she bit her lip to stop the traitorous smile that threatened.

"You know, you favor grandmother a great deal. She never could stay angry with me, either. She always wanted to laugh."

Alison groaned, laughing in spite of herself. "I'll bet you were a real monster when you were a kid. You and John were probably partners in crime."

His answering grin told her all she needed to know. But he said, "Grandfather Morgan's property was in the country then, so there were plenty of places to get into trouble. One summer we were shooting off bottle rockets and almost burned the barn down. It was the last time we did that. From then on fireworks were off limits." He laughed, shaking his head. "It's not much farther to the top," he went on. "C'mon, I'll help you." When he took her hand to pull her up the dozen or so steps that remained, he exclaimed, "My gosh, your hands are cold!"

"Cold hands, warm heart," she quipped. His touch was sending shivers up her arm, despite how she strove to ignore the fact. "At least they're not hot like yours."

As they reached the top of the path, his gaze lingered on her upturned face. "I suppose you have a saying for that as well."

"Mmm hmm," she nodded. "Hot hands, dirty mind."

His shout of laughter warmed her; she felt a blush sting her cheeks.

"Is that another of Aunt Gwen's sayings?" he chuckled.

"Oh, no. It's based strictly on personal experience."

His eyebrows shot up. "So you've been holding out on me. You're not a shy little innocent after all."

"I never claimed to be inexperienced," she denied. "You came to that conclusion all by yourself. I've endured my fair share of wrestling matches. The heavy gropers are the worst!"

"I'll have to remember that the lady likes finesse." His eyes searched her face, then his arm unexpectedly circled her shoulders, turning her toward the view of the city that made the climb worthwhile. "I won't try any smooth moves while your resistance is down from your week of work," he said. "But I warn you, once you're rested, you're fair game. Anything goes."

His words caused a shiver down her spine despite her attempts to suppress it in case he felt it. "Thanks for the warning," she replied lightly. "I'll be on my guard. Dark alleys and deserted streets will be strictly avoided. Should I wear a long-sleeved flannel nightgown and a chastity belt as well?"

"Heaven forbid!" he exclaimed, a look of mock horror on his face. "Such things were invented for the sole purpose of tormenting mankind. Thank heavens chastity belts went out of fashion centuries ago. As for flannel nightgowns, they should be outlawed!"

"Would you want women to catch cold?" she queried impishly. "New York winters can be terribly rough."

"There are other ways to warm women up, and I don't mean electric blankets!" At her laugh, he eyed her sternly. "If you're not careful, this conversation is going to lead somewhere other than where you'd like." His hand swept the view before them. "Now, look. Then we can eat. I'm starved!"

"Somehow that doesn't surprise me," she retorted dryly. She followed his command, then allowed him to direct her to the shorter of the two paths. In record time they reached the car, removed the loaded basket and found a picnic table in the shade of a stately pecan tree. The contents of the basket were soon spread out, and Alison stared in delight at the vast array of food: ham sandwiches, potato salad, coleslaw, pickles, cherry tomatoes, wine, peaches.... "Did you do all this?" she asked.

"Only the sandwiches. The rest was generously provided by the neighborhood delicatessen and grocery store. Here, have some wine." He reached for the bottle, only to discover there were no glasses. "I knew I'd forgotten something. Looks like we'll have to drink out of the bottle."

"I don't mind," she assured him.

After quenching her thirst, she watched as he, too, drank from the bottle. There was something intimate about sharing a bottle of wine; and Alison couldn't draw her eyes from him. She was suddenly glad he had insisted on this outing. She had been alone too much lately, thinking too much about this very man. At least when she was with him she didn't have to wonder whom he was spending his time with. "How was New Orleans? Was your business successful?"

He reached for a sandwich after handing her one. "Not particularly. In fact, I'm beginning to think it was a waste of time. Mr. Carlson won't listen to reason. He wants a fifth of the profits—which is ridiculous. I tried to tell him ninety-five percent of my revenue goes back into the field and that I can't afford to give him that big a cut. But he won't listen. How the hell is this country ever going to be energy self-sufficient if the independents give away most of their profits just so they can drill?"

"But what about the major oil companies?" Alison asked. "Don't they do exploratory drilling?"

"Sure they do. But their overhead costs are out of this world, which means they can't always afford to drill smaller wells. Independents don't have the overhead, so they can take a chance on a small field. That's why they find so many more wells than the majors."

Alison ate her sandwich thoughtfully. John had said Christina more or less had control over the deal between her father and Jason. If she was running interference for Jason, she was doing a pretty sorry job of it. She wouldn't earn Jason's love by standing in the way of his work. Had something gone wrong between them?

She was startled out of her musings by the touch of his finger on her arm. She blinked, looking at him in confusion. "I'm sorry. What did you say?"

"I was just wondering how work is going on the house. Have you had any difficulties?"

"Oh, no," she assured him. "In fact, everything is going better than I expected. The windows will be installed Monday, and someone is coming to work on the ceilings. After that I can start on the wallpapering. Mr. Halston is still working on the plumbing; he should finish early in the week. I still have to get a carpenter to build a banister and repair damage to some of the woodwork."

"Sounds like you've really been busy. I'm impressed." He took another drink of wine before offering her the bottle. "You know, I've never really understood your desire to keep the place. In today's market, it's nothing but a white elephant, yet you're determined to hang onto it. But why? Just as inspiration for your writing?"

Alison struggled to find the words to explain her feelings about the mansion. "There are several reasons. You know I was raised by my aunt. I never realized until I saw the mansion that I never really fitted into Aunt Gwen's home. It was almost as if I was just passing through. Oh, she loved me and she never made me feel unwelcome. Maybe it was just in my head. I wanted a family so badly, and she couldn't give me that.

"Anyway, when I saw the mansion, everything just sort of fell into place. I didn't know grandmother, and I know she didn't live at the mansion long, but it's a tangible link to her. I guess you could say it represents my roots. My own great-grandfather and my own grandmother worked there. With a little imagination I can see them there, picture them walking where I walk. It makes them both so much more real.

"And then, as you say, it's inspiring," she

went on. "The personification of the plantation in my manuscript. I've done a lot of research for this book, but research doesn't compare to actually visiting the places you write about. Research can't tell you that the third step on the stairs creaks or that when the mountain laurels are in bloom the scent of grapes is everywhere. It's an incredible resource, besides being a magnificent house. And it would be a wonderful home for a family. I can just see kids and dogs running all over the place—there's so much room."

Jason studied her thoughtfully, frowning at the wistful expression on her face and the longing in her voice. A shuttered look dropped over his own face. Alison noticed how withdrawn he seemed when she finally looked up. He was watching her, aloofness cooling the blue of his eyes. Perplexed by his sudden change, she tilted her head inquiringly. "What's wrong?"

"Nothing." He started to repack the basket. "Speaking of your writing, how's it coming? Have you been able to get much accomplished?"

"Oh, yes." As she handed him the containers of potato salad and coleslaw, her eyes glowed with excitement. "Characterization was my major problem, but I think I've just about got it solved. Once I made Arabella into a more believable character, everything else worked itself out. Strong, independent women aren't just a product of the twentieth century, they've been around for years. So even though Arabella is the daughter of a plantation owner, she's not a sweet, simpering miss. She grew up on the plantation with three brothers, so she's got to be something of a tomboy. Sometimes she forgets to be a lady."

The aloofness she had noticed in Jason's eyes faded with her lively description. She now looked up to find him regarding her teasingly. "And what about the hero? I suppose he's arrogant enough to put this bold girl in her place, which is, of course, his bed."

"Don't you ever think of anything but sex?" Alison asked in irritation.

"Can you deny that the girl ends up in bed with him?"

Alison laughed in defeat. "No, but there's more to the story than one love scene. The hero's name is Miles Hayden. He's sort of a combination of Robert Redford, Burt Reynolds and Errol Flynn. He's very daring, but then he has to be—he's a spy. I think I told you he's pretending to be a requisition officer for the Confederacy while he reports the location of supplies and ammunition to the Yankees. Of course, he's not above using people, and that's where the conflict develops between him and Arabella. She discovers he's a spy and threatens to tell her father. So he kidnaps her and takes her with him. That's when it really gets juicy!"

The corners of Jason's eyes crinkled with laughter. "How are the love scenes going? Has my expert instruction helped at all?"

It helped me fall in love with you. The words trembled on Alison's lips. Her heart was suddenly pounding in her ears. But with a pretended air of indifference, she shrugged. "I haven't really got into those scenes yet. Anyway, I'm the wrong person to ask. I'm too close to it. I can't be objective."

"You'll have to let me read it," he stated. "If it doesn't sound right, we'll have to get in some more practice."

"It'll sound right, believe me," she retorted. He didn't know it, but those farcical lessons were a thing of the past. Any further demonstration of his lovemaking would be more than she could stand. Purposefully she changed the subject. "I've been reading grandmother's diaries."

"Oh?"

His response certainly wasn't encouraging, she thought wryly. She lifted her chin and met his wary gaze. "Yes. They've helped a lot in my writing. Did you know that Edward Smythe was engaged when he met her?"

At his nod, she sighed. "It must have been very hard for them, concealing their love from his parents. Especially since they were meeting right under their noses. What happened, Jason? Why did they split up? I know from a letter I found in the attic that grandmother was accused of something she didn't do. What was it? Who—"

The pressure of his mouth suddenly halted her words, and all thoughts of questioning him flew right out of her head. She didn't know why he was kissing her—she didn't care! A delicious warmth spread through her veins, and she didn't even notice the table edge biting into her side as she leaned closer to Jason, returning his kiss with an ardor that surprised them both. She sighed in disappointment when he reluctantly released her mouth, his darkened eyes going over her face possessively. "I'm giving you fair warning," he said huskily, "from now on every time you ask me questions about those damn diaries, I'm going to kiss you. I don't care if we're in the middle of a grocery store!"

Just the thought of being ruthlessly kissed in the middle of the frozen-food section sparked Alison's sense of humor. "Promise?" she asked, her eyes dancing with laughter.

"Lady, you can bet money on it!" His hand reached for hers, his fingers linking them together. The smile he gave her would have melted Antarctica, Alison decided. She found herself grinning in response, her head in the clouds.

Moments later they were back in the car. The low-slung sports car, sleek and powerful, was like a cat on a leash, straining to escape. When the speed limits of the park were left behind the car jumped forward eagerly, its high-performance engine quickly gobbling up the miles.

Again Alison found herself downtown. A sign reading Market Square caught her eye, and she turned eagerly to Jason. "Are we going shopping?"

He grinned at the light of excitement shining in her eyes. "I never met a woman yet who didn't like to go shopping. C'mon, brown eyes, this is the Mexican market. You can browse to your heart's content, and even barter with the shopkeepers the way they do in Mexico."

As she stepped into the cool interior of the building, Alison's eyes shone in appreciation of the colorful sight that met them. Glazed flowerpots of assorted sizes were nestled in macrame hangers outside the many small stalls that comprised the market. Piñatas of scarlet, orange, lime green and royal blue made bright splashes of color against the walls. Eagerly she pulled Jason into a shop, exclaiming over the delicate porcelain flowers captured in small glass boxes of unusual shapes. Her fingers caressed the roughness of suede vests lined with wooly sheepskin. Jewelry of silver and turquoise was shown by an eager shopkeeper, who glowed when she praised the workmanship but sighed with disappointment when she failed to make a purchase.

With Jason by her side she went through each and every shop, so engrossed in the varied merchandise that she failed to notice his interested gaze studying her. He watched the changing expressions flit across her face—curiosity when she spied treasured antiques that reminded her of childhood, laughter at wooden ducks that continually dipped their bills into glasses of water, delight with a ceramic cow that hung on a leather strap, its tag proclaiming it a cowbell.

"Would you like to have it?" Jason asked of the last item.

She glanced up to find him staring down at her, an enigmatic expression on his face. She glanced at the bell before shaking her head. "No, thank you. I was just thinking what a cute gift it would make. Maybe I'll come back in a couple of months to do some Christmas shopping. I'm sure Susan would like it."

As they walked out of the shop, he looked at her inquiringly. "Susan was your roommate?" At her nod, he teased, "Was she another Victorian miss like you?"

"Susan?" She laughed at the image of Susan dressed in frills and crinolines. "Hardly. She's one of the top models in the country and doesn't have one old-fashioned bone in her body."

"Didn't that make complications? I would imagine it would be difficult living with someone whose life-style was so different from your own."

A twinkle appeared in her eyes as she gazed up at him guilelessly. "*Our* life-styles are completely different. Do you think it would be difficult living with me?"

His lips parted in an amused grin, his eyes darkened by something other than laughter. "I'm sure I could adjust to seeing you walk around in those sexy pajamas." His fingers came out to flick the end of her nose. "If you're through looking, let's get out of here."

His hand closed around her arm, but she stopped abruptly to look over her shoulder. "Wait." Slipping free of his hold, she walked to a nearby shop to talk to the clerk, gesturing to the colorful piñatas hanging over her head. When she reached for her purse, Jason was there, his fingers closing over hers. "What do you want to buy?"

She motioned to a large strawberry piñata that the clerk was taking down. "But Jason, I'll buy it. It's for Susan's niece. She loves strawberries."

When he continued to ignore her protests, handing the man the money for the piñata, she frowned in irritation. "Jason, will you please listen to me! I can't let you pay for a birthday gift. . . it's not even for me."

She watched in mute surprise as he picked up the piñata and headed for the exit of the market. She hurried to catch up with him, clutching his arm to stop him. "You can be so exasperating sometimes!" She held out the money. "Are you going to take this or not?"

When he refused to answer, her eyes narrowed dangerously. "If you don't take it, I'm going to put it in your pocket myself," she warned.

Something flickered in the depths of his eyes before amusement replaced it. He stopped his long strides and turned to face her, smiling lazily. "I dare you," he challenged.

Her resolve wavered briefly, but then she lifted her chin. "I don't walk away from a dare." Swiftly, before she had a chance to back down, she gripped the money with trembling fingers and slipped it into the pocket of his camel-colored slacks. Yanking her hand back as if it was burned, she turned on her heel and strode quickly away, ignoring his command to come back.

His long strides quickly reduced the distance between them. Tanned fingers gripped her arm to spin her around, and she found herself gazing into his laughing blue eyes. Chuckling at her anger, Jason smoothed the frown from her brow before allowing his fingers to trail down her flushed cheeks. "What are you so mad about? It was only three dollars. Forget it."

She stomped her foot. "I will not forget it! It's not the money, it's the principle. I don't like being overruled, and that's exactly what you're doing. I'm warning you, I'm getting sick of it! You leave for a whole week—with Christina, I might add—and then you come back and start giving me orders again. And I won't have it! Those other women you date may like the macho act, but I don't. So save it for them. I'm not impressed. I don't need you to put my life in order; I've been doing quite well up to now, thank you. So quit trying to take over!"

Far from making him angry, her tirade only seemed to afford him greater amusement, though only the faint twitching of his lips revealed the fact. He was staring at her with an almost fascinated expression on his face, his eyes moving from her flushed cheeks to her flashing brown eyes. His fingers slid down her arm to her wrist, sensuously caressing the sensitive skin. "You're the strangest girl. Any other woman would be mad if I didn't spend money on her, but you blow up because I spend a lousy three bucks."

"I keep telling you I'm not like the other women you date." Her eyes locked with him. "I don't play games, Jason. When I stopped to look at the piñata, I wasn't angling for you to buy it. I had the money to pay for it."

"I know you did. But I wanted to buy you *something*, even if it was a stupid piñata." His smile was totally unrepentant. "Next time I'll ask. Though I might not pay any attention to your answer. Now, Miss Independence, can I take you to dinner or are you going to object to that, too?"

Her eyes, which had only moments before been seething with anger, were now alive with laughter. "Dinner! How can you be hungry? We just ate. I swear that's almost all you think about!"

"We ate three hours ago. And that was just a snack. But if you'd rather wait a while, I know another way to pass the time." His voice dropped to a sensuous whisper, sending shivers down her spine.

A blush tinged her cheeks, but she retorted innocently, "You know, I've suddenly got a ravenous appetite. Let's go somewhere for dinner."

Jason shook his head in pretended disgust. "I had a feeling you'd say that."

A short while later, he again parked the car and helped her out. "Tonight we dine among the stars," he announced grandly, taking her hand. Before them the tall, cylindrical Tower of Americas rose high into the clouds, its slowly revolving restaurant, when they took the elevator to the top, offering a bird's-eye view of the city.

Alison was entranced with the view out the floor-to-ceiling windows of the restaurant. The sun had just slipped beneath the horizon, leaving in its wake a brilliant orange streak that gradually softened to pink, shot through with finely spun clouds of lavender. The evening star twinkled brightly in the gathering dusk, and by the time they'd been seated at a window table the streetlights of the city had come on, casting a golden hue over everything.

During the course of their meal, the restaurant revolved a full 360 degrees, bringing them back to their starting point. And Alison was thoroughly intoxicated with the view, with the wine and with Jason. She was floating ten feet off the ground and she didn't care who knew it. How could she ever have thought him arrogant? Determined, yes. Self-assured, no doubt about it. But arrogant? He had charmed her out of her earlier mood; now she couldn't even remember what she had been upset about. She only knew that being in his company was the nearest thing to heaven she had ever experienced. She didn't want the evening to end.

She met his gaze across the table and smiled tremulously. "Thank you for bringing me here, Jason. It was a lovely dinner."

He pretended surprise. "And I thought you were going to chew me out for not consulting you about the choice of restaurant." He shook his head in wonder, his dimples flashing as he grinned at her. "It's amazing what a little food can do for a person's disposition. Even a shrew can become docile."

"It must be the wine," she retorted, "it's mellowed me." Her eyes glowed as she studied him guilelessly. "Though I can't say the same for you. I warn you, if you're going to be obnoxious again, I'm going to retaliate in self-defense."

"Go ahead," he laughed. "But my method of counter-retaliation may not be to your liking."

They hardly spoke on the ride home. Instead the sound of violins drifting from the radio enveloped them in a romantic cocoon. Leaning her head against the headrest, Alison closed her eyes. She was tired but happy. The few disquieting words they had exchanged had been unable to mar the overall success of the day. She knew beyond a shadow of a doubt that she loved Jason with all her heart and would like nothing better than to spend the rest of her life with him. But she could not and would not be willing to share him with any other woman. He liked her, at times desired her, of that she was sure. But he also seemed to like and desire Christina Carlson. . . .

A frown creased her brow. Damn! Why did she have to think of that woman now?

Further troubling thoughts were pushed away, however, as the car came to a stop in front of the cottage. There was a light shining in the living room, its illumination welcoming in the darkness. Alison noticed it absently. She didn't remember leaving a light on; Jason must have done so.

As she got out of the car, she glanced up the hill to the mansion. Although there was no moon, it was a cloudless night, and the muted lights of the city clearly revealed the shape of the old house. The eclipsing darkness muted the shabbiness, giving the building a certain regality that the light of day destroyed; tonight there were no broken windows, no cracked and peeling paint. Miraculously the house stood as it had a hundred years before, proud and majestic, untouched by the ravages of time.

"It's a beautiful sight, isn't it?"

Alison jumped at the soft words spoken so close to her in the darkness. She had been staring at the mansion, unaware that Jason had walked around the car to stand at her side. His hand came out to caress a dark curl that lay against her cheek. His eyes were on her, not on the house, when he spoke. "Beautiful and romantic. In fact, it's perfect for a book."

For the life of her, Alison couldn't get one

word past her tight throat. She had been a victim of many of Jason's moods, but never before had she had the full force of his sensuous magnetism directed at her. Her skin tingled where he touched her, his fingers gliding from her neck to her shoulder. His eyes caressed her—her hair, her eyes, the curve of her cheek, before lingering on her mouth. When his hand tightened to pull her closer, she offered no protest, swaying into his arms. His lips feathered over the smoothness of her cheeks before hovering near her mouth. "Here's something else you can put in a book," he whispered thickly an instant before he took possession of her lips.

Like a drug, his kiss robbed her of her will and numbed her senses to everything but him. His masculine scent enveloped her as surely as his arms did. Desire left her a willing victim, and she needed no prompting to respond to his embrace. Alison melted against him, her arms encircling his neck as he kissed her, his hard muscular frame the only solid object in her reeling world.

CHAPTER NINE

THE PORCH LIGHT FLARED; like a searchlight it found and illuminated the embracing couple. "Jason, darling! I was beginning to wonder if you were ever coming home," a drawling voice complained, apparently unconcerned with the passionate scene she was interrupting.

Alison stiffened, the huskiness of the feminine voice grating on her nerves. Automatically she pushed herself out of the arms that had held her so close only seconds before. Her eyes were wide with shock and her knees threatened to buckle as she stared at Christina Carlson in stunned disbelief.

The glare of the porch light turned the woman's hair to spun silver, her green eyes glinting like a satisfied cat's. Not the least embarrassed by her intrusion, she sauntered farther onto the porch, blithely ignoring Alison to cast the full force of her smile at Jason. And for the first time, Alison became aware of the perfection of Christina's features. She *was* lovely. Her skin was smooth and unlined, stretched taut across high cheekbones. Tall and graceful, she had wisely chosen a green dress that just matched the color of her eyes. Cut along deceptively simple lines, the garment subtly displayed her sinuous figure.

Turning away in confusion, Alison failed to see the look in Jason's eyes or the set of his jaw. But she heard him demand, "What the devil are you doing here? And how did you get in?"

"Don't you remember, darling?" Her eyes shifted to Alison as she dangled a key before his eyes, a teasing smile playing on her lips. "You gave me the key in New Orleans. Surely you haven't forgotten? Remember, we were in your room and—"

"No, I haven't forgotten," he cut in. "But apparently you have. We were not in my room, but at dinner with your father. You were supposed to come back here to pick up those reports I had left by mistake. But you never came, Christina. What happened?"

"Now, Jason, don't be angry. You can be so nasty when you're mad. It was all a misunderstanding—you know, just one of those little mix-ups that can't be helped."

As if suddenly aware of Alison's presence, she cast her an embarrassed smile. "Oh, I'm sorry. You must be Jason's little cousin from New York. He told me he was going to take you sightseeing. Did you have a good time? Jason's such a dear, he always takes newcomers to all the tourist attractions—he feels it's his duty to welcome them to town." Holding out her hand, she smiled a smile that never quite reached her eyes. "I'm Christina Carlson, an...old friend."

Alison had been willing to accept this woman, if not as a friend, then surely as an acquaintance with whom she could converse civilly. Now she could see that was impossible. All the pleasure she had received in Jason's company slowly seeped away, destroyed by Christina's words. Duty! Was that all today had been?

Blinking back the tears that suddenly stung her eyes, she chanced to meet the older woman's gaze and was stunned by the venom reflected there. Recoiling from the hatred directed at her, Alison felt hot anger course through her. Couldn't Jason see what this woman was trying to do? Was he so enamored with her that he couldn't see through the facade of friendliness to the jealous core beneath? The shuttered expression on his face told her nothing. Obviously she would have to protect herself from Christina's jealousy.

Stepping onto the porch, Alison smiled sweetly, sardonic amusement glittering in the depths of her eyes. "I've heard so much about you, Miss Carlson, I feel as if I already know you. But I don't know how you got the idea Jason and I are cousins. Did he tell you that? He must have been teasing because we aren't even remotely related."

She turned her gaze to Jason, who was watching them warily. "I hope you don't mind my explaining the situation to Miss Carlson, Jason. After the kiss she just witnessed, I wouldn't want her to accuse us of having an incestuous relationship." Her lips quivered traitorously at his choke of laughter, but she carefully avoided meeting his eyes. Turning back to Christina, she smiled coolly. "You understand, Miss Carlson. This thing between Jason and myself is. . . well, it's just bigger than both of us."

Christina's eyes snapped and her lips thinned in anger as she struggled for control. But she quickly regained her composure. Walking over to Jason, she linked her arm through his. Then she glanced at Alison. "Of course, dear. I understand how infatuated girls become with older men. It's a phase of growing up."

Seething with rage, Alison was on the verge of telling Christina just exactly what she could do with her older-man complex when the sophisticated blonde turned to Jason and pouted prettily. "Please, darling, can't we go somewhere we can be alone? We have so much to discuss. I'm sure Alison will excuse us." Her glowing eyes and parted lips held a seductive promise. "New Orleans was so beautiful—the candlelit suppers and romantic atmosphere. How could I possibly think of business? You were always there to distract me."

Alison tried desperately to keep her features expressionless, but she knew it was a losing battle. She was trying to forget that Jason had even gone to New Orleans, but Christina insisted on flaunting the details. She was a fool to even pay her the least heed. The woman obviously saw her as a threat; she'd say anything to discourage her. But was she lying?

Alison's eyes swept from Christina to Jason and back again, and suddenly it was more than she could bear. She had to get away, to be alone, so she could think clearly. "Excuse me," she mumbled huskily before hurrying into the house, not caring that Jason suddenly frowned in bewilderment.

Hot tears blurred her vision and tightened her throat. Stumbling to the couch, she was about to sit down when instead she stiffened, her nostrils flaring at the cloying muskiness of Christina's perfume. The odor seemed to have invaded every corner of the house. Regardless of the air conditioning, Alison hurriedly raised the windows, allowing the sweetness of the night air to sweep through the house. Mumbled voices drifted in to her; abruptly she made her way to the small back porch where she would have neither sight nor sound of Christina or Jason.

Standing in the concealing darkness, her fingers clenched the porch railing fiercely. It was time she took a good hard look at her relationship with Jason. And his relationship with other women. Christina had implied their relationship was intimate, yet Jason had not been overjoyed to see her. He had even accused her of lying about how she got the key to the cottage. Alison frowned. How many keys were there to the cottage, anyway? The whole world seemed to have a key to *her* front door!

Determinedly she dragged her thoughts back to Jason. Christina couldn't be sure of his feelings or she wouldn't be so antagonistic. So where did that leave Alison? She knew all the reasons why she was crazy to hope for anything more than an affair. He hadn't led her on. There had been no false promises, no indication that he wanted anything more than a flirtation. His objective was to get her into bed, while hers was to win his love. She wouldn't achieve that by chasing him. If he could elude the clutches of an expert like Christina Carlson, what chance did Alison have?

But she wasn't chasing him. He was the one trying to lure her into his bed. What would happen if she stood still and let him catch her? Her senses leaped at the thought. He was slowly wearing down her defenses anyway. If he loved her, there would be no contest. Could she trust the occasional flicker of tenderness she glimpsed in his eyes? If only she knew what to do! Her love made her vulnerable. . . she wanted just to melt into his arms and forget the world. Maybe she should do that and forget about tomorrow.

One thing was definite—she couldn't continue to hide on the back porch. Until she came to some sort of a decision, she would go on as she had, enjoying his friendship and his kisses without letting him see how much she loved him. It wasn't going to be easy.

She took a deep steadying breath before retracing her steps to the front porch. When she spied the two figures standing by the car, she hesitated, loath to interrupt them. But when Jason glanced up and caught sight of her, she was compelled to speak. "Jason, would you mind bringing in the piñata for me? I'll wrap it tomorrow so it can be mailed first thing Monday morning."

"Sure, I'll bring it right in." Against the direct light of the porch lamp, he squinted at her. Alison was glad that her face was in shadows. Christina, however, was clearly illuminated. She had stiffened at Alison's approach, and her eyes flared with resentment for a moment before she quickly veiled her irritation.

Jason was nodding toward the house. "Since you insist on discussing this tonight, Christina, why don't you go in the house with Alison while I get the piñata from the car. We can have some coffee." Grinning almost wickedly, he looked at Alison. "You don't mind making coffee, do you? Christina seems to have a problem that must be solved tonight."

How he was enjoying this! Alison fumed. Having two females spitting and clawing over him must be infinitely rewarding to his male ego. Oh, how she would like to tell him what he could do with his coffee! Momentarily she wavered. But her anger would only amuse him and make her look like a fool in front of Christina. She wouldn't give either one of them the satisfaction. Instead, she swallowed the angry words and turned a cool smile on their visitor. "Of course not." Opening the screen door, she motioned to the living room. "Won't you come in, Miss Carlson? It won't take me very long to make the coffee."

Christina headed ungraciously into the house. Stopping just inside the living room she gave Alison a cool glance. "I don't want any coffee, thank you. And I have no desire to make inane conversation with you. My business is with Jason, and it's private!"

Biting back the ready words that sprang quickly to her lips, Alison dug her nails into her palms for several indignant seconds. Then she forced herself to relax, a falsely sweet smile on her lips and the light of battle in her eye. "I'll ignore your comment about inane conversation, Miss Carlson. I can only assume you're referring to yourself, since you don't know me well enough to make a judgment."

At her outraged gasp, Alison's smile broadened. "I always thought Texans were famous for their hospitality, but you make me wonder. Didn't anyone ever tell you it's ill-mannered to be rude to someone in her own home? You're taking unfair advantage, Miss Carlson, because you're a guest. I wouldn't mistreat a dog in my own home, but don't push your luck."

"Why, you...you conniving little fool!" the Texan woman cried. "Do you honestly think this little ruse of yours will work?"

At Alison's obvious confusion, she scoffed. "Oh, come off it! You're no more interested in fixing up that old house than I am. You're using the situation to get Jason. But you *won't* get him. He may take what you offer—what else would a man do when you continue to throw yourself at him? But it's me he wants. You're wasting your time."

Despite herself, Alison could no longer contain her anger. "If Jason had the bad taste to want you, then I *wouldn't* want him!"

The squeaking of the screen door effectively interrupted the argument. Jason stood in the doorway, the piñata under his arm. There was no way he could have missed her last dramatic statement. His eyes lingered on Alison's flushed face. "Something wrong?"

Alison felt her face flush deepen. "I. . . I was just going to make some coffee," she muttered.

Christina's manner had instantly changed. Her earlier hostility was replaced by a patronizing friendliness that set Alison's teeth on edge. "Please don't make any for me, dear. Coffee would keep me awake for hours. Jason will fix me a drink; he knows exactly what I like."

"I'll bet he does, too," Alison replied innocently enough. "Would you like coffee, Jason?"

"Don't make any just for me." Setting the piñata in a corner, he walked to the small bar to pour Christina her drink. Grinning over the glass of Scotch he held in his hand, he teased her with his eyes. "But I'll take a piece of that chocolate cake I spied this morning. Did you make it?"

She took a deep breath and managed a smile in return. "Yes. Sure you don't want coffee to go with it?" At the shake of his head, she reluctantly turned to her uninvited guest. "How about you, Miss Carlson? Would you like a piece of cake?"

"No, thank you." The woman's eyes swept over Alison. "So you bake, too. How. . . sweet." She looked around the neat room.

"You seem very domesticated, Alison. I'm surprised. I didn't think girls bothered with such things these days. From what I've seen of the younger generation, alcohol, drugs and sex are the main interests."

Alison replied smoothly, "I leave all that to my elders, Miss Carlson. Perhaps you'd care to tell me about it sometime. If you'll excuse me, I'll get Jason's cake."

Well, she'd done it again! Viciously she cut into the cake, secretly wishing it were Christina's throat. She refused to feel guilty about what she'd said. It gave her infinite satisfaction to know she had put Christina in her place. And it wasn't as though she hadn't had provocation.

An almost hysterical laugh bubbled in her throat. This was so idiotic, trading insults with Christina Carlson. If Alison could just keep her emotions at bay and not lose her temper she might be able to enjoy this banter. It wasn't often that she sharpened her claws on other people, but Christina more or less forced her to defend herself.

As she returned to the living room moments later, Jason asked, "Would you like something to drink, Alison?"

"No, thank you." Her gaze flickered to Christina, who was seated on the couch, her feet curled under her. She looked as if she was prepared for a long stay, and Alison was suddenly too weary to care. "I've had just about enough for tonight. I. . .I think I'll go to bed. You can lock up when you leave. Good night." Nodding to Christina, she crossed the room and hurried up the stairs, anxious to be alone, free of the tension the other woman's presence had created.

TWO DAYS LATER, standing in the den of the mansion, Alison watched as the new floor-to-ceiling windows were installed. It was amazing what new glass could do to improve the looks of a building, she decided. Without the broken windows the mansion no longer looked dead.

To a newcomer it still probably looked pretty awful, with its walls stripped to the bare plaster and all the woodwork and floors stripped for sanding. Walking through the front door was like walking in on a stranger half dressed. But to Alison it was beautiful. Mr. Halston was just about finished with the plumbing; the sound of water running through the new faucets was music to her ears.

Dodging around the scaffolds that held the men working on the ceiling, Alison walked slowly up the stairs. There she inspected with interest the work being done on the bedrooms. Once the ceilings were replastered, the wall-papering could begin. She had hopes of finding old-fashioned patterns that would retain the mansion's Southern atmosphere, but she wasn't sure she could afford them. If she spent too much on wallpaper, she'd have to hang it herself. And with ten-foot ceilings, that was going to be a real pain in the neck.

She stepped into the master bedroom and found her thoughts drifting to her grandmother's diaries. Last night she had read of the breakup between Edward Smythe and her grandmother, and she was still reeling from what she had learned. The beginning of the end of their relationship had started in this very room. Alison Ford Morgan had been called to the master suite to explain why several pieces of Mrs. Smythe's jewelry were missing. Totally ignorant of the crime, she had been stunned, not at first realizing that the alleged theft was a deliberate attempt to destroy her in the eyes of the man she loved.

Edward's parents had actually been aware of the affair and had seen it as a harmless summer romance. But when Edward had decided to break his engagement to a well-known debutante, they could no longer ignore what they felt was an impending scandal. Since Edward would not voluntarily stop seeing the family maid, they'd taken matters in their own hands and had literally framed her: they'd planted several items of jewelry as well as some of the family silver in her room.

Alison walked to the window seat and sat down. It had happened years ago, but owing to her grandmother's vivid descriptions she could picture it with ease. In their elaborate plans to save their son from folly, the Smythes had given little thought to their maid. They had never dreamed that she would fight them, that she herself would bring in the police to call their bluff, or that she would tell reporters it was all a hoax to prevent Edward from marrying her. The scandal they had hoped to avoid hit the front page of the papers.

But their ploy had worked. Edward had found the ensuing publicity distasteful and embarrassing. In his eyes, one person had been responsible for the scandal—Alison Ford Morgan. He'd found it impossible to believe his parents would ever do the despicable things she accused them of. She was trying to shift the blame, he decided, so obviously she was guilty. Fear of being disowned had also encouraged him to renounce his love for her. He returned to college without a backward glance, and the gardener and his daughter had been fired.

It was a tragic story, the consequences far-reaching. When Alison Ford Morgan had left the mansion in disgrace, she had been carrying her lover's baby....

Alison was still trying to adjust to it all. Edward Smythe was her grandfather! His actions had been nothing but cowardly, yet the pressure exerted by his parents must have been tremendous, the threat to disown him a real one. It would have taken a stronger man than Edward to stand up to them. He had not known of the pregnancy, and it had been pride that had kept her grandmother from telling him. She and her father had moved to Dallas, where, to protect herself from gossip caused by the scandal, she'd assumed the name Ford. Years later she'd returned to San Antonio—as a divorcée, and no one had known the mysterious Mr. Ford had been just a figment of her imagination.

Alison glanced outside the window at the spreading oaks that shaded the lawn. If things had been different, her grandmother would have married Edward. Her own mother would have grown up here.

Her grandmother had eventually forgiven Edward—she had mentioned that in her diary—but how she had suffered! The man she had given her heart to had renounced her at the first sign of trouble, leaving her to raise her child alone. No wonder Jason despised him.

She frowned. This was not the time to think of Jason. She had too much to do without wasting time wondering where he was or who he was with. Since he hadn't bothered to call her, she supposed the wonderful rapport they had had during their day together was gone....

Enough, Alison, that's enough, she told herself fiercely. *Time to get back to work.*

With determination she got to her feet and strode quickly downstairs. By the time she reached the pantry, she was again in control of her wayward emotions. Flashing a tremulous smile at the plumber, who was installing the new hot-water heater, she said, "I'll be in the basement, Mr. Halston, if you need me for anything. I seem to have misplaced my note pad, and that's the only place I haven't looked."

As she reached the bottom step to the cellar moments later, she looked up from her thoughts and frowned in annoyance. The basement was dark, the only light that there was spilling down the stairwell. She reached automatically for the switch, but the unresponsive click reminded her that the electricity had not yet been repaired in this area of the house. Only the laundry-room lights were functioning properly.

Swearing softly, she hesitated, glancing over her shoulder at the stairs. She didn't want to climb back upstairs just for a flashlight. If her note pad was down here, it would be in the laundry, which she should be able to find by feeling her way along the wall. Bravely she stepped out of the shaft of light into the darkness.

Stygian blackness obliterated everything, only the roughness of the wall beneath her hand assuring her that she had not stepped into another dimension. Realizing it was useless to try to see what was before her, she relied on touch to guide her through the maze of hallways and small rooms that comprised the basement. Her heartbeat echoed loudly in her ears; fervently she prayed that the darkness didn't harbor small rodents or bugs. Finally, turning a corner in the labyrinth of dark corridors, she reached the washroom and switched on the light. She briefly searched the room, stopping at the sight of the black pocket-size pad lying on the table. Stuffing it reassuringly into the hip pocket of her jeans, she returned to the open doorway and peered unenthusiastically into the waiting darkness. Taking a quick, steadying breath, she cast the room into total darkness again.

The corridor, black as pitch, seemed twice as dark as before. Down in the bowels of the house the silence was eerie, and a shiver of fear crawled up her spine. Suddenly she couldn't wait to get out of there. She reached for the wall and started to run, uncaring that she might lose her way. She rounded the corner into the main hallway at a dead run and plowed into something, nearly falling down in the process. A scream escaped her lips and her eyes widened in horror as she tried to see into the blackness.

Strong fingers gripped her arms, steadying her. "Hey, where are you off to in such a hurry? You almost knocked me over!"

Before she had time to answer, two warm arms came around her to press her against a very male form. She stiffened, trying to see, but the darkness was obliterating. Her heartbeat had accelerated to an alarming rate, and her heart seemed to be knocking wildly against her ribs. Tentatively her hands moved from the broad chest where they rested to the rugged planes of the face she loved so well. "J-Jason?"

Soft, throaty laughter caressed her, playing along the sensitive skin of her neck seconds before he kissed the hollow behind her ear. His voice was muffled against her hair, bringing her nerve endings to an instant awareness. "You were expecting someone else? Sorry to disappoint you."

"Who said I was disappointed?" she asked, giving a deep sigh of relief. The unseen monsters retreated into the dark crevices of her too vivid imagination, leaving her safe and laughing in his protective arms. With a laugh she slipped her own arms around his neck to give him a fierce hug. "You'll never know how glad I am to see you!"

His arms tightened when she attempted to withdraw. "Come back here, woman," he chuckled. "You can't greet a man that way and then try to run away. It's not fair!"

Before she could even contemplate his words, his head lowered unerringly to find her mouth in the darkness.

She stood rigidly for a second, remembering her resolve to hide her feelings from him. But his kiss was butterfly soft, his tongue tracing the outline of her lips until they were throbbing with desire. All thoughts were swept aside by the fiery emotions his caresses generated. With a moan she melted against him, clinging to him, her parted lips inviting him to deepen the kiss. But he only laughed. Raining soft kisses across her eyes and cheeks, his mouth hovered teasingly, his warm, moist breath mingling with hers. Almost angrily, she stared up at him, although the darkness was all-concealing. "Are you going to kiss me or not?"

Laughingly, he replied, "Just waiting for you to ask, sweetheart."

A quick firm kiss, infinitely frustrating in its brevity, was pressed to her lips. "Will that do, or were you hoping for something a little more satisfying?"

She knew she was playing with fire, but she couldn't resist. "Do you think you *can* satisfy me?"

"There's only one way to find out." Instantly his mouth captured hers possessively. She was molded to his hard frame, her breasts crushed against his chest, his splayed hands at her lower spine holding her firmly against him. His mouth demanded a response, and she gave it willingly.

When he finally raised his head, she was clinging to him shamelessly. His hands caressed her cheek, his thumb sensuously rubbing her throbbing lips as he said huskily, "One of these days, my girl, you're going to push me too far. C'mon, let's get out of here before I forget you're still an innocent." Slowly releasing her, he kept his arm around her shoulders to keep her close to his side as they made their way toward the stairs. "By the way, what are you doing down here in the dark?"

His nearness was doing strange things to her nervous system, the threat to carry her off to his bed appearing more and more appealing. She strove to shore up her weakening defenses, trying for nonchalance. Shrugging, she retorted flippantly, "Soliciting. It never hurts to practice." When his arm tightened, she held him off laughingly. "I'm just teasing. Actually, I was looking for my note pad. I must have left it down here last week." She tried to peer through the darkness to see his face. "Were you looking for me?"

"Yes. Have you had anyone out to look at the pool?"

Her eyes flew to his as the couple reached the muted light of the stairs. "Why, no. I thought our agreement was only for the house."

"It was. But it's been a scorching summer. We might as well have the pool checked out. We could be using it."

She nodded. Why hadn't she thought of that? The heat was killing her. "No problem. I'll call around and see what can be done."

"Good." Reaching the top of the stairs, he quickly kissed her on the forehead. "I've got to get back to the office. See you later." Grinning, he turned on his heel and sauntered away, leaving her staring bemusedly after him.

"DON'T YOU HAVE ANYTHING ELSE in a vinyl? These colors would clash terribly with the tile and fixtures. And I'd rather have something that can be washed...like vinyl." Alison's brown eyes pleaded with the clerk to solve her problem.

Smiling regretfully, the clerk shook her head. "I'm sorry, miss, but this is all we have at the moment. We are expecting another shipment in a few days. If you'd like to wait...."

Nibbling her lower lip in indecision, Alison studied the rolls of wallpaper before her. She had been looking at samples for days, and she was sick to death of it. Decisively she tapped several different patterns and smiled at the clerk. "I'll take this for the dining room and these two for bedrooms. The bathrooms and other bedrooms will have to wait until you have a bigger selection."

Several moments later, with her purchases under her arms, she stepped from the air-conditioned coolness of the home-decorating store into the blistering heat of a Texas summer. Like an almost physical slap in the face, the heat robbed her of her breath. Her eyes squinted in the glare, and frantically she reached for her sunglasses before hurrying to her car. "Mad dogs and Englishmen," she muttered. Now she really understood what they meant about going out in the noonday sun. And Jason had warned her the heat could last into nearly November.

Dear God, how could she survive it? The interior of her car was like an oven; for the thousandth time she futilely wished for the coolness of air conditioning. As the sweat beaded on her brow and her fingers tentatively gripped the hot steering wheel, she thought longingly of the cool refreshing water of the swimming pool waiting at home. It had taken a lot of work on her part to get the pool ready, but it was definitely going to be worth it. Just the thought of it had been keeping her going all day, reviving her spirits whenever they began to wilt.

Her one wish now was to get home and relax in the cooling depths.

The cottage was deserted when she reached it; hurriedly she climbed the stairs and changed into her swimsuit. With towel in hand, she quickly strode up the hill to the mansion, walking through the overgrown side garden to the back of the house. Her eyes shone like the clear depths of the water, catching and reflecting the sun's rays.

On the point of running toward the pool, she suddenly stopped short, her eyes wide with disbelief at the sight of the couple lying side by side at the edge.

She swallowed, momentarily stunned by the expanse of skin each of them had exposed. Obviously Christina had not been in the pool; her platinum hair was sleek and smooth, not a strand out of place. Only the bare essentials of her anatomy were covered, and those by wholly inadequate triangles of cloth linked together by fragile strings. Jason was by her side, his bronzed skin gleaming from the drops of water that clung tenaciously. His eyes were closed, a contented look on his firm lips. Alison's gaze wandered to his broad shoulders, the thin covering of dark hair on his chest, his flat stomach.

"I'm so glad you took my suggestion, darling," Christina purred as her hand reached out to link fingers with his. "It was silly for this pool to sit here empty when we could be enjoying it."

The words echoed in Alison's ears. *Her* suggestion! Fierce, hot anger gushed through her, threatening to erupt. How dared he! With all the other things she had to do, she had taken time out to call the pool service company. Because she had thought that she was doing it for him, she had remained home the day the servicemen were to come, wasting hours of precious time because they didn't arrive until late in the afternoon. And the blisters she had collected raking up those stupid leaves! All for that... that bloodsucker!

A vindictive desire to disturb the contented scene before her suddenly brought a sparkle of pure mischief to her eyes. Dropping her towel soundlessly to the ground, she hastily stepped out of her sandals. Then she set off at a run, cannonballing into the water only a few feet from where they lay. The spray shot upward, arcing into the sky before falling onto her unsuspecting victims.

Kicking back to the surface, Alison hastily pushed the hair from her eyes and turned toward the side of the pool. Predictably, Christina was shrieking in dismay, her blond hair matted and clinging to her face. "Jason, just look what she's done to me! And I have to go to a charity dinner in an hour. I'll look like a drowned rat!"

With wide brown eyes, the picture of innocence, Alison watched as Christina toweled her hair. Feeling that at least a token apology was called for, she said contritely, "I'm sorry, Christina. I didn't mean to ruin your hairdo. You can use my blow drier."

"You...you little brat!" For once Jason's presence could not stem the woman's anger. "You think you can pull one of your childish stunts and then just say you're sorry. Well, it won't work!"

Her criticism stung more than Alison cared to admit. Realizing Christina was past reason, she turned to Jason. "I really am sorry, Jason. I was so hot, I just didn't think."

His thoughtful blue eyes studied her, and then he winked at her. Jumping to his feet, he cast Alison a mocking glance. "Whether it was deliberate or not is immaterial. I'll go change so I can take Christina home. Enjoy your swim."

Chagrin coursed through her at the unexpected turn of events. Damn! Damn! Damn! Here she was, condemned to a lonely swim when she could have been sharing it with Jason. *And Christina,* an inner voice reminded her. Scowling into the water, she started swimming slowly across the pool. As much as she hated to admit it, she had to accept the truth of Christina's statement. She *was* acting like a child. But wasn't Christina doing the same thing? She, however, simply clothed her jealousy in sophistication. Men could be so blind!

CHAPTER TEN

ALISON PUSHED BACK from her typewriter irritably, yanking the paper out of the carriage and crumpling it into a ball. She tossed it toward the trash can and, when it missed, swore softly under her breath. Restlessly she got up and paced the tiny office, finally coming to a halt by the window. From there she gazed unseeingly toward the mansion.

Was Jason avoiding her? She hadn't seen hide nor hair of him for four days, ever since that stupid incident at the pool. Christina's angry words had struck home, and Jason had witnessed it all. Had he agreed that she was childish? She had been so determined to conceal her feelings, yet at the sight of Christina she felt green with jealousy. No wonder he was avoiding her—she was probably behaving just like all the other women in his life did.

She turned her back on the view and sighed in disgust. She was ruining a perfectly good day with all this pointless speculation. Work on the mansion had ceased, at least for the moment.

The paperhangers would arrive tomorrow, so she was left with some unexpected freedom. Her mind, however, would not free her thoughts for writing. The one day she had to devote to her career, and she was wasting it brooding about Jason!

"I've got to get out of here!" Her own words, spoken aloud, convinced her she needed to escape, and she hurried to the desk. With pencil and extra paper in hand, she picked up the chapter she had been working on, along with a dictionary and a thesaurus. A change of scenery was just what she needed. In the years she'd been writing, she'd discovered that that was the best solution to writer's block. It didn't necessarily improve her writing, but it opened her mind to new ideas. And right now any subject other than Jason was a new idea.

The screen door slammed behind her, and she was halfway down the steps when the phone rang. She groaned. What now?

For a minute she considered ignoring it. If she had left two minutes earlier she never would have heard it anyway. But what if it was important, she wondered. What if it was Jason? She sprinted back into the cottage and answered the phone breathlessly. "Hello."

"Alison?" a feminine voice asked hesitantly. "I don't know if you remember me, but my name is Lana Harper. I cleaned the cottage for you one day."

"Yes, Lana. Of course I remember you. You did a great job, too." She hadn't forgotten she had suspected Jason of cradle snatching either. "Is there something I can do for you?"

"Well, actually, it's for Jason. He needs some geological logs that my brother, Jim, has. I'd take them out to the office, but I really don't have time today because I have to go to the Medical Center. Jason suggested I leave the logs at the cottage, and he'll be in some time soon to pick them up."

"That's fine," Alison assured her. "I haven't locked the door and Jason pretty much comes and goes as he likes anyway. But why are you going to the Medical Center? If you're sick, let Jason come and get his own logs and don't worry about it."

"Oh, no," the younger woman laughingly objected. "I'm as healthy as a horse. It's Jim who has the appointment. Last month he had an accident at a drilling site and almost lost a couple of fingers. If it hadn't have been for Jason, who administered first aid and rushed him to the hospital, he would have. Jason's help with the hospital bills really kept us from getting in a bind, too. I've been cleaning house for him to repay him. At first he didn't want me to, but when we refused to let him help us if we couldn't do something to pay him back, he gave in."

"I hope your brother's all right," Alison said once she'd got over her initial shock. She didn't know why she was so surprised. She should have known Jason would be a rock in a crisis. And although he might appear indifferent sometimes, it was only a cover for his generosity and thoughtfulness.

"He's doing much better," Lana replied. "I wish I could tell you what time I'll be by, but you know how doctors' appointments are. It could take thirty minutes or two hours."

"Don't worry about it. I'm going out right now, and later I'll be going to the movies with John Peters. But if I'm not here, you can leave the logs in the mailbox."

When Alison had hung up she hurriedly picked up her manuscript and books and escaped outside. Once out of earshot of the cottage, she relaxed. The beauty of the summer day surrounded her, lifting the tension from her shoulders, and she automatically slowed her pace.

Just when she thought she knew Jason, she mused, he did something that stumped her. She hadn't expected him to be so sensitive to Lana's—and Jim's—pride. Aunt Gwen had always said, "Still water runs deep," and Alison was certainly beginning to suspect that was the case with Jason. The occasional ripples of emotion that swept across his features were only a fraction of the feelings that seethed beneath his usually mocking exterior.

With her thoughts still centered on Jason, Alison wandered aimlessly around the side of the mansion. When her willful feet led her to the fountain, she sank down at the base of a nearby oak with a contented sigh. This was what she needed—solitude. The cottage was out of sight, the mansion looming above her, and the cicadas were buzzing monotonously. And in the distance, the image of the city wavered in the heat. The widespread branches of the oaks shielded her from the direct rays of the sun, and Alison was glad she had ventured outside, even if it was hot. But even the heat wasn't too bad because of the cooling breeze that whispered through the trees.

She picked up her manuscript and read over the recent changes she had made. The heroine, Arabella, had already been kidnapped by Miles and had been spirited away from everything that was familiar to her. She was currently torn between her loyalty to the Confederacy and her growing love for her captor. Alison found her thoughts centering on her grandmother....

Arabella Clayton *was* Alison Ford Morgan. The fictional character had all the boldness and determination of the real one, refusing to bow to defeat despite the circumstances. As her grandmother had refused to allow the Smythes to intimidate her, Arabella refused to conceal from her family Miles's true identity. Because of this, they both suffered heartache that might have been avoided. Her grandmother might have married the man she loved had it not been for the scandal. Arabella would have known of Miles's love for her much sooner if she hadn't forced him to resort to the desperate action of kidnapping her.

Alison laid her manuscript on her lap and leaned her head back against the reassuring strength of the tree. With her eyes closed, she tried to visualize what she would have done had she been in her grandmother's shoes. Of course, she had the advantage of hindsight, so she couldn't really be objective. But she was almost positive she wouldn't have meekly complied with the Smythes' command to leave. Her grandmother had also acted under the misconception that Edward loved her as much as she loved him. He might have loved her, but he had valued his wealth and position more.

A cooling breeze ran across the grass, caressing Alison's face before rustling through the loose papers on her lap. With a startled cry, she opened her eyes and reached vainly for the pages that were caught by the wind. Horrified, she watched as several of the sheets landed in the water of the fountain. For one stunned moment she was rooted to the spot, unable to move. But when one of the pages started to sink, she tucked the rest of her manuscript under the thesaurus and jumped to her feet.

Sprinting to the edge of the fountain, she waded in without hesitation, trying not to think what might be under the water. It wasn't too difficult to avoid thinking about lurking marine creatures: she was too preoccupied with retrieving the pages. All those long hours of work lost! How could she have been so stupid? She was so close to completing the revisions, and now this had to happen. Why did something always go wrong every time she was about to reach her dreams?

She watched in dismay as several pages sank beneath the surface. One lone sheet still floated on the opposite side of the fountain. The water lapped around her knees as she hurriedly tried to rescue the paper before it, too, sank into the water. Her fingers reached for it....

"Alison!"

Startled, she jerked around to see Jason descending the stairs cut into the side of the hill. At the same time her feet slipped on the mossy bottom, and she started to slide. She grabbed for some support but her fingers met thin air. As her feet flew out from under her she fell with a splash, her head grazing the concrete side of the fountain. Pain shot through her, a searing flash that momentarily stunned her. She tried to regain her footing, but the sudden movement sent her head spinning. Weakly she sank into the water.

"God, Alison, are you all right?"

Her eyes snapped open at the husky note of concern in Jason's voice. She closed them again immediately, however, wincing in pain. This was just great! She was soaked to the skin, covered with slime, and her head was throbbing like a blinking light. Hot unshed tears pricked her eyes. Why did Jason always seem to see her at her worst? She shook her head automatically in silent protest and instantly regretted it. "Oh, my gosh!" she groaned. Her fingers gingerly reached up to touch the tender spot and were engulfed in a warm grasp. Cautiously she opened her eyes and squinted up into Jason's worried blue eyes. "What are you doing here?"

He ignored her question, his expression tense as he critically examined her white face. "You just scared the hell out of me! I couldn't believe it when I saw you wading in the fountain. I'm really sorry I startled you. Do you think you're all right?"

"Pretty sure," she replied, accepting his help to get to her knees. Without bothering to ask, Jason lifted her gently out of the pool and set her on a nearby bench. Then he began with exquisite tenderness to examine her scalp.

"My manuscript!" she cried suddenly, trying to get up, but Jason's hands forced her back down. Helplessly her eyes filled with tears. "Jason...my manuscript...part of it fell in the water. I've got to get it out."

"Is that why you were in the fountain, rescuing that damned manuscript?" he asked incredulously. The concern in his voice was tinged with anger. "What would have happened if I hadn't come along? You could have knocked yourself out and drowned!"

"If you hadn't surprised me, I wouldn't have fallen in the first place!" she retorted, stung by his words. "And it's not a damn manuscript. My writing may not set the world on fire, but it's just as important to me as your *damn* oil wells are to you!"

"Touché." The anger in his eyes was pushed aside by concern when she closed her eyes in pain. His arm slipped around her shoulders as she tried to stand up. "Careful. You might have a concussion. I think I should run you over to the emergency room just to make sure you're okay."

Alison grabbed her spinning head. "You'll do no such thing. I'm perfectly all right. I've just got the grandfather of all headaches."

She could see by his worried expression that he wasn't convinced. Her eyes pleaded with his.

"Please, Jason, I'm fine. After I clean up and take a couple of aspirins, I'll be good as new."

He held up three fingers. "How many?"

"Three, Dr. Morgan. And no, my vision isn't blurred and I'm not nauseous—lucky for you," she teased lightly. "Now can I please go back to the cottage?"

His fingers moved across her cheek to push her dripping hair back from her face. "All right. But I'm going to stick around for a while to make sure you're okay." He started to help her toward the cottage, but when she swayed unsteadily, his arms came around her again, despite the wetness of her clothes. He chuckled suddenly, pulling back and wrinkling his nose at her. "There's no way to put this delicately, Alison. Your new perfume leaves a lot to be desired. In other words, sweetheart, you stink. If you're going to insist on swimming in the fountain, it'll have to be cleaned."

She grinned gamely, trying to ignore the dull pounding in her head. "Don't clean it on my account. It's not big enough for me *and* the goldfish."

Jason obviously wasn't fooled by her grin; he was still looking worried. The blow to her head had done more than rob her face of its usual healthy color: it had left her feeling fragile and vulnerable as well. His arm, which circled her shoulders, tightened gently. "You're going home, young lady. And after you've cleaned up, you're going to relax for the rest of the day."

He urged her toward the cottage but she stopped him as she remembered her books and the part of her manuscript that had not blown into the fountain. "Would you carry my things for me? After today's fiasco, I don't trust myself."

He went over to pick up her papers, then helped her back to the cottage. "I'm sorry about your manuscript," he said. "How many pages did you lose? Do you have copies of them?"

Alison started to shake her head then thought better of it. "No, those were the originals. I won't make copies until I finish the rewrites." She sighed as they reached the porch. "I think I lost about six pages. I guess I'll just have to try to remember what those pages contained and rewrite them. But now I'm going upstairs to take a bath. This smell is killing me."

Jason followed her into the living room, grinning at her bedraggled appearance. "Need anyone to scrub your back?"

"No!" In her present jittery state that was the last thing she needed. "I may have received a blow on my head, but I haven't taken leave of my senses. Why don't you go check the mailbox to see if Lana came by with your geological logs or whatever it is she was supposed to drop off. That's why you're here, isn't it?"

"Partly," he admitted. "Go on upstairs and take your bath before that stuff dries on you. Are you sure you don't need any help?"

This time his offer was sincere, and she hastened to reassure him. "I'm sure, Jason. Quit worrying." To set his mind at rest, she climbed lightly up the stairs, not allowing her shoulders to sag until she was out of sight of Jason's watchful eyes.

Her head ached with such intensity it was an effort to keep her eyes open. And the smell of her slime-covered clothes was making her sick. She hurried into the bathroom as fast as her pounding head would allow and turned on the taps, filling the tub with warm water. Her powdered bubble bath was just the thing for the job, she decided, pouring a good amount of it into the tub. With awkward haste she stripped off her sodden clothes and slid into the soothing depths. She frowned at the ruined garments in disgust for a moment before the enervating warmth worked its magic on her bruised body. Immersed up to her neck, she leaned her head against the back of the tub and closed her eyes with a tired sigh.

The water relaxed her, soaking the tension from her weary bones. The pounding in her head, though, didn't ease. Deliberately she made her mind go blank, hoping the ache she was trying to ignore would go away. Instead she found herself drifting into a lulling sleep. She didn't fight the sensation. She didn't have the strength to lift a finger, let alone stay awake.

Minutes or maybe hours had passed when suddenly the bathroom door banged open. "Alison? Are you all right?"

Alison sat up with a start, shrieking in alarm. She was disoriented from the sleep that had taken her unawares, but not so disoriented that she missed Jason's bold gaze burning her skin. Hastily she slipped beneath the bubbles, which had somehow dwindled to a paltry few.

"What are you doing in here?" she gasped in outrage, the throbbing in her head increasing with renewed vigor. The water lapped gently against the rounded swell of her breasts, and a fiery blush flooded her pale cheeks with color. Her eyes were almost black with anger. "Get out of here! Right this minute!"

When he remained undaunted, she said threateningly, "Jason, I'm warning you, if you don't get out of here, I'll—"

"Oh, pipe down," he laughed. "You can't carry out any threats at the moment, and you know it."

When she could only sputter in rage, his grin widened. "You know, you're the most suspicious woman I know, but why? I've never done anything to make you leery of me. I only came in here because I was worried about you—

I knocked but you didn't answer. You've been in that tub for over an hour."

She groaned at his continued stubbornness. "Well, as you can see, I'm fine. I just fell asleep. Now will you please get out of here?"

When he only shook his head and advanced farther into the room, her glance flew wildly to her shield of bubbles, her only protection against his raking gaze. Before her very eyes the bubbles were dissipating one by one. "*Please*, Jason!" she said with clenched teeth.

Sitting on the side of the tub, he reached out to touch her collarbone, savoring the silken wetness of her skin. The fire in her cheeks raged out of control. As she slipped farther into the water, the bubbles now tickling her chin, he laughed. "There's no reason to be so modest, Alison. I've seen the female anatomy before."

"I'm sure you have," she snapped, glaring at him futilely, "but not this female's anatomy. It's strictly off limits and not accessible to the viewing public!"

Teasingly his eyes refuted her words, inspecting the bubbles languidly. He was so close she could smell the male scent of him, a clean outdoors fragrance that assailed her senses. When his gaze traveled to her face to linger with maddening deliberation on her parted lips, she was spellbound, unable to break the sensuous trance in which he held her. His hand cupped her cheek, his thumb tracing the outline of her mouth before caressing the fullness of her lower lip. His eyes were riveted to her mouth as he said huskily, "How's your head?"

Alison blinked. "What?"

Chuckling softly, Jason tenderly touched her bruised forehead. "When you hurt yourself, you really do a first-class job. That's going to be a beautiful shade of purple tomorrow."

"It still hurts," she confided. "And you're not helping matters. You're beginning to be a real pain in the—"

"Neck," he supplied laughingly. Before she could even begin to guess his intention, he leaned over and gave her a quick, burning kiss on the mouth. As he released her lips, his fingers caressed her cheek before dipping into the water that covered her breasts. When she gasped, he whispered, "You'd better get out of that cold water before I have to warm you up."

Stunned into silence, she watched as the door closed behind his retreating figure. The click of the latch broke the spell that held her and she groaned in despair. How much more of this could she take? This constant warring of her emotions was tearing her apart, bit by bit destroying her resolve. Each kiss, each caress, tore another brick from the wall of protection that surrounded her heart. Her love was making her defenseless. She was close to being a willing participant in her own seduction without even knowing Jason's true feelings.

A heavy hand pounded on the door. "By the way, Alison, you'd better be out of there in five minutes or I'm going to come in after you."

"All right, all right!" she called irritably. Hurriedly she washed her hair and rinsed her body. Stepping out of the bathtub, she toweled herself dry, then shrugged into her robe. Wrapping her hair in a turban, she cast annoyed glances at the paneled door. Who did he think he was? He had no right to give her orders. But he didn't make idle threats, she knew. With the towel still covering her hair, she opened the door slowly, glancing down the hall cautiously. She wouldn't put it past him to be lurking somewhere. The coast was clear, however, and she hurried into her room.

Several minutes later, dressed in jeans and a red gingham blouse, her face free of makeup, she entered the living room to find Jason sitting on the couch reading her manuscript. Her brow lifted in surprise, but before she could say a word, he pointed to the coffee table. "Two aspirins and a glass of water—just what the doctor ordered. That should knock out your headache. Would you like a cold washcloth for that bruise? It might make it feel better."

"No, thanks. The aspirins will probably be enough." She forced herself to remain unruffled when his eyes swept over her, but she wasn't too successful. She walked stiffly across to the coffee table and swallowed the aspirins. When her eyes turned back to Jason, he was looking at her manuscript. She really didn't mind that he was reading it. She needed someone's opinion besides her own. "Well, what do you think?"

"It's good."

"Don't sound so surprised," she objected, frowning. "Didn't you think I could write?"

"A lot of people call themselves writers, but that doesn't necessarily mean they're any good at it." He set the stack of typed pages on the low table in front of him. "I don't have to ask if you've been reading the diaries. It's obvious. The heroine sounds just like grandmother."

"Do you really think so?" Alison asked excitedly. "Lately I've felt as if I really knew her. I guess that's why I used her as a model for Arabella's character. I knew how she'd react in any situation."

"You've done a beautiful job. She would have been flattered."

Alison sat down in the chair opposite him, curling her feet under her. "Did grandmother like your parents?" The question popped out before she could stop it. That blow to her head must have loosened her brain. She cringed, waiting for the sarcasm with which he usually answered her questions.

Although his expression was guarded, the response she had expected was not there. "I don't think she was overly fond of them."

Encouraged by the unexpectedness of his reply, she asked hesitantly, "Do you feel the same way?"

He shrugged. "Why this sudden interest in my family?"

"I've always been interested. I just didn't think you'd answer my question." She looked at him mischievously. "But now that I'm one of the walking wounded, you can hardly refuse."

"Don't count on it," he retorted with feigned sternness. Leaning back against the cushions of the couch, he grinned. "I had you pegged for a reporter the minute I saw you. You've been asking questions ever since. Go ahead, today I'll humor you. But don't be surprised if you get a 'no comment.'"

"Did your parents ever come to visit you after you came to live with your grandfather?"

"Occasionally. They used to come at Christmas and sometimes during the summer. For a while, I even went with them during summer vacation. But after I got older, I quit going."

"What does your father do?" Alison asked, unable to believe he was being so cooperative.

"He's an importer. That's why he travels around a lot." He looked at her in exasperation.

"Don't you want to talk about something else? This is boring."

"You're just trying to squirm out of answering," she accused him laughingly. "It's not boring at all. I don't know anything about your childhood. Do your parents love each other?"

"I doubt it."

She could tell from the shortness of his answer that she was treading on thin ice, but she couldn't resist one last question. "Have you ever been in love?"

"Yes," he replied promptly, grinning wickedly at her start of surprise. "She was the most beautiful redhead I've ever seen, and I adored her. She was twenty-three. And I was nine. She was my third-grade teacher."

Alison grimaced. "Be serious, Jason. Have you ever been in love?"

"No comment."

"That's not fair! You...."

A knock at the door interrupted them. "You stay where you are," Jason instructed. "I'll get it."

He opened the door to admit the visitor, and Alison winced in sudden remembrance. John... how had she forgotten their date? She looked up to meet his gaze across the width of the room. Color flooded her pale face. "John, I'm so sorry. I completely forgot about our date. I... I...."

"She fell in the fountain and cracked her head," Jason supplied when she started to struggle for an explanation. "You can see from the bruise on her forehead she's in no shape to go anywhere."

John was immediately concerned. "Are you all right? You don't look so good—you're awfully pale. Maybe you should see a doctor—or at least lie down."

"I'm fine," she protested. "You and Jason are worse than a couple of old hens. I've just got a slight headache. I'll be fine by tomorrow."

When John started to object, Jason advised, "You might as well save your breath, John. She's as stubborn as a mule." He turned to Alison, his eyes locking with hers. "I've got to go. John will keep you company. How about dinner tomorrow night? A little TLC might make you feel better."

Totally floored by his unexpected invitation, Alison nodded dumbly.

He grinned. "Good. I'll play chef. I doubt if you'll want to go out with that neon sign on your forehead, so we'll eat here."

As he turned and walked out the door, Alison tried not to think about his reference to tender loving care. It conjured up dreams she was afraid to believe in. Deliberately she turned back to John. "I really am sorry, John. I can't believe I forgot."

"That's okay. It's a wonder you even remember your name. That must have been some fall. Was Jason there?"

"He had just arrived. He came by to pick up some geological logs that Lana had dropped off." She frowned at his thoughtful expression. "What's the matter?"

He shook his head. "Nothing. I was just wondering if Jason's trying one of his old college tricks. He seems to be here quite a bit."

"What do you mean?" Alison demanded. "Of course he drops by. He's half owner, you know."

"I know. I guess it's just a coincidence he's always here when I show up." Evidently convinced, he smiled reassuringly. "I'm probably just being paranoid. Forget I said anything."

CHAPTER ELEVEN

"FORGET I SAID ANYTHING." John's words kept echoing in her head. How could she forget? He had unwittingly encouraged her doubts, and she found herself becoming suspicious of the many coincidences that had thrown her and Jason together. The night she had met him at John's office, Jason had deliberately asked her to dinner before John had had a chance. And the night of Nancy's barbecue he had arrived at the cottage to take her out, conveniently overlooking the fact that he hadn't even asked her. And then yesterday.... Was his interest in her based solely on the fact that John had befriended her? Was she the prize in some sort of competition? The irony of it all was that she wasn't even interested in John as anything but a friend. There *was* no competition. Jason won hands down.

Alison blinked rapidly. She was so confused. Nothing added up. Any man contemplating the seduction of a woman simply to prove that he could do it had to be a monster. She couldn't believe Jason was that heartless, or that he was indifferent to her. The alarm he had shown when he discovered her in the fountain was real. It had to be based on a stronger emotion than mere liking. It had to be!

With a tired sigh, she got to her feet and picked up her manuscript. It was finished. John's suspicions and her headache had completely destroyed her sleep the night before. She had tossed and turned until she was exhausted, but her doubts had persisted. In desperation, she'd got up in the middle of the night and started typing. The pages she had lost came back to her more easily than she'd expected, and except for the dull pain in her head and in her heart, she might have enjoyed what she was doing. Instead she found it a necessity, a retreat from her torturous thoughts.

But at least her manuscript was finished. Carefully she packaged it, deliberating for long moments whether or not to include return postage. She knew it was a courtesy, but it seemed pessimistic to her—almost as if she was admitting defeat before she even mailed it. Finally she decided to include it, hoping against hope it wouldn't be used. What would she do if it wasn't accepted?

What would she do if it was? It sounded ridiculous, but she was almost as afraid of success as she was of failure. A contract could completely change her life and open up a whole new world to her. She'd spent hours at her typewriter, so close to her work it was impossible for her to judge its merits. Publication acknowledged the fact that her writing was commercial, that she was doing something right.

C'mon, Alison, get on with it, she chided herself. She picked up the weighty package and stepped onto the front porch.

"Oh, no! Not more water!" she groaned at the sight of the steady downpour of rain that was being quickly absorbed by the thirsty earth. The sky was heavy and dark, a rare day indeed for a usually cloudless Texas summer. Everything was gray and gloomy, silent except for the incessant patter of rain.

The steady drum of droplets on the roof would have normally delighted her senses, but today she could find no joy in it. She was tired and depressed and confused, and she certainly didn't want her manuscript to get wet! The contents of the old-fashioned umbrella stand just inside the front door came to her rescue, and within seconds she was plunging into the rain. Her tennis shoes were immediately soaked, but she didn't care. She wasn't going to wear her best shoes in this downpour!

Once safely in her car, she set her manuscript on the passenger seat before throwing the dripping umbrella in the back. Moments later she was at the post office watching the window clerk literally *throw* her manuscript into a cart with a dozen other packages. She winced. Would it get to New York in one piece? And once there would it land on the slush pile and be ignored for months?

She returned to the cottage, leaving her shoes on the porch to dry before she padded barefoot into the living room. What was she going to do with herself today? She wasn't really needed at the mansion. The paperhangers knew which design she wanted for each room, and the carpenter she'd hired to build a new banister certainly didn't need her help. She didn't really want to go out in the rain again anyway. Her manuscript was in the mail, so she had nothing to work on.

Her eyes rested on her grandmother's final diary, still lying on the coffee table where she had last left it. She'd barely started reading it. After she'd discovered the reason for the breakup between her grandmother and Edward, her manuscript had distracted her from finishing it. Now she picked it up eagerly.

There were large time gaps in the journal entries now. The years after Edward's betrayal had obviously been difficult for Alison's grandmother, even harder because of the death of her father. She and her baby daughter were alone in the world, with no one to help them out of their financial difficulties. After a while, though, the burden seemed to have eased, but there was no explanation in the diary for their sudden shift in fortune.

Alison was confused by the turnabout, but she soon forgot about it as she read of her own mother's childhood. Her grandmother had never regretted having her baby, and it was clear that nothing on earth could have convinced her to part with her. Her world had centered on the girl, and all the love she was unable to give Edward she'd showered on his child. Which explained why she had been so overly protective....

Tears welled in Alison's eyes. Her mother's death had come as a terrible shock to her grandmother. A particularly poignant passage revealed all her heartache and pain. Too late, Alison Ford Morgan had admitted that she was wrong. She had been devastated by the loss of her only child, bitterly regretful of all the wasted years. She'd been at her lowest point, unwilling to face the loneliness of the future, when Jason's widowed grandfather had come into her life again after an absence of several years. Need and friendship had drawn them together, and marriage had made their reunion permanent. Then Jason had landed on their doorstep.

Jason's own description of her grandmother's feelings for his parents had been a gross understatement. She'd had no use at all for them. She hadn't understood how a couple could abandon their own child to people he didn't even know, even if those people were his grandparents. Jason had been the rope in a tug-of-war, first drawn to his parents even though they had deserted him, then pulled the other way, as his growing love for his grandparents swung his loyalty toward them.

At first the situation had been impossible. Jason's mother had often used her son as her means of revenge. But her continual threats to remove Jason from his grandparents' care had eventually backfired. His uncertainty about where he belonged had caused problems for him in school and at home, and Alison Ford Morgan had put her foot down. Jason's mother had been given an ultimatum: either his grandparents became his legal guardians or he would live permanently with his mother. Jason's residence with the Morgans had become legalized.

Poor Jason, Alison thought. No wonder there was no love lost between him and his parents. They had given him little cause to respect, let alone love, them. It was his grandparents who had eventually received his love. And they'd received a lot more. He'd proved to be a godsend to them, bringing a sudden spark of joy and vitality into their lives.

It was understandable that after a period of time Jason's feelings for his absent parents would have given way to indifference—one that undoubtedly masked a bitter hurt. Alison tried not to think of what that hurt could mean to her. For years he had not allowed himself to get close to anyone but his grandparents and a few friends. Would she be allowed to join the select group? Christina had known him for years and—presumably—had yet to earn his love. Why did she herself have any reason to think she might be luckier? Did a whispered word of endearment, a note of concern in his voice or a supposed desire to further her "education" point to love? Her eyes turned back to the diary....

The years her grandmother had spent with her husband had been happy ones, the love they'd shared deep and sincere. But it had not been anything like the love she had had for Edward. Her first love had burned with an intensity that was overpowering, a bright, blinding flame that for one precious summer lit up her world. She had never recaptured it.

Nor did the purchase of the Smythes' mansion years later help in any way. All she'd experienced from it was heartache. Her memories were clouded by the scandal that had shattered her life, and after one visit to the aging mansion, she could never bring herself to go there again.

As Alison read the last entry of the diary, she

felt she finally understood why her grandmother had willed her journals to her. She had wanted to not only share her life with the granddaughter she had never known, but she had also wanted to leave her as a legacy all the wisdom she had gained from her experiences. Obviously she did not regret her love for Edward or for the child she had borne, and she'd expressed it beautifully.

> The moments of true love in this life are fleeting. They should be grasped with both hands and experienced to the fullest because they do not last. Like the mist in the valley, they vanish with the rising sun.

Alison stared at the flowing script. Aunt Gwen would certainly argue with that! She herself couldn't dismiss it lightly. There was a very real possibility that Jason was interested in an affair with her and little else. John's suspicions certainly pointed that way. Could she accept an affair and give her love to Jason without reserve? At the moment, even moved as she was by Alison Ford Morgan's testimony, she didn't know.

THE RAIN OF THE MORNING gave way to the sunshine of the afternoon, drying the steaming ground and creating a muggy humidity that soon had Alison's dark curls in disarray. She put the last diary with the other volumes, still disturbed by the question they raised, and went upstairs to shower and dress before Jason arrived. She was in no mood to try to impress him. Whatever she wore would clash with that ugly bruise on her forehead anyway. Absently she pulled on black gabardine slacks and a lace-collared flame pullover, not even noticing how the black pants emphasized her sinuous slimness or the way the knit top hugged her waist and breasts.

Downstairs again, she wandered into the office in search of a way to fill the time until Jason arrived. She would write, she decided, fill the page with words that would block out her thoughts of Jason.

She sat down at the typewriter, and for a few long moments was immobile. Her imagination was fixed on an image it refused to relinquish—coal-black hair that glittered in the sunshine, glinting eyes so blue you could drown in them, and a wide generous mouth that could take her to heaven. Then she began to type.

What seemed like hours later she was staring at the words she had composed on the blank page before her. The description she had written was so clear and accurate. And she knew Jason's image was engraved indelibly on her heart and mind, as well. She wasn't one to give her heart lightly; when she did, it was without reservation. Was she destined, like her grandmother, to spend the rest of her life loving a man she couldn't have?

The shadows had lengthened on the lawn, and the fierce heat of the day had begun to lessen when Jason finally appeared. His suit coat was slung over his shoulder, his tie undone and his collar open when he walked into the house, stopping short when he noticed Alison sitting at her desk. His eyes narrowed and scanned her face when she hastily wiped at the tear that clung to her cheek.

"What's the matter?" he asked in concern.

She could hardly say, "I love you and it's making me miserable." Instead she lowered her lashes to conceal the pain in her eyes. She needed desperately to appear cool and unconcerned before him; it would be such balm to her troubled spirit to know that she could remain unaffected by him. But her body refused to cooperate. With one gesture, one word, he destroyed her control. Her heart was either in a euphoric state of joy or in the icy depths of despair. No one had ever had such power over her emotions before, and Alison found it frightening.

Lifting her chin, she met his gaze, her pride demanding that she conceal her feelings from him. "It's my head. I guess I hit it harder than I thought. It. . . it still hurts." Feeling the color riding high in her cheeks, she was unable to continue holding his gaze. Her eyes fled from the watchful skepticism of his.

She jumped guiltily when he sat on the corner of the desk and lifted her chin with his finger, forcing her to meet his gaze. "Are you sure that's all it is? There's nothing else bothering you?"

Laughing shakily, she pulled away from his grasp. "Of course not. What else could be bothering me?"

Questioningly he searched her face, unsatisfied with her reply. Just when she felt she could endure his gaze no longer, he leaned back and grinned seductively. "Poor baby! Should I kiss it and make it all better?"

When she hastily drew back, he laughed. "Don't worry. You're safe. . . for now. My concern is strictly platonic."

Alison eyed him suspiciously, unable to believe what she was hearing. She raised her hand and laid it on his forehead. "Are you feeling all right? Maybe you've been working too hard."

Chuckling, he grabbed her hand from his brow and stood up, pulling her to her feet beside him. "I'm not the one who's been working too hard. Come on. You're going to take the night off while I cook dinner."

"You?" she laughed cynically. "I know you

volunteered last night, but I didn't think you meant it."

He pulled her into the living room, where he scowled down at her in pretended annoyance. "Are you doubting my culinary abilities? I'll have you know, young woman, that this is a privilege bestowed on very few people. You should be honored, you should be thanking me profusely instead of giving me smart remarks."

His hands settled on her shoulders and he pushed her down onto the couch. "Now sit and go with the tide, sweetheart. That's much easier than always fighting me."

The smile he gave her literally weakened her knees, and she found herself on the couch, watching his retreating back. If she had only him to fight, she was quite sure there would be no battle at all. But she was fighting herself as well—those strict old-fashioned morals instilled in her during childhood—and she wasn't sure what the outcome would be. Living for the moment, without thought of tomorrow, was fine for others, but could she turn her back on her childhood and all its teachings, and adopt the more permissive morals of contemporary society? And if she did, what of next week, or next year, when he walked away without a backward glance? Could she survive such heartbreak?

A glass of chilled wine was suddenly held in front of her, startling her out of her musings.

She couldn't suppress a grin when she noticed the apron tied around Jason's waist. "What, no chef's hat?" she teased. "I warn you, I won't put up with a TV dinner! I'm expecting a first-class meal!"

Shaking a spoon at her, Jason retorted, "Lady, the cook doesn't take any back talk. You'd better watch it or you'll find yourself doing the dishes!"

"Oh, no! The boss gave me the night off."

A slow grin spread across his face. "The boss—that's got a nice ring to it. I'm glad you recognize who's in charge around here." As he headed back to the kitchen, his smile flew across the room to caress her. "Enjoy your wine."

The appetizing aroma of grilling steak soon drifted to her, teasing her taste buds until her stomach was growling in protest. It had been hours since lunch, a simple sandwich, and judging by the darkness gathering outside, it was getting late. No wonder she was hungry! She was on the point of investigating the kitchen when Jason appeared in the doorway, a secretive smile lighting his eyes. "Is everything okay out here?"

"Yes, of course." Her expression was quizzical as she scanned his face. "I was just coming to see if you needed some help."

"No, ma'am!" he said emphatically. "This is my treat tonight, and you're not going to lift a finger to help. Okay?"

At her reluctant nod, he turned to go, then glanced back over his shoulder speculatively. "Promise me you won't get up from that couch until I come for you."

"Jason, for pete's sake, what is this all about?" she asked in exasperation.

The stubborn set of his jaw was the only reply she got. Sighing, she shrugged her shoulders. "All right, I promise. Though why you insist on treating me like an invalid beats me. I just bumped my head. And to tell you the truth, I'm starving."

He grinned boyishly. "Just humor me for once?"

It was again several minutes before he returned, minutes in which the only sounds were those of Alison's own movements. At last she glanced toward the kitchen, but from her position on the couch she could see little. What was going on? Unable to take the suspense any longer, she jumped to her feet—and came face to face with Jason.

"I thought I asked you to wait until I came for you," he said accusingly.

She blushed at his tone. "You did. But, Jason—" her eyes lifted to his questioningly "—this is getting ridiculous. What's going on?"

Taking her arm, he led her out to the front porch. "Come on. There's something I want to show you."

Glancing over her shoulder at the cottage, she hesitated. "What about dinner?"

"It'll keep. Now will you just quit arguing and come with me?" he asked in exasperation.

Nodding silently, she allowed him to take her hand and lead her down the porch steps. It was dark out, but the path they took was easily recognizable to her, even at night—it was the route to the mansion. As they neared the house, she longed to ask him where they were going, but wisely she refrained from doing so. Obviously he knew what he was doing, and he would probably not appreciate any more questions from her.

Darkness enveloped them, but with an almost catlike ability Jason remained on the path, miraculously avoiding trees and underbrush alike. Alison followed him, her hand gripping his and her eyes glued to his dark, shadowy back. As they topped the last small rise her eyes widened at the sight of a flickering light and at the muted strains of music drifting on the night air. She stopped in her tracks, tugging Jason to a halt beside her.

When he looked down at her inquiringly, she whispered, "Jason, listen. There's music coming from the mansion. And a light. It must be prowlers! Shouldn't we go back to the cottage and call the police?"

His smile flashed in the darkness, his soft

chuckle caressing her. "Prowlers don't bring a radio with them, silly. C'mon." Pulling her after him, he quickly covered the distance to the mansion with his long strides.

Stepping a moment later from the tree-shaded path into the portico, he turned to watch Alison as she glanced around. An appreciative gasp escaped her as she took in the sight before her. Then her eyes flew to Jason, only to be inevitably drawn back to the small circular wrought-iron table nestled under the protective eave of the mansion. Set for two, with a small bowl of daisies in the center, the table was perfect for a romantic dinner. Lighted candles flickered and danced from pewter candle-holders, their flames reflected in the shining glass top of the table. Everything sparkled—the crystal wineglasses, the polished pewter, the silver. From the open windows, the soft sounds of Nat King Cole drifted to her, making the mood complete.

Tentatively she approached the table, her fingers gliding along the smoothness of the glass. Tears suddenly filled her eyes at this totally unexpected gesture of Jason's. Turning back to him, she smiled radiantly, her eyes bright with unshed tears. "It's beautiful. Did you really do all this for me?"

At his nod, she asked, "But, why?"

"I promised you a little tender loving care."

Walking toward her, he pulled a chair out for her, then leered down at her in obvious exaggeration. "I'm also setting you up for seduction, brown eyes. If my manly charm doesn't work, then the candles and romantic music ought to do the trick. What do you think?"

A soft blush stole into her cheeks. "You certainly picked the right music. How did you know I liked Nat King Cole?"

"Just a hunch. I'm glad you approve."

"Oh, I approve, but it wasn't really necessary. Your manly charm was working nicely."

Sitting opposite him Alison searched the bronzed planes of his face, trying to fathom this sudden turnabout. Was he serious? The candlelight was muted; its glowing light created secret depths in his eyes, depths she could not penetrate. He was watching her with equal intensity, deepening the blush in her cheeks when his eyes lingered on her mouth. "Does that mean my timing is right for once? Do you finally want me as much as I want you?"

His assumption was too close to the truth; instinctively she shied away from his probing question. Teasingly she pretended to consider it before retorting provocatively, "That's for you to find out."

Picking up the wineglass he had just filled, he raised it in a salute to her. "If that's a challenge, I accept."

The dinner went smoothly. Their steaks were cooked to perfection, and Jason did his utmost to keep her entertained. Alison had been afraid he would persist with his seduction of her, but her fears proved groundless. She didn't know whether to be relieved or disappointed when he kept the subject on much less intimate topics.

"I hope you're not disappointed because we're not having anything fancy. The last time I had a gourmet meal it was a disaster, at least for my grandmother."

Alison looked at him in interest. "Why? Did she burn it or something?"

His eyes danced with laughter. "Nope. She made the mistake of letting grandfather do the shopping. She wanted to make a fancy duck dinner one year for Thanksgiving, so she sent him to the store with a list of things she needed, including the duck. He didn't see any sense in buying one when we already had one on the property. The only trouble was it was my pet duck Donald."

"Donald?" Alison snorted. "It figures. But surely your grandfather didn't kill your pet?"

"Yes, he did. But Donald really deserved it. That duck was mean! John and I witnessed the whole thing, and we were sworn to secrecy. If grandmother had found out, you see, she would have had a fit. But we all forgot about John's big mouth."

"Oh, no. What happened?"

He laughed in remembrance. "John and his family came to dinner, and everything was going fine until John decided he wanted seconds. I don't know if he forgot his promise or if he did it on purpose, but he lifted his plate to grandfather and asked for another piece of Donald!"

Alison choked with laughter. "What happened? Did everyone know Donald was your pet duck?"

"Oh, they knew all right. And I've never seen such a mad dash from the table."

Alison laughed until tears slid down her cheeks. Under the soothing effects of the music and of Jason's crazy childhood stories, she felt herself relax completely. He kept their glasses filled, though she hardly seemed to notice, and by the end of the meal a warm glow of happiness had enveloped her.

She was swirling the wine in her glass, enjoying the reflection of the candle's glow in the rich burgundy color, when she suddenly became aware of Jason by her side. Taking the glass from her he coaxed, "Come and dance with me under the stars."

Alison's heart caught in her throat. His request was sweet, seductive and tempting. She wanted nothing more than to dance with him, she realized; she wanted to eliminate the distance between them, to feel his arms holding her close. It would make their eventual parting that much more painful, but at the moment she couldn't resist. Deliberately she ignored her common sense to say, "I don't know if I should trust you. I've got a feeling you're closing in for the kill."

His husky laughter was his only reply, and she found herself giving him her hand, allowing him to pull her up into his arms. Resisting his efforts to mold her against him, she spread her hands against his chest to keep herself away. "I'll dance with you only if you'll promise not to hold me too close."

With a straight face he agreed, though his eyes were dancing with many unspoken messages. Allowing the distance to widen between them, he asked, "How's that? Is it close enough, without being improper, but far enough away, without being insulting?"

Laughingly she squeezed his hand. "It's perfect."

The music swirled around them, casting its spell, until they seemed to be in a world of their own making. On an island of candlelight, they were surrounded by an ocean of darkness. With each dance, the distance between them lessened automatically, until there was no distance at all. With her cheek resting against his heart, Alison didn't even wonder how she came to be there. When he released her hand to wrap both arms around her, she offered no objection, but slipped her arms around his neck, a contented smile on her lips. While they were wrapped in each other's arms, their steps slowed, then stopped altogether, until they were simply swaying with the romantic strains of the music.

Jason pressed his face into her soft curls, inhaling her fragrance. His arms tightened, and his lips swept her brow and cheek before nibbling at her earlobe, sending shivers of delight across her skin. "How about it, honey?" he whispered into her ear before pressing a kiss to its shell-like perfection. "Don't you think you're ready for the advanced course?"

CHAPTER TWELVE

ALISON STIFFENED. The decision she had been avoiding all day was being forced upon her, and she was no closer to making a rational decision now than she had been that morning. Jason's closeness wasn't making the situation any easier; she couldn't think straight when she was in his arms. She tried to pull away, but she had only drawn back a few inches when his arms locked around her, refusing her escape. Her eyes lifted to his, her uncertainty clearly visible. "The advanced course...I suppose your bed is the classroom?"

His sapphire eyes were watchful, barely concealing the smoldering fire of his desire. His arms drew her closer. "I can see I'm going to have to convince you." He lowered his head to explore her neck with his lips. "Don't be afraid, sweetheart. Don't you know by now you can trust me? Just relax."

How could she relax when his touch sent the blood rushing through her veins? Trust him.... God, didn't he know how much she wanted to?

She closed her eyes, leaning against him weakly, unable to fight this deliberate assault on her senses.

His lips moved to her face, exploring every inch of it with soft, light kisses. His hands began a slow, subtle investigation of her back and hips before sliding around her body to capture her breast. Alison's nerve ends screamed in awareness, and she was suddenly frightened by her own response. She didn't want to make a decision in the heat of passion. She needed breathing room so she could think. "Jason..." she gasped.

His mouth cut off her words before she could begin, his tongue slipping between her parted lips to take his fill of the sweetness within. And then she was lost. The full force of his sexual vitality encompassed her, his seductive prowess easily stripping away her resolve and making her aware of her needs as a woman. She felt her lips soften and tremble beneath the mastery of his, and she couldn't remember what she had wanted to say to him. Her hands clutched at his shirt as her legs trembled in reaction.

Breaking off the kiss, Jason stared down at her, his eyes narrowing at the sight of her parted lips and her passion-darkened eyes. As if unable to stop himself, he captured her mouth in a long drugging kiss before picking her up and starting off toward the cottage with long sure strides.

The soft light of the flickering candles they left behind as he stepped into the shrouding darkness of the night, carrying her effortlessly.

The raging desire that enflamed her heart left no room for the nagging doubts that were desperately trying to resurface. She loved Jason, and she was tired of fighting him. This was what they both wanted; even her grandmother would have approved. *You can't put restrictions on love,* Alison told herself decisively; it would die if it wasn't given freely. This was her chance to be happy with the man she loved, and she wasn't going to turn her back on it. She loved him, and nothing else mattered.

They approached the cottage, and Jason, still holding her in his arms, pushed the door and stepped inside. In the bright lights of the living room his eyes searched her flushed face, her anxious eyes, her kiss-bruised mouth. Sitting down on the couch with her on his lap, he reached behind her to switch off the lamp, leaving only one light to cast a soft glow in a corner of the room. His arms closed around her as he moved his head toward hers and whispered huskily, "I've wanted to hold you like this from the first moment I saw you." His lips covered hers possessively, stealing her breath.

Alison's thoughts tumbled over themselves in sudden agitation. Stark reality had returned when Jason carried her into the brightly lit living room, effectively quenching her desire. All her doubts had come rushing to the fore, and she could no longer ignore the suspicions that John had inadvertently raised the previous day. Tears of confusion burned her eyes, and with a wrench she tore her mouth free. "What about John?" she choked. "If you want to make love to me just so you can cut him out, you might as well stop right now!"

Jason blinked, momentarily confused by the unexpectedness of her question. "What the hell are you talking about? What has this got to do with John?"

She wanted desperately to believe that his indignation was real, that all her suspicions were groundless, but she had to know for sure. "I'm talking about the game you played in college—when you tried to steal each other's girl friends," she explained.

"That was years ago! This has nothing to do with John," he exclaimed. "I've made no secret of the fact that I want you. I thought the feeling was mutual."

Suddenly his eyes revealed his own suspicions. "Why are you throwing up roadblocks all of a sudden? Are you getting cold feet? Or is this just an act to get more copy for your book? I would never have figured you for a tease."

"I'm not a tease!" She was staggered by his accusation. Suddenly there was a wall of distrust between them, built higher by the accusations they were throwing at each other. Why had she started this? Jason had retreated behind an unapproachable facade and he showed no signs of relenting. How was she going to reach him?

Without any warning, she heard her grandmother advising her not to let love escape. She had to tear down that wall between them before it became permanent. Purposefully she stood up and turned to face him, her eyes meeting his squarely. "I mailed my manuscript this morning. But even if I was 'getting copy,' which I'm not, you have no right to complain. That's why you started those ridiculous lessons in the first place, wasn't it? To give me the experience I needed to write better?"

In spite of himself, he grinned. "Touché." The grin faded as he studied her. "All right, you're not a tease. But why are you standing over there? What's all this about? Are you going to let me make love to you or aren't you?" His last words were husky and almost raw with—with what? Vulnerability? Deep emotion?

Alison swallowed, her grandmother's words ringing in her ears. She took a hesitant step toward him, knowing now that if he touched her he would know exactly how she felt. Struggling for words, she choked, "I am," but when he started toward her, she panicked. "Wait! I've got to say something first." She twisted her hands together. "I don't think I could say it if you were touching me. I...I...." She looked at him helplessly. "I can't say it."

"Yes, you can," he said softly. "You can tell me anything. Say it."

Her eyes locked with his. "I...I love you, Jason."

Her words came out on a whisper, but he heard them. A light flared deep in his eyes as his hand reached out for hers. "Come here," he growled huskily. He grabbed her wrist to pull her closer, and she toppled into his arms. His eyes blazed, scanning her defensive face before he took her mouth in a hungry kiss that ignited the flame of passion deep within her. His hand slipped under the clinging material of her top, trailing a scorching fire as he reveled in the silkiness of her skin. Kissing her ear, he murmured her name over and over again, his lips wandering down the sensitive cord at the side of her neck, caressing and tasting, melting her last faint doubts. Then he turned back to her mouth, quickly parting her lips to taste the full, intoxicating sweetness there, while his fingers expertly worked at the neck opening of her blouse.

Her world was reeling out of control. Like a leaf floating on a raging river, she was helpless against the passionate currents sweeping over her. Before she realized what he was doing, the creamy skin of her breasts was revealed to him. When his lips followed the path his hands had blazed, she couldn't hold back the low moan that escaped her lips, or prevent her nails from digging into his muscled neck....

Dear God, what was he doing to her? She was on fire for him, her fingers fighting with the buttons of his shirt until they gave, pushing the silken material aside so that her hands could glide across his hair-roughened chest. She longed to make him feel what she was feeling—an all-consuming need that blocked out the rest of the world. Her senses gloried in the touch and scent of him; she couldn't get enough. He was initiating her into a world of sensuous delight, and her mind no longer had control of her responses. All her resolutions were gone, incinerated in the flames of his desire. His lips retraced their path to her parted lips, kissing her hungrily when she answered his passion with that of her own, their embrace deepening until they were enveloped in a raging inferno.

Shifting her in his arms, Jason followed her down to the soft cushions of the couch. His weight pinned her beneath him, his arms wrapped around her. Alison welcomed him, straining to be closer, to breach the physical barriers. When his wandering hand went to the waistband of her slacks, her eyes, velvety soft with desire, pleaded with him.

"It's all right, babe," he answered her, kissing her eyes, her cheeks, the corner of her mouth. As he cradled her in his arms, his lips again covered hers passionately, possessively. She was swept along on the wave of his desire until she no longer cared what was right or wrong, as long as he relieved the terrible longing that was building up inside her.

His heart pounded in her ear, the reassuring beat almost engulfing her in its insistence. But when Jason pulled away from her, reality came slowly flooding back, leaving her blinking in surprise. Someone was banging at the door, so persistently it couldn't be ignored.

Raking his fingers through his disheveled hair, Jason glared angrily at the front porch. "Who the hell can that be?" Frustration was in his every move as he glanced from the door to Alison. His eyes blazed over her, his hand coming out to cup her cheek as he smiled crookedly. "Make yourself decent, sweetheart, we've got company."

Hot color rushed into her cheeks. Hastily she sat up and straightened her clothes, watching as Jason again ran his hand through his hair. With a muttered oath, he strode quickly to the door and yanked it open, nearly pulling it off its hinges in the process. He stiffened at the sight of the visitor and growled, "What do you want?"

Unperturbed by Jason's rudeness, John stepped into the living room with a boyish grin on his face. "A little courtesy would do for starters." As he was still unaware of Alison's presence, his teasing eyes inspected his friend's disheveled appearance, the rumpled hair and unbuttoned shirt. He whistled softly. "What happened to you?"

Sitting unnoticed on the couch, Alison blushed crimson. In agitation she automatically reached for her hair, trying to smooth her wildly tousled curls. Catching the movement out of the corner of his eye, John cast a curious look toward the sofa. His incredulous gaze bounced from her to Jason and back again.

If it hadn't been such an embarrassing situation, Alison could have almost giggled. It was the first time she had ever seen John at a loss for words. A painful flush tinged his cheeks as he muttered, "Damn! I've put my foot in it now!"

Jason snorted wryly. "You certainly have. You and your rotten timing!" One glance at Alison's bemused face wiped the start of a smile from his mouth. "God, I need a drink!" Walking to the liquor cabinet, he motioned to the array of decanters. "You want anything?" At John's curt nod, he picked up a bottle and poured a liberal dose for each of them, then splashed half that amount into another glass and offered it to Alison.

Keeping her eyes lowered, she stared at the glass he held out to her and shook her head. "N-no, thank you, Jason. I don't want anything."

His eyes narrowed, taking in her drooping shoulders and fluctuating color. "Drink it," he snapped. "You look like you could use it."

With a sigh of defeat, she took the proffered glass and swallowed the contents. Liquid fire coursed down her throat, burning its way to the pit of her stomach. She choked, her eyes watering with tears. When Jason obligingly pounded her on the back, she glared angrily at him. "What was that?"

"Whiskey," he chuckled. "You're not supposed to drink it like Coke."

When her coughing subsided, he turned back to John, who was watching them quizzically. "Well?"

John grinned sheepishly. "I'm really sorry for interrupting, but I knew you'd want to hear my news as soon as possible. Old man Carlson phoned. He's letting you have the lease—on your terms! He tried reaching you at the office, but when he couldn't get you, he called me." His glance slid to Alison, who was pointedly refusing to meet either man's gaze. "I tried phoning you here, but when you didn't answer I thought you might be up at the mansion."

Alison struggled to remain cool and unconcerned, but it was a hopeless effort. Trembling with emotion, she finally set her glass on the coffee table and rose to her feet, forcing herself to meet John's eyes. "Please don't worry about it, John," she assured him. "You didn't interrupt anything that didn't need interrupting."

She had to walk past Jason on her way upstairs, and she flinched at the sudden blaze of anger in his eyes. Lifting her chin, she murmured, "If you'll excuse me, I'll leave you to your discussion. Good night." Quickly she slipped from the room and fled to the haven of her bedroom.

Once inside, she hastily locked the door before sinking onto the edge of her bed. She pressed the palms of her hands to her hot cheeks as realization swept over her. Dear God, what had she nearly done? The wine and the music, combined with Jason's lovemaking, had overpowered her doubts. She had almost made the biggest mistake of her life—she had told him she loved him. But he had made no move to tell her of his own feelings, except for the fact that he wanted her.

Wanted! Didn't his feelings go any deeper than that? He'd had plenty of opportunities to express his love before John's untimely arrival, but he had not. The love was all on her side.

He hadn't even bothered to deny her accusations that he was playing a game. Instead he'd simply sidestepped the issue. She should have run like a rabbit the minute she'd laid eyes on that candlelit table. If ever there was a scene set for seduction, that was it.

Her heart cringed at the coldbloodedness of his actions. He didn't even have the excuse of loving her. Were it for love, she could forgive him. But lust! How that word chilled her, hacking her heart into tiny pieces, leaving an aching void in its place. Tears clouded her eyes, filling the brown depths until they spilled over, silently sliding down her pale cheeks as she sat on her bed in the darkness.

For what seemed like hours she sat in a dazed world of lost emotions. But no matter how she avoided it, she knew she had to make a decision. What was she going to do? Tonight she had been spared, but what of tomorrow? With Jason dropping by as often as he did, she had little doubt that another opportunity would present itself to him. Next time she would be no stronger than she had been tonight, and Jason would be more determined than ever. Despite her grandmother's advice, she could not give herself to a man who didn't love her. She would move out of Jason's life completely before she'd let him touch her without love.

Alison's shoulders straightened as she realized she'd come to a decision. She absolutely couldn't stay there any longer. The situation had become intolerable, and she had to flee before she gave in to emotions that were too powerful for her to control. She had once teased Christina, claiming that the thing between Jason and herself was bigger than both of them, and it was. Jason was using her, no doubt because she was close at hand and available. Well, she would not be used any longer! If John hadn't arrived when he had, she would without a doubt have been in Jason's bed; she would've had no one to protect her from herself. She must get out while she could.

Dragging a small overnight bag from her closet, she studied her clothes, trying to decide what to take. All the while her thoughts centered on the two men downstairs. Dear John, why couldn't she have fallen in love with him? It would have been so much simpler than these constant war games between herself and Jason. John was so safe and lovable, coming to her rescue when she needed him, being a friend when he wanted to be so much more. But as much as she liked and admired him, he didn't make her heart jump in her breast at the mere sight of him, and she didn't spend every hour of the day wondering whom he was with.

She packed a few essentials, leaving the majority of her things to be collected later. Switching on the bedside lamp, she wrote a short note to Jason. She was unable to leave without giving him some sort of explanation.

> Jason, I've come to the conclusion that tonight was a terrible mistake. In the future, it would be better if we avoided each other as much as possible, so I'm moving out of the cottage. You can reach me through John.

Signing her name, she stared at the missive for several moments before collapsing on the bed in tears.

The seconds dragged by, prolonging the final wrench of leave-taking. With blind eyes she lay staring at the ceiling. Eventually her eyelids grew heavy, blinking with the strain to stay awake. On the verge of sleep, she suddenly became aware of voices on the front porch. She got up and glanced quickly out the window. John and Jason were standing within the illuminating circle of the porch light, talking quietly.

Her time of departure had arrived. She left her note propped on the bed, picked up her small case, and slipped quietly from the room. Tiptoeing down the stairs, she froze in alarm when one of the steps groaned in protest, but the murmur of voices continued. Releasing her breath, she quickly and silently made her way down the rest of the stairs. Within seconds she'd gone through the living room to the kitchen, her fingers closing over the knob of the back door to ease it open.

Outside, the ignition of John's car's engine broke the silence of the night, carrying easily to her. The overgrown bushes at the side of the yard were dark voids of shadow, concealing everything with their thick leaves. Fighting her way into them, Alison shifted uneasily as she tried to see in the darkness, suddenly leery of coming face to face with something frightening. But the silence reassured her. Stealthily she made her way around to the front of the house. From fifty yards away, concealed by shrubbery and darkness, she watched as John put his car in gear and drove off. The screen door banged after Jason as he returned to the house, switching off the downstairs lights.

Her fingers gripped her overnight bag tightly, the handle cutting into her palm. The house was like a beacon in the night, and she could imagine Jason's movements. By now he would be knocking at her bedroom door, wanting to pick up from where they had been interrupted. Sure enough, the light flared in her room, crossing the blackness of the night to stab her in the heart. She could almost hear his muttered expletives as he read her note.

She could easily trace his path through the house as, one by one, the lights sprang on upstairs. The futile search continued downstairs until the house was ablaze with lights. Again the porch light rent the darkness, accompanied by the loud slamming of the front door.

Jason strode quickly onto the porch, and even from her hiding place she could see he was in a towering rage. A quick glance assured him that her car was still parked at the side of the house. He scanned the darkness, searching for a glimpse of her, but even his fierce eyes couldn't pierce the opaqueness of the night.

"Alison!" he yelled loudly, startling her so that she almost jumped and revealed her hiding place. When only a chorus of frogs answered his call, he cursed softly. "Dammit, I know you're out there! Quit hiding like a child and come in the house, so we can discuss this like two rational adults."

Shaking her head silently, she ordered her heart to ignore his command. *I can't,* she cried to herself, the pent-up tears burning her eyes and throat. How could he speak of discussing anything like two rational adults when he knew she lost all touch with reality the minute he was near? She couldn't allow him to take her love as well as her self-respect, giving nothing in return.

The night was silent except for the sounds of nature, and still he waited, as if he was trying to decide whether to search for her or not. When it became obvious she had no intention of answering him, he hit his clenched fist against the railing. "All right, have it your way!" he declared. "I hope you enjoy your infantile games!"

Storming into the house, he slammed the door and flicked off the porch light. When he showed no signs of leaving the cottage, she knew he intended to wait her out. Well, he would have a long wait.

Like a shadow, Alison slipped through the blackness of the night. The force of her heartache almost blinded her, but she needed no guiding hand to lead her over the well-worn path she had already taken once that night. Near the mansion she halted beneath the spreading arms of an ancient oak to stare with wounded eyes at the portico. One of the candles was still alight, its persistent flame dancing to the sound of Nat King Cole. The song was about the magic of love....

With jerky movements, Alison forced herself to approach the table. She reached to snuff out the candle, but realized suddenly that Jason might be able to see its faint glow from the cottage. So she let it burn, turning her back on the scene as she entered the house. He couldn't hear the music, however. Quickly pulling the cassette tape from the portable recorder, she cut off the poignant song in mid-phrase. She needed no mechanical devices to remind her of what she had lost; the refrain persisted in the deep recesses of her mind, playing over and over again torturously.

She walked through the dark house, not caring that there was no light to guide her. In her dazed state it was unimportant where her feet led her. What was important was that she move around, expend so much energy that she would be too tired to think, to feel. Her wanderings led her into the library, empty of books, but still somehow a sanctuary to her troubled spirit. She paced restlessly the length of the long room, her churning emotions making it impossible for her to even think of sleep. Now that she was out of the cottage, she didn't even know what she intended to do. Go back to New York? She flinched at the thought, her eyes moving around the darkened room. She couldn't go back and leave this behind.

If she was running from anyone, it was herself. Until she came to grips with the conflict raging within her, she would avoid Jason at all costs, regardless of what he or anyone else thought. She couldn't think straight when he was around; her emotions kept getting in the way and all she wanted was to be in his arms. So retreat was the order of the day. Although it was cowardly, it was infinitely safer than a head-on confrontation.

The blackness of the night passed at last, the first faint streaks of dawn growing brighter with each passing moment. The sun peeked over the horizon, shooting the sky with arrows of red and gold.

Alison viewed it through bleary, red-rimmed eyes. Her muscles ached with weariness. In her troubled vigilance, she must have walked for miles, all within the confines of one room. Though she could not greet the morning with joy, a tired feeling of relief coursed through her as she watched the bright red orb in the eastern sky gradually shift to orange before turning to the yellow rays that would heat the Texas skies. Its presence signaled the beginning of another day.

From her vantage point at the mansion, the cottage appeared deserted, and Jason's car was nowhere in sight. At some point during the long night he must have given up on her. And she, caught up in her own private hell, had not even noticed. Her heart throbbed with pain. She had never felt so alone in her life. Like her grandmother, she seemed destined to suffer heartache. How ironic that they should both fall in love, then lose that love, at this very mansion!

With Jason's departure, there was no longer any reason for her to hide out in the mansion. Wearily she clutched her small bag and hurried down the hill to her car. Opening the door, she hesitated, her pain-filled eyes staring at the cottage hungrily. All of her earthly goods, including her heart, were in that house, but she could not walk in and regain possession of them. It would be too painful.

Instead she drove almost automatically to John's law office, pulling into the parking lot just as his secretary was opening the office. When the woman invited her in for coffee, Alison gratefully accepted. John arrived some time later to find the two of them chatting. Alison was drinking her second cup.

He didn't attempt to hide his astonishment at her appearance. "Alison, what are you doing here? My God, you look exhausted!"

She gave him a wan smile. "Thanks! I...I have to talk to you, John. Could we go into your office?"

Instantly he slipped his arm around her shoulders and guided her down the hall. "Of course! Here, sit down."

Hunching beside her on the small loveseat, he eyed her anxiously. "Are you all right? What's wrong? You know I'll help if I can."

Sniffing, she reached for a tissue in her purse and wiped her eyes. "Oh, John, I'm so miserable. Last n-night...I—"

"Look," he interrupted, "I want to apologize for last night. I had no idea you and Jason...

well, I shouldn't have come barging in like that."

"No," she protested, "don't apologize! I want to thank you."

At his look of surprise, she felt a blush fire her cheeks. "It wasn't what you thought. I mean, it *was*, but...oh, I don't know what I mean!" Jumping to her feet, she strode quickly away from him in agitation. Staring blindly at the impressive collection of law books behind his desk, she said, "It was all a mistake. Jason's only interested in an affair, and I won't settle for that."

John's brow lifted in surprise. "Did he tell you that? He actually said he only wanted an affair?"

She laughed shortly. "Not in so many words. He didn't have to. He's been trying to get me into his bed ever since I met him."

Something flashed in the green depths of his eyes. "I can't believe this, Alison. Oh, I know I was suspicious, too, but when I saw him last night I thought I was mistaken. Surely he can't be stupid enough to think you're in the same category as Christina...and that's a compliment!" Rising to his feet, he strode quickly to his desk and reached for the telephone. "I'm going to call him right now and set him straight."

Before he could respond Alison snatched the receiver away and replaced it in its cradle. "No, don't! Just leave it, John. Thanks for the offer, but it wouldn't help. You can't make Jason change his way of thinking and neither can I. It doesn't matter anymore, anyway. I moved out of the cottage last night."

"You did what? But when? And where did you stay?"

"When you were leaving, I slipped out and went up to the mansion. I stayed there all night." She fiddled with the phone cord before glancing at him hesitantly. "I left Jason a note telling him he could reach me through you. You don't mind?"

"Of course not," he assured her. "I told you if you ever needed me, to just call."

She smiled in relief. "Thanks, John. I don't know what I'd do without you. I couldn't cope with Jason right now. So if he calls, I don't want to see him."

"You're not going to continue working at the mansion, are you?" The phone interrupted them, and he glared at it in annoyance before picking up the receiver. At the sound of the caller's voice, his eyebrows rose and he winked at Alison. "Jason, how are you?"

Alison blanched, backing away from the desk as if he could see her through the phone. When John smiled at her, she shook her head frantically.

Still grinning, he repeated, "Alison? Why, no, I haven't seen her. Isn't she at the cottage?"

A wicked grin parted his lips as he listened to Jason's response. "If I see her, I'll certainly tell her you called," he agreed sincerely. When he hung up the receiver, he laughed aloud. "Boy, is he hopping mad! If I were you, I'd give him at least two weeks to cool down. In the state he's in now, he's liable to murder you!"

Still chuckling, he almost rubbed his hands together in gleeful satisfaction. "This is great! Just great! Don't get me wrong; Jason and I are practically like brothers. But for years I've watched women drop at his feet. It was disgusting! Then you came along with your beautiful brown eyes and a smile that would set a dead man's heart to beating, and suddenly the situation was reversed. I love it! He's been too arrogant by half; it's about time someone put him in his place!"

"I'm not doing this to get back at Jason, John. I'm doing it for myself. I...I just couldn't take any more. I have pride, too."

"I know you do, Alison." His expression grew serious, but his eyes still twinkled. "What do you intend to do now?"

"I've got to find a place to live." She gave him a sheepish grin. "I was hoping you could help me."

His eyes lit up. "How about with Nancy? I'm sure she'd love to have you stay with her a while."

She shook her head regretfully. "Tony's parents are visiting. I couldn't intrude. Anyway, I need to be by myself for a while, to sort out my feelings. Just a small one-bedroom apartment would be fine."

"Okay, if you're sure." Motioning her to sit in the chair near his desk, he pressed the intercom button and asked his secretary to join them. "Among the three of us, we're bound to come up with something," he explained.

CHAPTER THIRTEEN

"WELL, THAT'S THE LAST OF THE LOT." Dusting his hands, John looked around the limited space of the living room in satisfaction. Cardboard boxes were piled in a corner, wrinkled newspaper discarded haphazardly underfoot from the cartons Alison had already started to unpack. The bare walls and rugless floors gave the room an almost naked appearance, and the old-fashioned couch and chair had seen better days. With a rueful grin on his face, John motioned to the mound of odd-sized possessions. "Did you bring all this stuff with you from New York?"

At Alison's nod, he exclaimed, "How did you get it all in your car?"

Alison laughed in remembrance. "It wasn't easy. What I couldn't get in the back seat had to go in the trunk. It's a good thing I didn't have a flat on the way. It would have taken an hour to unpack everything just to get to the spare tire." She glanced at the small dimensions of the room. "Don't forget how small this place is. Not that I'm complaining," she assured him.

"It's small, but it's been a lifesaver. I can't thank you enough for helping me find it. And for moving my things for me." The spark of laughter in her eyes flickered and died, to be replaced by the longing that had been present for days. "Was...was Jason there when you packed my things?"

Settling on the ancient velour sofa that dominated the room, John motioned for her to sit down before he said dramatically, "Was he there? Does Texas have longhorns?" His amusement could not be contained. "I had a feeling he'd be there. He blew up when I refused to tell him where you were. I've never seen him so mad! I'm sure glad I took Nancy along for protection."

"Nancy was there?" she asked, blinking in surprise. "But why?"

"I asked her to pack your clothes. And was I glad I did!" He laughed at the memory. "She really gave Jason a piece of her mind! Even told him you'd probably be there today if he hadn't been such an idiot. Any fool could see you were falling in love with him. But what did he do? Treated you like a one-night stand instead of the woman he's been looking for all his life!"

Color washed Alison's face. "Oh, no!" Did the whole world know about that night? No wonder Jason was mad. "What did he say?"

"He laughed." John shook his head in bewilderment. "I don't understand it. One minute he's so mad he can't see straight, and the next he laughs. He agreed he didn't handle the situation right, but he couldn't understand why you walked out without telling him off. Evidently you were never shy about venting your anger."

So he only agreed that he had treated her badly, not that he loved her, too. Despair weighed Alison's spirit. Tiredly she tried to explain the situation to John. "I was convinced that we wanted different things from a relationship, you see. I thought a little breathing space would clear my mind so I could see things straighter, but nothing's changed. Jason would rather have his freedom than be tied down to any woman, including me. And I won't be his mistress. There's no future in it."

Pointedly she changed the subject. "How about some iced tea after all that hot work? It won't take me a minute to fix it."

Later, after John left, she looked around the small apartment and tried in vain not to compare it to the cottage. Nothing would be gained by that except more painful memories. She had to make herself forget. But when she looked at the tiny living room, she didn't see the dilapidated couch, or the chair that didn't match it. Instead she saw a room twice that size, a comfortable early-American sofa where she and Jason....

Abruptly she shied away from that agonizing recollection. She inspected the kitchen, though it couldn't really be classified as a room because only a counter separated it from the living room. She wouldn't have to worry about dropping any blue willow china here; it was all still at the cottage.

A salty wetness trickled down her cheek, and suddenly Alison realized what she was doing. With an impatient swipe at her eyes and cheeks she went into her tiny bedroom, trying not to notice how it was crammed with a twin bed of questionable durability and a scratched dresser. The closet was almost bursting its seams. She had never thought she had a lot of clothes, but those she had would have a rough time squeezing into the small space.

Alison spent the rest of the day trying to make the apartment homey, but curtains and knickknacks could only do so much. By evening it still looked as if it was furnished with antique leftovers. She gave up in disgust.

THE DAYS PASSED with a dragging loneliness that pulled at her heart. She avoided the mansion completely, knowing full well that Jason would expect to find her there. Instead she telephoned the workers involved and explained what needed to be done, thereby keeping her whereabouts secret. They in turn reported to John when the work was completed. He inspected it to make sure it would meet Alison's specifications and paid them.

It was an unsatisfactory arrangement as far as Alison was concerned. She longed to be in the thick of things instead of stuck away with no idea what was happening. But John's report that Jason had showed up once when he was inspecting the place more than convinced her that this was the only possible solution.

She gazed at her typewriter bleakly. It looked terribly out of place on the kitchen counter, but there was nowhere else to put it. Not that it mattered; she hadn't written a word since she'd left the cottage. The companionship of her fictional characters was gone, mailed to New York, and she couldn't find the energy to create new ones. Her mind was blank, empty of everything except despair. She had moved to the tiny garage apartment to escape Jason, but her stubborn thoughts remained with him. He held her heart more than he would ever know.

Agonizing, heart-wrenching pain coursed through her, bringing a sob to her tight throat. Had her grandmother's separation from Edward been this terrible? How had she survived it? The loneliness was unbearable, with the future a great yawning gap. Alison could think of nothing that would ever lighten her heart. Jason didn't love her, and she couldn't accept anything less than his love. There was no reason to think that either of them would ever change....

A knock at the door startled her. She felt the blood drain from her face as she saw a masculine outline through the curtains covering the glass window of the door. A trembling seized her, making it impossible for her to move. When the knock was repeated, and John yelled, "Alison, are you all right?" she expelled her breath in a rush.

Hurrying to the door, she unlocked it and pulled it open. "Oh, John. I'm so glad to see you. Please, come in."

Stepping into the apartment, he scanned her face searchingly, then frowned. Obviously she looked pretty haggard again. His long, lean fingers gently wiped away a crystal tear that clung to her cheek. "Tears? What's happened now? Don't tell me Jason's discovered your whereabouts?"

"Oh, no." She motioned to the couch. "You'd better sit there. The springs in the chair must have given way. The couch is safer."

When they were both sitting, she met his gaze bravely. "Nothing's wrong, John. Really. I... I guess I was just lonely."

"It's no wonder," he retorted gruffly. "You keep yourself cooped up in this apartment like a hermit! If you'd get out more, you might be able to put Jason out of your mind."

"I can't," she whispered, hardly able to get the words out. "Don't you realize, John, it doesn't matter where I am or who I'm with? If I were in a crowded subway in New York or alone at the North Pole, he would still be with me."

"All right, so you're in love with the guy," he retorted flatly. "I know it and you know it. But does Jason know?"

"Yes! And it didn't make a bit of difference!" Her cheeks were bright with color. "I told him, but he still wanted just an affair. Face it, John. I have. He doesn't love me."

"How do you know?" he demanded. "Just because he didn't say so doesn't mean he doesn't. I don't think he's ever been in love before. Maybe he was working up the nerve to tell you when I burst in on you. My God, how could he *not* love you? I'm crazy about you!"

The fierceness of her expression quickly softened to compassion, "Oh, John, I'm sorry. I do love you as a friend, if that's any consolation."

He shrugged. "It's about as much consolation as kissing my sister, but it's better than nothing." Taking her hand, he studied her seriously, all amusement gone. "Really, Alison, I think you should talk to Jason and discuss this thing with him. If not for yourself, then for him. I've known him for a long time, and I know he feels more for you than he's letting on. He won't even go to New Orleans to discuss that oil lease with Mr. Carlson, and you know how important that is to him. Any time he starts letting his work slide, something's wrong.

"And I've never seen him in such a foul mood. He snaps at everyone and everything. This afternoon I went to the mansion to give it a final check over. Jason came in and started questioning one of the carpenters about your whereabouts. When he told him you had contacted him over the phone, Jason was livid. He said a few choice words that shocked even me, and believe me, I thought I'd heard everything. He went storming out, probably to the nearest bar."

His eyes pleaded with her. "Alison, you've got to talk to him. My God, if you love him as you say you do, don't you want to put him out of his misery?"

"Why? So he can make *me* miserable?" she cried, her eyes clouded with anguish. "I suppose it doesn't matter what kind of private hell I'm going through as long as Jason is happy. Give him what he wants!"

Her eyes were accusing when they turned on him. "You don't know what it's like, John. It's easy for you to say give in to him. Don't you think it hurts me to keep away from him? I love him. But he doesn't love me! I'm just a challenge, another one of those little games the two of you used to play in college. But I'm different. *I* got away, and that's why he's so mad! It galls him to think that a woman actually refused to go to bed with him."

She paced restlessly before him. "Once he finds me again, this whole charade will start over again, the fox and the hare, until he finally snares me in his bed. That's why I'm going to avoid Jason Morgan at all costs. Because afterward, when I regained my senses, I would be in a worse hell than I'm in right now. I'm sorry, John. I can't do it. I won't be used."

Seeing his arguments were getting him nowhere, John relented. "All right. Maybe you're right. I'm sorry. But I still think you're not giving Jason very much credit. I know him better than just about anybody, Alison, and I don't really think he would do what you're suggesting. Hell, you're a nice girl! Anyone can look at you and see you're not the type to jump in and out of bed with guys as if you were trying out different brands of shampoo! And as for our high jinks in college, that was a different matter altogether. Those girls knew exactly what we were up to. Regardless of what you think, Jason would never deliberately seduce an innocent girl just for the hell of it. He's not like that."

When she started to protest, he raised his

hand to stop her. "Okay, I know you don't agree. Why don't we drop the subject and go out to dinner?"

Even before the words were out of his mouth, she was shaking her head. "I'm sorry, I just couldn't." At his look of disappointment, she smiled halfheartedly. "I'd be rotten company."

"Are you sure?" His eyes swept her figure. "You look like you've lost weight again. Are you eating right?"

She laughed away his concern. "Don't worry, John. I'm not about to pine away. I wouldn't be that stupid." Not wanting to talk about herself, she changed to a less personal topic. "Have the men finished working on the mansion? How does it look?"

"Great! You've really done a marvelous job. I'm sure Jason approves."

When her eyes flickered in pain, he said solemnly, "You're going to have to face him sooner or later, Alison. After all, you *do* own a house together, and the work on it *was* completed today. Everyone's been paid. Now you and Jason have to decide what to do with the place. You can't just leave it there to fall back into disrepair. Something's got to be done."

"I know." Agitated by his persistence, she jumped to her feet and went to stand by the room's only window. Her fingers touched the frilly curtains as she imagined her last visit to the mansion—the flickering candles, the daisies...Jason. She repeated huskily, "I know. And I will speak to Jason. Just give me a d-day or two." Turning around, she cast him a brave smile to hide the trembling of her lips. "I'll go tomorrow to see the house, then I'll contact Jason. Okay?"

"Okay." Rising to his feet, he walked over to her. Her eyes were overly bright with tears, her smile forced. "Would you like me to be present when you see him?"

Momentarily Alison considered his offer, ready to grab it as a drowning person does a lifeline. But her innate sense of fairness would not allow her to use him so callously. Regretfully she shook her head. "Thanks, John, but I couldn't bring you in on this any more than I already have. It might jeopardize your friendship with Jason. It will be better if he and I meet privately without bringing in a third party. Surely we can maintain a veneer of civilization for such a short space of time."

BUT THE NEXT DAY she was not so sure. She awoke with a feeling of dread, a sense of impending doom for which she could find no immediate explanation. As sleep receded and awareness gradually returned, however, she rolled over in her narrow bed with a low moan of despair. How could she face Jason? One touch, and she knew without a doubt she would melt in his arms, powerless to resist him. She could fight his anger with her own, but his passion reduced her to a quivering mass of desires. She had been a fool to succumb to John's pleading. He didn't understand; he didn't know what he was asking of her. To see Jason again while her emotions were still so volatile was sheer madness!

She wouldn't do it. A spark of defiance flared within her, and her jaw set stubbornly. Why should she put herself through such torture? What would it accomplish? Only more heartache, and she'd had just about all of that that she could take. She needed no reminders of what she was missing. Her heart was permanently singed by a flame she had come too close to. Unlike the moth, she would not keep courting the heat until it destroyed her. She was no masochist.

Coward! an inner voice taunted her. *What are you afraid of—life? Love? Or perhaps yourself? You're not running from Jason; you're running from the feelings he awakened in you. But you can't hide forever in an ivory tower. Loneliness is frightening and will make a cold bedfellow. Don't be a fool!*

Torn apart by the conflict raging within her, she frittered away the precious hours of the morning in indecision. Her emotions were on the rack, pulled first one way, then another. Her mind bitterly protested the urgings of her heart, advocating instead that she avoid a meeting with Jason. But her heart was not to be denied, and shortly after noon she found herself contemplating her wardrobe in search of an outfit that would bolster her courage.

She found it in a dusty-rose blouse and floral-print skirt that tied at the waist. During her summer in San Antonio the Texas sun had turned her skin to the golden hue of honey and had streaked finely spun strands of sunshine in her dark curls. Her cheeks were blooming with color, her hair in soft short curls around her head. Her eyes were wide with apprehension, looking even larger when she darkened her lashes with mascara. Sweeping her lips with rose lipstick, she stole a final glance in the mirror. At least she had no need to be ashamed of her appearance.

Not long afterward she drove through the gates of the estate. Carefully she avoided looking at the cottage, after one quick glance assured her that Jason wasn't there. As she parked in front of the mansion, she had the oddest feeling, as if she was coming home. The building was imposing in the summer sunshine, but she knew that with the right person sharing it, the place could become a warm and loving home.

An inner quaking took hold of her as her eyes swept the portico, but all signs of the romantic dinner she and Jason had shared had long since been swept away. On trembling legs she advanced to the intricately carved double doors and pushed them wide.

No litter met her eyes this time, no destruction to wrench at her heart. The faded and tattered wallpaper had been removed, replaced with the warm muted colors of antique gold and powder blue, rose, off-white and jade. Miraculously, through the application of new wallpaper and paint, the mansion had been restored to its former elegance and charm. The old parquet floors had been sanded and revarnished to achieve their original beauty, and now shone from the sunshine spilling through the new windows.

In a daze of delight Alison walked through each room, her heels clicking loudly on the wooden floors, a pleased smile lighting her face. Everything was perfect, exactly as she had envisioned it the first time she walked through these halls; only furniture was needed to make the picture complete.

Her wanderings led her upstairs, where the transformation of the bedrooms was all that she had hoped it would be. Wainscoting had been restored, the varied rooms papered in quiet elegance. Dreamily she trailed her fingers along a window seat, imagining children romping and playing in these rooms, their voices lifted in laughter. And at her side, watching them grow, would be Jason, laughing and teasing, protecting and sharing, loving.

A stifled cry burst from her throat; reality came rushing in once again with a vengeance. *Fool,* she berated herself fiercely. Her emotions were tangled together in a web of hope and despair, a lost cause that she could not quite turn her back on. If he loved her, such a dream might be possible, but without him it was a nightmare, a never-ending ache of loneliness.

In an attempt to escape her anguished thoughts, she hastily climbed the stairs to the attic, blinking in surprise as another dream unfolded before her. The steep slanting roof created a coziness that the other rooms, with their high ceilings, lacked. Her imagination furnished the room in wicker, with tufted aqua cushions to match the tiny flowers of the wallpaper. It was a perfect hideaway, a comfortable, beautiful place to retreat from the world and to write. No unwanted telephone calls would reach her here, no unexpected visitors except those that knew of her secret place. But unless she and Jason were able to come to some type of agreement, such imaginings would come to nothing.

With dragging feet she retraced her steps,

hardly looking where she was going, so caught up was she in her tortured thoughts. She was midway down the last flight when she felt a prickle of apprehension. Someone was watching her. Her feet automatically stopped their descent as her eyes scanned the room below for sight of an intruder. Then she gasped.

Jason was standing in the doorway below, a strange light in his eyes as he watched her approach. He looked incredibly handsome, a three-piece suit hugging his muscular frame, his bronzed face clean-shaven and strong. Alison's heart tripled its beat, urging her to run to him and throw her arms around his neck....

It took all her efforts to resist her urgings. Her fingers bit into the new wood of the banister to hold herself back. With superhuman control, she met his gaze unflinchingly and continued her descent of the stairs at an unhurried rate. When she reached the bottom, she stopped halfway across the room and asked tightly, "What are you doing here?"

His gaze swept over her, taking in every aspect of her appearance. "In case you'd forgotten, I happen to own half interest in this place."

When she refused to comment, his eyes narrowed dangerously. "But that's not the reason I'm here. I've been here just about every afternoon waiting for you to show up. I knew this house was too close to your heart for you to abandon it completely. You were bound to come sooner or later.''

His eyes held her captive, not allowing her to break away. Mesmerized, she stood there while he advanced. When he was almost upon her, his hand reached out to touch her. It was then she uttered a cry of dismay. ''Don't touch me!'' she pleaded. Her trembling legs carried her a few feet away, as her traitorous body yearned for—and dreaded—his touch. It seemed an aeon before she was able to whisper, ''How do you like the house?''

Quietly he studied her face, his eyes wary and alert. Again he moved toward her, this time stopping only a foot away from her slim figure. His low voice sent shivers of awareness through her. ''It's beautiful. The colors are elegant, and the place is crying out to be furnished with antiques and Oriental rugs. It will make a wonderful place to live. You've really done a first-rate job. Congratulations.''

The tension flowed out of her at his words, leaving her strangely weak with relief. ''Oh, Jason, I'm so glad! I was petrified something would go wrong. Now we don't have to sell it!''

His blue eyes never wavered as he replied quietly, ''I'm sorry, Alison, but this changes nothing. I'm just as determined as ever to sell the estate.''

"What?" The heady feeling that had only seconds before transformed her suddenly turned sour. She knew the blood drained from her face, she could feel it. She stared at him speechlessly as the questions jumped around in her head. Finally she stuttered, "B-but what of our agreement, our bet? You promised you wouldn't try to force the sale if I could restore the house within the budget we agreed on!"

"To hell with our agreement!" he retorted.

Alison was shattered. His arrogance stabbed her in the heart, wounding her so that she wanted to cry out in pain. Unable to endure his presence a moment longer, she brushed hurriedly past him into the library, slamming the door after her. The tears she had held at bay came pouring out, silent sobs shaking her slender body. How could he? He had deliberately led her on, had encouraged her even, while he had absolutely no intention of keeping his promise. How could she love such a cad? He was cold-blooded and unfeeling, a monster!

The door behind her opened. Hastily she wiped at her cheeks with the back of her hand. Ignoring his presence, she stared unseeingly out the window. Jason's glance traveled around the quiet luxury of the room before settling on her averted face. He seemed completely unconcerned with her anger. "Is this where you were going to write?"

Momentarily, she met his gaze. "No," she retorted coldly. "Since you insist on selling this place, I can't see what concern it is of yours where I write!"

His eyes danced with ironic laughter. "I guess you're right!"

His mockery snapped the tight control Alison had on her temper. Her eyes blazed as she turned to face him. "Do you know what I think of you? You're despicable! This bet between us was nothing but a sham, a disgusting trick on your part to get my hopes up just so you could knock them down. Well, you're a sadistic brute with nothing in your veins but ice water!" To her horror, she heard her voice begin to shake with tears and she could do nothing to stop it. Pivoting away, she choked. "No one h-has the right to de-destroy another person's dreams!"

His hands came around her waist and pulled her firmly back against him, despite her struggles to stop him. She stood stiff and unyielding within the circle of his arms, but he seemed unperturbed as he bent his head to kiss the nape of her neck. "What are your dreams, Alison?" he asked against her ear.

His warmth was destroying the coldness that surrounded her, but stubbornly she tried to build it back up again. "If you think I'm going to tell you, you're out of your mind!"

His muffled laughter sent warm waves crashing over her. "I probably am out of my mind, but you *are* going to tell me." At her continued silence, his arms tightened about her threateningly. "If you don't tell me, I'm going to kiss you until you do. Who knows, we might be here all night."

Goaded beyond endurance, she spat, "Dammit, all right! But if you laugh I'll never forgive you!" Refusing to look at him, she said huskily, "I...I wanted to...l-live here...and have b-babies...and write in a garret!" Sobs were welling up in her throat, demanding release. Struggling wildly, she choked, "Let me go, damn you! You've had your kicks."

Gently but firmly Jason easily subdued her, clamping her against him until she could hardly move. "Be still, you little wildcat! I just want to know about your plans. Does this home, with the babies and you writing in the attic, include a husband? I know modern liberated women don't need husbands to have children, but somehow I can't see you doing that. Think what Aunt Gwen would say!"

When she refused to answer, he laughed softly. "We'll come back to that later. Don't you want to know the asking price?"

His mouth was caressing the sensitive cord of her neck, his hands burning her rib cage through the thinness of her blouse. Her senses were clamoring wildly, and she could hardly concentrate on what he was saying. Looking over her shoulder at him, she frowned in confusion. "W-what?"

Their mouths were inches apart. Pressing a quick kiss to her parted lips, he repeated, "Don't you want to know the asking price for the mansion? You may want to buy me out."

Another wave of coldness washed over her. She fought to escape his clutches, but his grip only tightened, refusing her freedom. Defeated by his strength, she said bitterly, "Oh, sure, Jason! I'll just go down to the bank tomorrow and withdraw the two million or so dollars this estate is worth! Would you like a check or money order? Or perhaps you'd prefer cash. Would you like it all in ones?"

His laughter filled the room. "You know, you're adorable when you're angry. Like a kitten spitting fury. But I much prefer you when you're purring, darling." At her start of surprise, he grinned. "I don't know why you're being so stubborn. What I'm asking is really quite reasonable."

His closeness was pure torture, she would do or say anything to be free of him. "Oh, all right! What are you asking for the mansion?"

Turning her in his arms, he pulled her close against him with one arm, while his other hand lifted her chin, forcing her to meet his gaze.

"All I ask," he replied huskily, "is that you let me love you—"

Wrenching herself from his hold, she stared at him aghast. "How can you?" she whispered brokenly. "You don't really believe I would prostitute myself for this house?"

Amazement quickly turned to anger as he jerked her back into his arms, pulling her up hard against him. "You're damn right I don't believe that!" he ground out fiercely. His eyes were as dark as the sea in the grips of a violent storm. "Let me finish what I'm trying to say! I'm trying to tell you I love you, and you're jumping down my throat for making an indecent proposal!"

When her eyes widened with shock, his face softened into unbelievable tenderness. He caressed her cheek before his fingers moved into her hair to cup the back of her head and lift her face to his. "I thought I'd never say this to anyone, but I love you. I think I have ever since you walked in on me that first day, looking so shocked and adorable. In case you haven't noticed, I've had the devil's own time keeping my hands off you! Why do you think I've jumped at any excuse to drop by the cottage? I couldn't stay away."

Unable to believe what she was hearing, Alison shook her head. "Jason, don't do this just to save my pride." A sudden thought struck her, and she went on. "Has John been talking to you?"

"I would hardly call it talking," he laughed wryly. "I've been on the receiving end of an ongoing lecture for the past two weeks. I fought it all the way, but I finally had to admit he was right. I've been in love with you for weeks, and I'd be a fool to let you go."

Those were the words she had never expected to hear. Suddenly, miraculously, the pain of the past few weeks vanished, and she wanted to melt against him. "What about Christina?" she asked, bewildered.

"I've never cared for her. Because of business I had to force myself to be civil to her for two months. I wouldn't even have done that if I hadn't known how jealous it made you."

"Jealous! I was never jealous—"

"Liar," he teased softly. "You didn't know it, but you didn't have a thing to worry about. Even in New Orleans, which, I might add, was strictly business. I had no idea she was going until she sat down next to me in the departure lounge. And all those hints she threw at you about our being together constantly were nothing but lies. Her father was there the entire time."

"But what about the swimming pool? I was so hurt when I heard her say it was her suggestion to have it cleaned. I thought I was doing it for you."

Cradling her closer in his arms, he nuzzled her neck. "I know, darling, and I'm sorry. You were doing it for me. Christina encouraged me to have it filled after I suggested it. Satisfied?"

She met his glance boldly, challengingly. "There's one other thing I want to know. How did you find out about grandmother's affair with Edward Smythe? Did you read the diaries?"

"I haven't forgotten my promise, you little witch."

No sooner were the words out of his mouth than his lips were on hers, tenderly at first, then with a growing fire. Instantly a flame ignited deep within her, and for minutes it raged unchecked, filling her with joy, with hope, with unfulfilled desire. She had long since lost control when he reluctantly released her lips and rained kisses over her face. "Oh, Jason, I love you so much," she breathed.

"I know you do, sweetheart. Why do you think I tried to seduce you?"

When she leaned slightly away to stare at him in puzzlement he pulled her back to her former position, his chin resting on her hair. "I was so damn frustrated—we were always arguing, and Christina was becoming a pain in the neck. I was holding my own, though, until I walked in on you in that bathtub. You have no idea how delectable you looked, all creamy and soft, with roses in your cheeks, that mound of bubbles. For weeks you'd been driving me mad, but that bubble bath really did it. I made plans all night. I fixed up everything at the mansion, got the wine chilled and the music ready, and I was all set. Forgive my intentions, sweetheart, but I was going to get you slightly drunk, somehow get you into my bedroom, strip the clothes from your beautiful body and torment you until you confessed you loved me as much as I love you. And I would have, too, if John hadn't walked in!"

"Shall we try again?" she asked boldly. "This time I promise not to run away."

"Don't tempt me, woman." He gave her a quick, hard kiss before releasing her unwillingly. Both of them were breathing unsteadily. "By the way," he said, reaching into his pocket and extracting a letter, "this came today in the mail. It might be important."

Alison took the envelope, a puzzled look on her face. She tore it open, her eyes scanning the contents quickly. Suddenly she shrieked, throwing her arms around Jason's neck ecstatically. "They accepted it! My God, Jason, they've accepted my manuscript! I'm going to be published."

He hugged her fiercely, his eyes reflecting her joy. "Congratulations, darling. But I can't say

I'm really surprised. Writing's so much in your blood."

Alison was so thrilled she didn't understand him at first. But after a moment she pulled back to look at him in surprise. "What do you mean, in my blood. What are you talking about?"

Jason smiled teasingly. "Patience, sweetheart. All in good time." His hand captured hers and he pulled her outside. She had to practically run to keep up with his long strides, and when he finally came to a stop in his bedroom in the cottage, she was gasping for breath. Suddenly a book was thrust into her hands. "Read the inside front cover," he instructed.

Alison frowned at the book. "Why? This is one of Abigail Peyton's best books."

"I know." He sighed, pretending impatience. "You are the most exasperating woman! Will you please just open the book?"

"Okay, okay!" She did as he asked, and abruptly the smile was wiped from her face. Her eyes flew to Jason's. "How...."

The warmth of his smile caressed her. "This is your own autographed copy. It's been waiting for you ever since grandmother got your letter. Abigail Peyton was the author's pseudonym, you see. Her real name was Alison Ford Morgan."

"What?" Her knees suddenly buckled, and Alison collapsed on the bed.

Jason immediately sat down beside her. "I discovered the secret when I was a kid, and she made me promise not to tell a soul. She had horrible memories of that scandal with the Smythes, and when she started writing, she was afraid she would be connected with it again. So she used a pseudonym. And she hated publicity. The day you arrived, I mistook you for a reporter who had somehow pieced the story together. I couldn't let that mess hit the papers again—grandmother had an excellent reputation as a writer, and I refused to let it be tarnished. And I knew you were coming to town and probably didn't know much about your relatives. I wanted you to have time to read the diaries before all the skeletons started rattling in the closet. I knew grandmother would give it to you straight."

Alison was dazed. "I can't believe it! I wondered why her financial situation eased, but this. . . I never even suspected!"

"When you told me you were a writer, I was floored. Now you know why." He stood up and reached for her hand. "Now that that's settled, let's get back to us. You are going to marry me, aren't you?"

Alison stared at him speechlessly. Numbly she let him raise her to her feet next to him. When she finally did get her voice back, she stuttered, "You w-want to m-marry me? But your parents. . . I mean, I thought you didn't ever want to get married."

His eyes were tender as they swept over her. "At one time, I didn't. But that was before I met a stubborn, nosy, bullheaded writer who was thoroughly enchanting and refused to let me get away with anything." He kissed the tip of her nose. "These last few weeks have been pure hell, but I must admit they opened my eyes. You're nothing like my mother, and I'm the exact opposite of my father. We can make it work. I lost you once; I'm not taking any more chances. I'm not letting you out of my sight again. C'mon."

When he tried to drag her out of the bedroom, she stopped, grinning impishly. "Why are you in such a hurry? You've been trying for weeks to get me into this room."

With a growl he pulled her into his arms and kissed her lingeringly on the lips. "You little witch. Every time I put my arms around you in this house, someone interrupts us. Well, it won't happen again because we won't be here. We're flying to Vegas so I can get a ring on your finger before you have a chance to change your mind. After that, I plan to lock myself in a hotel room with you for at least a week—maybe a month. When I get you in my bed, darling, I'm going to make damn sure no one walks in on us! Christina and John have interrupted us for the last time!"

Her eyes were teasing as they roamed his face. "I should have known. This is all just another excuse for crawling into bed with me!"

He pressed her slender curves to his hard frame and his mouth hovered over hers as he taunted softly, "Just try to keep me out, brown eyes!"

Enter a uniquely exciting world of romance with the new

Harlequin American Romances.™

Harlequin American Romances are the first romances to explore today's new love relationships. These compelling romance novels reach into the hearts and minds of women across North America...probing the most intimate moments of romance, love and desire.

You'll follow romantic heroines and irresistible men as they boldly face confusing choices. Career first, love later? Love without marriage? Long-distance relationships? All the experiences that make love real are captured in the tender, loving pages of the new **Harlequin American Romances.**

What makes North American women so different when it comes to love? Find out in the new **Harlequin American Romances!**

Send for your introductory FREE book now!